Hot Cross Buns at the Little Cornish Bookshop

Jennifer Bibby is an author of warm and heartfelt community romances. Her debut novel was a contender for the 2022 RNA Joan Hessayon award. A lifelong lover of stories, she enjoys exploring the everyday lives of modern women through literature. Jennifer is happiest by the sea and loves dinosaurs, travel, classy cocktails and medieval history.

Also by Jennifer Bibby

The Cornish Hideaway
Christmas at the Little Cornish Bakery

Hot Cross Buns at the Little Cornish Bookshop

Jennifer Bibby

ZAFFRE

First published in the UK in 2026 by
ZAFFRE
An imprint of Bonnier Books UK
5th Floor, HYLO, 105 Bunhill Row,
London, EC1Y 8LZ

This is a work of fiction. Names, places, events and
incidents are either the products of the author's imagination or used fictitiously.
Any resemblance to actual persons, living or dead, or actual
events is purely coincidental.
A CIP catalogue record for this book is available from the British Library.

Paperback ISBN: 978-1-78512-667-3

Also available as an ebook and an audiobook

1 3 5 7 9 10 8 6 4 2

Typeset by IDSUK (Data Connection) Ltd
Printed and bound by CPI Group (UK) Ltd, Croydon, CR0 4YY

The authorised representative in the EEA is
Bonnier Books UK (Ireland) Limited.
Registered office address:
Block B, The Crescent Building
Northwood, Santry
Dublin 9, D09 C6X8
Ireland
compliance@bonnierbooks.ie
www.bonnierbooks.co.uk

*For the readers. For anyone who has picked this book
up as a way to escape.*

Prologue

The closer they got, the more Effie began to relax. Huddled in the back of her parents' car, her university belongings packed up and stuffed in beside her, Effie was a storm of emotions. Disappointment at failing to get to grips with the city life she'd so desired mixed with relief that she was returning home to her beloved Cornwall. They'd travelled mostly in silence, the radio turned down low, her mum making small talk as the miles rolled by. Effie still had her graduation dress on, a deep navy blue that felt far too formal. She could still feel the indents on her head from her mortar board, and her face ached from the false smiles she'd forced.

So that was it. Three years done and dusted and what did she have to show for them? A nice middle of the road 2:1 degree in English Literature. A dissertation that had kept her up to the small hours in frustration the past three months. A few numbers in her phone she knew she'd never use. Air-kisses and empty hugs as they'd handed back their gowns and filed off to whatever their futures held.

Effie ran through them in her head. Jobs in journalism, internships in publishing houses, a summer spent backpacking around Thailand. Everyone had buzzed with the joy of being unleashed into the world, whilst Effie had hovered there, frozen, terrified by a future she had zero plans for. Out the corner of her eye she had spotted Brad, all chiselled jaw and flawless floppy hair, handsome as a romcom hero. Effie's heart cracked at the thought of him. The memories of their brief romance that had spanned her final year, a romance that she had pinned her future on.

Even now she was embarrassed to think of the plans she'd hung on their rickety frame. Brad was heading back to Manchester to work in some vague start-up business with a few school friends. Effie wasn't sure of the exact details, but, then again, neither was Brad. Effie had tied herself in knots trying to convince herself that Manchester would be a fun, cosmopolitan place to live and she'd have Brad to show her around. She began to apply for jobs in bookshops and libraries. Even though she'd disliked the busyness of London, Effie had convinced herself Manchester would be different. She wasn't sure how, but it was a hope to cling to.

That had been her plan until Brad had sat her down a week before graduation to let her know she didn't feature in his plans. It had been fun and all that, he'd said, but it was time to go their separate ways, he didn't want to be tied down during his next chapter. The only thanks Effie could give was that he'd broken up with her before she'd told her parents her plan to move with him. How on earth had she got her wires so crossed? The only thing that soothed her was the thought of going home to Cornwall.

Effie had still been choking back the sting of being dumped as she'd put on her graduation robes. Brad had been sitting in the row in front of her during the ceremony, but he'd given her no more than a brief nod before resuming bants with his friends. Effie had sat there, her future in tatters, as everyone around her thrummed with the excitement of life. Glancing at her watch, she had realised that she only had an hour left of faking it in this world, before she could leave. The relief washed over her like a wave.

Effie focused on that metaphorical horizon until the sea appeared on the literal one. Her heart rate slowed, her body relaxed, she could put London behind her now. Pretend it never happened. Build something here. But what?

Her dad pulled the car up outside the little cottage they lived in. Home, the feeling flooded through Effie, all warmth and familiarity. They sat for a few moments in silence.

'I think I'll go and stretch my legs,' Effie said.

'Don't you want—' her mum began only to be cut off by her dad.

'Let her go. It's been a long day.'

Effie let herself out of the car and made her way through the town and down to the seafront. Penzance. A place she'd once yearned to leave was now the place she was thrilled to come back to. She breathed in the clean sea air. It was overcast, the sky and sea merging into one swathe of pale grey. A swimmer in the bay was moving methodically through the waves. She watched them for a while. When the woman emerged, she made her way over to Effie.

'You should give it a go, does you the world of good.' She was glistening with seawater but it was the exhilaration that shone in her eyes that captured Effie. She wanted to know what that feeling was like.

'There's a swim club,' the woman told her as she rubbed herself dry with a towel. 'Join us. Thursday mornings.'

'I might.' Effie found herself smiling. She loved to swim. Being held by water had always been her sanctuary. The sea had been the thing she'd missed most about being landlocked in London. The swimming pool had been a poor substitute.

'Here, have a flyer,' the woman pulled one from her bag and shoved it into Effie's hand.

The kindness brought a tear to Effie's eye. She made her excuses and, turning away, made her way along the promenade. Every step she took centred her. She crossed the road and headed back through the town towards home. As she walked, she trailed her eyes over shop windows, searching for vacancies. There was nothing until she came to Books by the Sea, her favourite childhood shop. Happy memories of choosing books to spend her birthday money on assailed her. As she went to push open the door, her eyes caught a small notice stuck in the window.

Shop assistant needed. Full time. Apply within.

The possibility of those seven words settled on Effie, restoring her faith that coming home to Cornwall was the best path she could have chosen. Who needed gap years or inflated family promotions when there was the possibility of selling books by the sea?

Chapter One

Eight years later

Effie paused, hand raised, ready to knock. For the millionth time she wondered why she'd received a summons to the office of Clive Trevellyn, owner of Books by the Sea. First thing on a dreary March Monday morning too. Stifling a yawn, having tossed and turned the previous night, her mind whirred as she tried to figure out what she had done wrong, sure she was going to get the sack, then panicking about what she'd do next. Effie loved her job in the bookshop. Books were everything to her. She didn't think she'd be above begging or bargaining to be kept on. Knowing there was only one way to find out, Effie knocked. A bit too timidly at first, before applying a bit more force.

'Come in!' Clive called.

Effie pushed open the door and slipped inside, tugging her rainbow knit cardigan around her like a comfort blanket. 'You asked to see me.'

Momentarily confused, Clive shuffled some papers. 'Er, yes, I did. Sit down.' He pushed the spare chair across to Effie, and she balanced expectantly on the edge of it. Clive fiddled with his tie. 'The thing is, well . . . do you want a cup of tea or anything?'

Effie shook her head, her stomach clenched. Whatever this was, she wanted it over with as quickly as possible.

'Right.' Clive rubbed his bald head. 'The thing is, I've been thinking of expanding for a while. Opening another shop,' he explained when Effie still looked at him blankly.

Wishing she'd said yes to that cup of tea, just for something comforting to wrap her hands around, Effie asked, 'A new shop?'

'I'd like you to run it,' Clive put simply, 'you're our longest serving member of staff, the customers love your window displays, you have experience. You love books more than the rest of us put together. I also trust you to get it up and running and make a success of it. What do you think? Your own shop, Effie. Well, technically it'd be my shop, but .. .' He shrugged.

Effie stared at Clive in disbelief as her brain sorted through what he'd just offered her. A chance to run a bookshop. Something she'd been dreaming about since she'd been a child lining her picture books up on her windowsill and selling them to her dolls. 'I don't know what to say.' Effie blinked back the tears. 'I was expecting to be sacked.'

'Don't cry! Sacked? Never. We'd be lost without you.' He pushed a box of tissues towards her. 'You are interested, yes? I've not got this hideously wrong, have I? You're well overdue a promotion and I think you'd be perfect to head up the new shop. You know what customers want, you work hard, you've always impressed me. Here, have a look.' He gathered up some paperwork and held it out to her.

Effie took the paperwork he passed her and flicked through the extremely flattering description of what appeared to be a dark, forgotten shop on Polcarrow seafront. It had potential, she guessed, and the sea view was to die for. She'd been to Polcarrow once as a child with her parents. It was tiny, some would even say forgotten. Was there a thriving literary community there that she knew nothing about? 'Why Polcarrow?'

'It's up and coming,' Clive explained. 'It was featured in *Cornish Life* last year and I wanted to get in there, open up a branch before anyone else nabbed the shop. It's perfect for another location of Books by the Sea, look at that view!' He tapped the paper Effie was holding.

'The sea view from the window is gorgeous,' she admitted, 'but it's a long way to travel every day.' She wasn't sure her little blue Corsa would be up to daily bounces along the narrow Cornish lanes and she wasn't the most confident of drivers.

'Ah, that. There's a flat too,' Clive explained, reaching across and flicking through the sheets until he came to the photos, 'you can stay there whilst getting the shop up and running. They come as a package.'

He really had thought of everything to make it an offer she couldn't refuse. Effie looked through the papers, the layout of the shop, the photographs of the cute pastel-coloured cottages on the harbour and swallowed. It would mean moving out of her parents' cosy fisherman's cottage, the only place she'd ever felt at home. Yes, she'd been promising herself every first of January that this would be the year she'd fly the nest . . . but . . . the reality always slipped like cold fingers under her collar. Maybe this was the shove she needed.

Effie gave the papers another flick through. It was cute. She'd be close enough to the sea to swim every day. She'd be master of her own shop, she'd be able to display whatever she wished, she'd be able to connect with a whole new host of readers. Effie exhaled. In her hands lay her big dream, one she'd created numerous Pinterest boards for, but as much as the excitement fluttered in her heart, moving away from everything she knew was still a huge, daunting step to take.

Effie fixed Clive with a curious look. 'Why didn't you offer this to Zach?' Zach was his wayward son, who flittered in and out of the shop when the whim took him, always acting like he owned the place, when he never lifted a finger.

'Erm, because I, erm, needed someone I could trust,' Clive managed, 'we both know Zach isn't the hardest worker. Anyway, he's wrapped up in some surf school thing at the moment. Zoey has the kids and Maddie is great but she doesn't have the same drive and ambition as you.'

Effie smiled – she always thought she was the complete opposite of ambition. She liked the safe quietness of her little routines. The temptation to just accept the job was strong but knew she had to consider the offer properly, lest she let herself get caught up with more than she could handle. Effie stood up and asked, 'Can I think about it?' She held the papers out to him.

Clive brushed them away. 'Keep them. Look over them. Of course you can think about it. I know I've dropped a huge surprise on you, but I know you'd be great at it.'

'When do you need an answer?'

'Friday. Come and see me Friday, half nine, and let me know. But, Effie, I really think you should do this, that it'll be good for you. Please think seriously about it. I've taken my time carefully considering this next step and I wouldn't be pursuing it if I didn't think it'd be a success.'

'Of course.'

'But can I ask you not to tell the other girls yet?'

Effie nodded and made her way out into the small corridor that separated Clive's cramped office from their break room. Closing her eyes, Effie took some deep, steadying breaths. A little shop, its door open to the harbour, the sound of the sea swishing, sunlight and stacks of novels, it was better than any vision board she'd cobbled together. She headed into the break room and, folding the papers in half, tucked them into her bag.

The sound of chattering from the shop brought her back to the present. As she stuffed her bag back into her locker, a wave of guilt washed over her. She usually discussed everything with Maddie, but although she meant well, she could be a bit nosey. Effie didn't want anyone else's input to influence her decision, knowing if this was her new door in life to open, she had to be the one to decide if she should step through. Anyway, Clive had asked her not to mention it to the others, so Effie squared her shoulders and headed into the main shop to check if anyone else wanted a cup of tea, since she regretted turning down Clive's offer.

Chapter Two

Effie pushed open the garden gate and whispered hello to the two garden gnomes that stood guard. They'd been there for as long as she could remember, her dad giving them a yearly makeover as the weather faded them. Effie had started to say hello and goodbye to them as a child and the habit had stuck well into adulthood.

Closing the gate behind her, Effie made her way up the garden path, which in a few weeks would be lined with bright yellow daffodils. She paused on the doorstep to take in the garden. Other than some bright bursts of pansies, it was still slumbering from winter. In a few weeks, as well as the daffodils, tulips would be bobbing their heads and then the roses would begin to bloom. If she left, Effie would miss everything springing back to life.

Pulling her key out of her pocket, she shook her head. If she took Clive's new role she'd only be in Polcarrow, it wouldn't be like moving away to university, to London, leaving everything familiar behind only to have her big city hopes and dreams shattered. She'd spent the day wafting around the bookshop in a daze, imagining herself in the tiny Polcarrow shop, the sunlight streaming in through the big bay window, the walls a rainbow of colourful spines.

After the disappointment that had been London, Effie hadn't considered moving away again, but at least she would still be in Cornwall, and after all, despite all her savings, it wasn't as if she had enough money to open her own independent bookshop. This really was the next best thing.

Effie unlocked the door and let herself in. The cosy comfort of her parental home was a warm, familiar embrace. Closing her eyes, Effie soaked up the homely atmosphere. The radio was playing rock classics at a gentle volume, fighting with the sound of the evening news on the television. She could hear her parents chattering away in the kitchen, from where a delicious aroma wafted. What would it be like to leave this behind?

Rosemary, Effie's mum, stuck her head around the door, her hair wild and her apron stained with tomato sauce. 'Evening, love, almost ready. Lasagne, your favourite.' She blew Effie a kiss before disappearing back into the kitchen. 'Brian, I asked you to make a salad!'

'I'll just go and get changed,' Effie called before heading upstairs to the sanctuary that was her bedroom. Painted pale pink and rammed to the rafters with paperbacks, almost all of them sweeping, swoony historical romances featuring earls or dukes or Vikings. Her desk was strewn with an assortment of notebooks, makeup and a half-finished jumper she was knitting for her dad.

It was purple-striped and currently a tangle of knots and dropped stiches.

Flopping onto her bed, Effie pulled the paperwork Clive had given her from her bag, and let out a squeal of delight. Her own shop! Well, not her own exactly. She could hardly believe it was happening, almost daren't. Maybe she should've accepted on the spot? What if Clive also went away and had second thoughts? Effie sat up, the terror that gripped her at that thought was proof enough that there was only one decision she could make. Propping herself up on her elbows, she surveyed her cosy little bedroom, her childhood playroom, her teenage haven turned grown-up sanctuary.

Would she be packing all this up to take with her? Or just the essentials whilst she got settled in? She should've asked more questions but she'd been completely stunned by Clive's proposal.

Effie glanced around her. Her life in this room was comfortable, well worn in. The faux sheepskin rug on the carpet that covered up a nail-polish stain, the shelf where all her childhood teddies sat watching over her, the dip in her mattress that held her whilst she slept. What would it be like to sleep somewhere different?

Although she'd considered leaving home, it had always been a sort of abstract dream, something she could casually make her way towards. Yes, there had been a very brief moment of time after university when she'd considered going to Manchester with Brad, but that was something she was embarrassed to look back on now. She'd been diligently saving and had imagined a nice little flat somewhere in Penzance but had never thought of moving as far away as Polcarrow, on the other side of the peninsula. She flicked through the paperwork again, her eyes studying the dated flat, but it looked habitable, and she could easily transform it into a home from home.

After kicking off her shoes, Effie changed out of her work clothes, which were nothing more glamorous than a pair of dungarees, her favourite rainbow knit cardigan and a floral shirt and into a comfy pair of flannel pyjamas, perfect for lounging around after dinner. Home had always been her sanctuary, somewhere she could safely remove all the layers she donned when she went out into the world. She had always been a quiet homebody, content to curl up on a sunny windowsill with a book. One dip of her toe into reality had been quite enough.

She placed the papers Clive had given her on her desk and jotted down a couple of questions to follow up with. Would this be temporary? A trial run? Or would she be expected to settle there, run the shop forever? A permanent move would be big, but when she looked up the distance between Penzance and Polcarrow, she realised it wasn't as far as she'd feared. Maybe not commutable, but easy visiting distance.

Once she'd freshened up, Effie made her way downstairs, pushed open the door and stepped into the homely kitchen-diner. The yellow walls were decorated with an eclectic mix of artwork and ceramics her parents had picked up over the past forty years. Effie loved listening to her dad, Brian, recount the stories of where various pots had come from. Morocco, the Greek islands, a flea market in Paris. He'd been a roadie for a minor rock band back in the eighties and Effie had inherited his love of a rambling guitar solo. He'd traded in black leather and wild nights for heading up the local arts centre.

'Come here, darling,' he said, spotting her. He pulled her into a hug. 'Good day at work?'

Effie snuggled into him. 'Yes,' she replied rather hesitantly, her tongue pricking with nerves at having to disclose her news. What would her parents think of the prospect of her moving out? She almost blurted it all out, but managed to keep the news to herself, wanting to enjoy dreaming about it just a while longer. She'd already mentally decorated the shop on her walk home, freshening up the white walls.

Rosemary plonked an oozing tray of lasagne in the middle of the table, followed by the salad. 'Come on, sit down, don't want it getting cold.'

'No chance of that happening,' Brian laughed, poking the bubbling cheese with a spoon, 'it's bubbling more than a volcano.'

Rosemary pulled the spoon from his hand and began to dish up, serving Effie first. Brian poured red wine into their glasses. He had grand ambitions to become a wine connoisseur, however, had made no secret that he couldn't tell a Shiraz from a Cabernet Sauvignon. Still, Effie lifted the glass, swirled the red liquid, took a sniff, followed by a sip.

'What do you think?' Brian asked, showing her the bottle. Chianti.

Effie took another sip. 'It's like . . . wine.' She wasn't doing any better on the taste testing either.

Laugher erupted. 'I think this is lost on us,' said Rosemary, taking a sip, 'tasty though.'

As they ate, they swapped stories about their days. Rosemary, a community nurse, running through how her regular patients were getting on, Brian nodding whilst trying to decipher more of the wine flavours before updating them on the latest youth project he was trying to get funding for. On the edge of her seat, Effie waited to share her news, happy to hold back whilst her parents discussed their days.

'Anyone want any more?' Rosemary indicated the lasagne that was left.

Brian sat back, patted his stomach. 'I'm stuffed.'

'Effie?'

'I'm stuffed too.'

Rosemary shrugged and sliced off a tiny sliver. 'We can have the rest tomorrow. I take it no one has any room for dessert?'

'Oh, there's always room for ice cream!' Effie grinned. They'd finished every meal with ice cream for as long as she could remember. In the summer they usually took a stroll out along the seafront, trying different flavours from the ice cream parlour. Effie liked the ones made with clotted cream, bursting with berries. Ice cream sampling had always been more successful than wine tasting.

Rosemary rolled her eyes and Brian began to clear the table. He returned with three bowls, the scoop and a tub of raspberry ripple – Effie's childhood favourite.

Once the ice cream had been eaten Effie pushed her bowl away and took a breath.

'Are you all right love?' Brian asked. 'You've been very quiet, usually you're full of bookshop chatter.'

Clenching her fists together, Effie glanced between her parents, a smile spreading across her face. 'I have some news. Clive is opening a new shop in Polcarrow and he wants me to set it up and run it.'

'Oh, love, that's marvellous!' Rosemary beamed. 'You're long overdue a promotion.'

'Polcarrow! I remember it, tiny place,' Brian said, 'the seagull stole your sausage roll right out of your hand. Isn't it a bit far? I mean, it's doable, but driving there and back every day. Are you happy with that?' They all knew Effie was an anxious driver.

'There's a flat above the shop. Clive said it comes with the lease and I could live there,' Effie explained, feeling a bit like she was talking about someone else's life.

Rosemary sat back down. 'You'd be moving out?'

Effie nodded with more assurance than she felt.

Rosemary and Brian exchanged glances, swapping a multitude of questions and emotions in a single glance. 'How do you feel about this?' Brian asked. 'Truthfully.'

'I, erm, I don't know,' Effie admitted, which was the truth. 'Clive sprung it on me. It was a bit of a surprise. But it will be like my own bookshop! You know how

I've always dreamed of owning my own shop and this is the next best thing. I've already got lots of plans for it.'

'Oh my love, that is so exciting.' Rosemary bustled around the table and bundled Effie into a hug.

Brian nodded. 'It's a fantastic opportunity. Look, Effie, you're almost thirty years old, we love having you here and you can stay here forever if you wish, but aren't you curious about what lies over the horizon?'

'Maybe a little bit,' Effie admitted, 'but you know I didn't enjoy moving away to university.'

'That was London. This is Polcarrow. It's thirty-five minutes away. The worst that could happen is that seagull comes back for a second bite of sausage roll,' Brian pointed out gently. 'Clive must think highly of you to trust you with this. You're long overdue a promotion too. You work so hard there.'

'You could come home any time, and we could come and visit you,' Rosemary reminded her before glancing at her husband. 'We've been thinking that maybe it's time you spread your wings a little more.'

Effie shot a look between her parents. 'You want me to leave?'

'No, love, don't be silly, we love you being here, us a cosy little three, but we've both seen so much of the world, it'd be a shame if you didn't even explore it a bit,' Rosemary pushed gently.

Effie nodded. 'I told Clive I'd think about it. He's given me until Friday. I didn't want to leap right in without properly considering it first.'

'Whatever you decide to do, Effie love, we'll support you,' Brian said, taking her hand and giving it a squeeze.

'Thanks, Dad.' She squeezed his hand back. 'But I think we all know what my decision will be,' she said, beaming happily at them both, the possibility of her future unfurling inside her.

Chapter Three

Effie had always been drawn to the sea, pulled by its power as if she too was part of the tide. All her teenage angst and woes had been worked through whilst wading through the shallows, the waves rippling over her toes, but she'd never quite dared to venture in above her knees. The sea was powerful, and like a lot of things, Effie was afraid of that power. As she'd grown older, she'd come to respect the sea, accepting it as a part of her Cornish roots, and now it was as much part of her as it was the landscape.

She'd started sea swimming after she'd come home from London. The city had clung to her skin, got under her nails, dulled her shine. The only way she knew to cleanse herself was to go, full body, into the sea. Effie still recalled the first wince as the cold water closed in around her, how on the count of three she'd submerged herself, leaving only her head above the surface, teeth chattering, gasping for breath, but feeling more alive than she'd ever felt before. Effie always felt a little mad to say the sea had purified her, but she truly believed it had.

However, that Friday morning she didn't have time for a dip before work. Instead, she stood on the promenade, takeaway tea in her hand, half a nibbled almond croissant in her pocket, staring out to sea. She breathed in and out with the tide, her gaze focused on St Michael's Mount further round the bay, and allowed the ebb and flow of the waves to soothe her.

It had been quite an emotionally stressful week as she'd considered Clive's offer, turning it over and over like sea glass in the sunshine, looking for imperfections, checking out its beauty. It had been difficult to keep the proposition from her colleagues and guilt over hiding such a large secret had niggled at her. Effie knew she had her parents' blessing, and it was their unwavering support that had helped her make her decision. Effie now held that response in her heart, all she needed to do was to gather up the courage and share it with Clive.

After crumbling the remaining half of her croissant for the circling gulls, despite knowing full well they shouldn't be encouraged to scavenge, Effie tossed her empty cup in the bin and made her way across the road and around the corner towards Books by the Sea, which was tucked just away from the seafront in the main shopping street.

Pausing briefly outside, Effie took in the dark blue sign, the window display she'd spent an afternoon setting up with Zoey, filling it with an assortment of children's books for World Book Day. They'd had a lot of fun dressing up as their favourite characters, Effie having chosen

Alice in Wonderland, and greeting the children as they came in to choose books with their vouchers.

Eight years she'd been here, unpacking boxes, filling shelves, listening to customers and holidaymakers share their stories. Monday morning coffee and pastries with Maddie and Zoey, the occasional quiz night and after-work drinks. A whole community bundled into one small shop. A life and contentment an eighteen-year-old Effie had thought she'd only find if she spread her wings.

And now? Well, there was only one thing for it. Time to seize her destiny. Pushing open the door, she stepped into the shop with its well-worn shelves filled on one side with brightly coloured new paperbacks and on the other, crammed with tattered, well-loved second-hand books. Effie breathed in the aroma of old paper and furniture polish, followed the light filtering through the window towards the counter, which was stacked with postcards, notebooks and pens. She'd loved visiting the shop as a child, had enjoyed getting lost within its eclectic collections. She still had her first ever Jane Austen that she'd picked off one of the shelves as a teenager, so finding a job here had been a dream come true.

'Good morning,' she greeted Zoey who was setting up the till for the day's trade, before making her way through to the little storeroom that doubled up as a closet and break room. Effie hung up her coat, put her bag in her locker, then, smoothing down her mermaid braid, clenched her fists and made her way down to Clive's office. This time she knocked firmly.

'Come in!'

Effie pushed the door open, stepped inside with more confidence than she'd had on Monday, and closed it. She didn't sit down, instead she stood, her back to the door.

'Effie! How are you? Have you thought any more about my offer?'

Effie nodded. 'Yes, yes I have.'

'And?' His face was hopeful.

'I have a question. Is this temporary or will I be there running the shop permanently?'

'I've taken the lease on for a year, so we can see how it goes, no pressure, but your future there will be based on the shop's success and since you're such a hard worker, I don't have any fears that we'll be closing after a year. So it'll be a year in the first instance. That's why I want you at the helm, to give it it's best chance. Of course, if things go awry, we'll all have to reconsider, but I'm confident that won't happen.'

Satisfied with his response, Effie continued, 'Will I be running it alone? What about breaks and holidays and things?'

Clive swallowed. 'Well, as I said, to begin with, setting it up, you'll be doing it alone. Just do what you need to, shut for half an hour. When it gets to high season we can employ someone in the holidays to help out and stuff. How does that sound?'

It was a vague answer but the excitement of opening the shop overruled any sensibilities over running logistics. Effie bit her lip, counted to ten and said, 'I accept. I'd be delighted to run the Polcarrow shop, it's too close to my own dream to turn down.' A joyful smile spread across her face, a smile Effie felt right to the core of her being. She knew she'd made the right choice. Her future glittered before her and rather than being anxious, Effie found that she was excited and hopeful.

'So, what's all this for?' Maddie narrowed her eyes at the tray of doughnuts Clive was hovering behind in the staffroom Friday lunchtime.

Jigging on the spot, Clive ignored her, instead asking, 'Is everyone here?'

Effie wanted to shrink into herself as Maddie performed a head count.

'Me, Zoey and Effie, so yes, unless you're expecting someone else?'

Clive checked his watch. 'Only Zach.'

Effie and Maddie exchanged a glance. Zach had been a thorn in Effie's side whenever he decided to grace the shop with his glowering presence. Thankfully, he was rarely present, only dipping in and out in-between travelling or pursuing his next mad scheme. Maddie just thought he was a spoiled brat, living off his dad's hard-earned money and that was why he was rude, but Effie knew differently.

'What's up?' Zach asked, as he stepped into the room, taking up all the remaining space. He ran a hand through his hair, the stubble on his face more from laziness than style as he cast his eyes around the room, narrowing them at Effie.

She tried not to squirm under his scrutiny, but it was difficult, they had history she'd rather forget. They'd been at school together. He'd been the popular head of the football team, all the girls had swarmed around him, but still, he hadn't been able to leave Effie alone. It was like her indifference challenged him. He'd enjoyed taunting her quiet bookish ways, but even though his cruel jibes had cut deeply, she'd never allowed him to see how much he'd affected her.

She hadn't known he was Clive's son until she'd been working at the shop a few months and Zach had waltzed in like he owned the place, destroying a display Effie had spent hours working on. Her heart had jumped at the sight of her teenage adversary but once again, she refused to let on that he was getting to her. The sly looks, the undermining of her efforts, were all tiresome, at least going to Polcarrow, she'd be out of his way. Effie just feared that her promotion would unleash a new level of torment.

Effie reached for a pink glazed doughnut and nibbled nervously, avoiding catching Maddie's eye. Maddie had been trying all week to wheedle out of Effie why she'd been in Clive's office on Monday morning. Effie was exhausted with the constant dodging of questions. Lying wasn't in her nature, and she'd started to run out of excuses.

'Right, OK.' Clive clapped his hands together. 'You've all got a doughnut? Good.' He offered the box to Zach, who shook his head.

Maddie rolled her eyes at Effie, who buried her face in her cup of tea. Why on earth was Clive so nervous?

He wasn't the one moving across the county to open a new shop.

'Anyway, the reason I've gathered you all here is that I'm expanding the business. A property has come up for rent in Polcarrow and I've taken on the lease. As the longest reigning member of staff, I've asked Effie to go over and set the shop up. Effie has such a good vision when it comes to this shop, so she's perfect for setting up a new one. I'm excited to see what she has in store. So, if we could all raise our, erm, cups.' Clive lifted his branded Books by the Sea mug.

Maddie and Zoey followed suit, chinking their mugs against Effie's, both looking as baffled as they had when they'd come into the staffroom.

'Sorry I didn't discuss this with you all, but I wasn't sure if I'd get the lease and I didn't want to get everyone's hopes up. I considered asking all of you, but Effie has the least commitments,' he explained awkwardly.

'No hard feelings, Clive,' Zoey reassured him as she helped herself to another doughnut. 'Although sometimes I'd love to get away from my two, Effie is your best bet.' Zoey worked part-time in the shop whilst her two children, Isaac and Caitlin, were at school. She regularly claimed she came to work for a rest and a hot cup of coffee.

Relieved that Zoey and Maddie hadn't caused an uproar over her promotion, Effie watched as Clive let out a sigh of relief and asked if anyone had any questions. Everyone shook their heads.

Effie caught Zach's eye. He looked as if the wind had been knocked out of him. 'Dad, what . . . How is this fair? I thought—'

'We'll discuss this in private.' Clive threw him a look before turning back to the others. 'There's plenty more doughnuts, please eat up.' Clive beat a hasty retreat, Zach hot on his heels.

The three women exchanged glances as the staffroom door slammed behind Zach.

Maddie, mouth full of doughnut, turned to Effie and mumbled, 'Pub, later. Looks like you have a lot to fill me in on and we have some celebrating to do!'

Grinning, Effie nodded. 'We certainly do.'

'So, spill the beans,' Maddie demanded as she plonked Effie's pint of cider in front of her, followed by a bag of cheese and onion crisps.

They were in their favourite pub, all old beams, rickety floors and crammed to the rafters with seafaring memorabilia. Effie liked to imagine smugglers gathering in the darker corners. Being so old and warped, the pub had its obligatory ghost stories, although Effie had never had even the slightest spooky experience.

Effie took a fortifying, delaying sip and reached for the crisps, tearing into them as she sorted out what she was going to say to her friend and colleague. Maddie's direct, no-nonsense manner made Effie feel as if she was constantly having to defend herself. They'd become great friends in the four years they'd worked together, bonding over a love of historical fiction and post-work Friday night pints. As Effie realised she would miss her and their little rituals, a cold sense of dread crept down her spine. She had made the right decision, hadn't she? The locals would be friendly, wouldn't they?

Effie opened her mouth but Maddie interrupted with, 'And I want to know what actually happened. Were you expecting this? We had no idea Clive was thinking of opening another shop.' Maddie sat back and took a sip of her red wine, a suspicious look in her eye.

'I had no idea either until he called me into his office on Monday morning.' Effie explained what had happened during their discussion. 'You know I've always wanted my own bookshop and this feels as close to that dream as possible. Look—' she pulled her phone out and showed Maddie photos she'd googled of Polcarrow '—isn't it adorable?'

Maddie flicked through them. 'Totally.'

'You're not upset I was offered the job instead of you, are you?'

Maddie shook her head. 'No, well, maybe a tiny bit, but I can't really up sticks and move like you can, anyway, I just want to come in, shelve some books, chat to some customers and go home. It's always been more a calling than a job with you, Effie. Clive made the right decision.'

Effie gave her friend a squeeze. 'Thank you. I'll miss you though. It might be a bit lonely by myself.'

'Imagine if there's a hot surfer dude or something,' Maddie said.

Effie pulled a face. 'Not really my type.'

'Hmm, really? Why do you think Clive didn't get Zach to set the new shop up?'

Relieved that Maddie wasn't going to interrogate her on her lack of a love life, Effie shrugged. 'No idea. I mean, he's not exactly got the drive to set up and run a business. He's never here! And whenever he starts something, he's always coming back for his dad to bail him out. I'm clearly the safer pair of hands.'

Maddie nodded and gave her a long look. 'It all seems so sudden though. You've always said you'd never move away again. I know Polcarrow isn't far . . . but . . .'

'I decided it was worth a try,' Effie explained. 'I'm almost thirty. I can't live at home forever. And since I can't actually afford to get a place of my own, the flat coming with the shop is a nice bonus. The more I thought about it, the more I started to look up tiny bookshops online, the more excited I got and the less likely I was going to turn the opportunity down. My own bookshop, Maddie, or at least I can pretend it's my own. I've already thought about how I'll decorate it.' This was at least true and had helped sway Effie's decision making. 'White with lots of bright colours. Maybe some nice chairs, or some rugs, yes, definitely some rugs. I saw these gorgeous floral curtains—' She knew she was gabbling nervously.

'Curtains aside, how do you really feel to have your big dream placed right in front of you?' Maddie cut in through Effie's bluster.

Effie met her eyes and her resolve crumbled. 'Curtains aside, a bit scared. Way out of my comfort zone. Not just the flat. Setting up the shop. I've never actually decorated anything before. Clive said I can have free rein, as long as I don't go wild.' She laughed. 'Me, wild?! But it's only half an hour away. It'll be fine, honestly. You'll have to come and visit. Please say you'll visit, I won't know anyone and I'll miss this.' She raised her glass.

'Of course I'll come and visit you! You won't be able to keep me away!'

Chapter Four

'Are you ready, love?' Brian called up the stairs.

Effie's dad had been waiting patiently by the front door for the past fifteen minutes whilst she ran up and down the stairs, faffed around checking, then rechecking her bags. She could hear him singing to himself as she frantically ran her eyes over her bookshelves. A bag of books rested at her feet, packed slightly haphazardly as she'd squeezed in her favourites next to a stack of unread titles. Did she have enough books to last her? It seemed ironic packing books when she was going to open a bookshop, but Books by the Sea didn't sell the sort of bodice-ripping books Effie devoured.

Of course, she'd read every Cornish-based romance to ever grace its shelves, took it as one of her duties, so that she was ever ready to recommend a new swooning love story to a holidaymaker, or local, looking for an extra spark in their life. Effie knew it was slightly over-dramatic to say so, but romance novels had practically saved her life when she'd been overwhelmed and lost by the vastness and unfriendliness of her university years.

At the time her student loan hadn't stretched to being able to purchase her own books, so Effie had wandered into the local library, signed up for membership and proceeded to work her way through the racks of bodice rippers at such an alarming rate that she'd struck up a friendship with Edna, the librarian, who happily stamped the books she took out and asked her all sorts of questions when she returned them. Edna, it turned out, was a prolific romance reader herself, but had no one to share her joy with until Effie stumbled up to the desk, arms full of books. Edna had taken one look at all the dukes and shook her head.

'The Vikings are sexier,' she'd said as she checked them out.

That was how Effie discovered Vikings. Yes, they were much, much sexier. She couldn't get enough of them – powerfully swooping in with their long hair and icy eyes, rugged and broodingly handsome. Why couldn't someone like that ever turn up in Effie's life?

Reaching onto her bookshelf, Effie grabbed another book, despite having her e-reader tucked into her backpack. A Kindle that she'd once calculated had over four years' worth of reading on it. Well, better safe than sorry. Like most bookworms, she preferred a paperback, the smell of the ink, the feel of the pages in her hands. She adored second-hand books, their covers and spines scarred by previous readers, the pages yellowed with age, the smell of other people's lives lingering between them. Her e-reader, however, had got her out of a tricky book-free situation on many occasions and was easier to carry around. Plus, Effie really had no idea how much space there'd be in the flat, as the photos had been rather small.

'Effie?' her mum called. 'You're only going half an hour away, we can bring anything you've left next weekend.'

'OK! Coming.' Effie shrugged her backpack on, picked up the bag of books in one hand and her bag of knitting in the other and made her way downstairs. Seeing her parents lingering by the doorway brought a lump to her throat. It was far too reminiscent of when she'd headed off to university. She'd been bouncing joyfully, her eighteen-year-old head full of excitement at what experiences awaited her. Hours of studying, her mind being challenged, her thoughts encouraged, groups of friends to drink red wine with into the early hours, someone she'd fall head over heels in love with; they'd be inseparable, and everyone would marvel at how deep and true their romance was.

None of it had materialised. All that she'd got from her three years in London was a mountain of debt, a bruised heart and an aversion to jacket potatoes with baked beans, this having been one of the only meals she could afford to cook regularly. Even her degree result had been middling.

London had knocked her, so much, that she'd returned to Penzance in a completely different shape, the shine rubbed off, her spark missing. Slowly, she'd rebuilt herself, but all her friends who'd stayed behind, or studied more locally, didn't want to hear the truth about Effie's grand adventure. After extolling how amazing her life was going to be, when she returned, tail between her legs, Effie had been reluctant to tell them the truth. She'd rather just forget London ever happened.

'Come here, love.' Rosemary held her arms out. Effie put her bags down and allowed her mum to pull her in tightly. 'I'm very proud of you for taking this opportunity, I really am. I think it'll be good for you.'

'Thanks, Mum,' Effie mumbled into her shoulder, biting her lip to stop the tears coming. *It's only thirty minutes' journey*, she reminded herself. At least technology and social media had moved on since she was at university.

'Dad's just packing up the car. I'd come with you, but I'm not sure there's space.'

'No, it's fine, really. I'll be fine,' Effie promised her, her voice surer than she felt.

'All ready?' Brian stuck his head round the door. 'shall I take them?' He nodded at the extra bags Effie had brought down.

Effie followed him out, watching as he squeezed the bags onto the back seat. The boot was full of new bedding, a selection of Effie's clothes and some food to keep her going. A frisson of excitement fizzed through her as she thought of making the flat homely and opening up her own shop by the sea. Effie's excitement at the task ahead of her managed to smother any fears she had about starting a new life. Her emotions had been all over the place as she'd packed her belongings and made plans to move. Surely Polcarrow would be far friendlier than London had been.

Effie took one last glance at the house, her mum standing in the doorway, cardigan pulled tightly, her hair long and wild, whereas Effie tamed hers into a French braid, before slipping into the passenger seat and flashing her dad a smile. They'd regularly gone on road trips when she'd been younger and her mum had had to work. Fishing trips, scrambling over ruins, paddling in the sea followed by ice creams.

'Ready?' he asked as she started the car.

Effie nodded. 'Yes.' As she said it, she realised she meant it.

Chapter Five

As they turned off the main road into the narrower streets of Polcarrow, Effie turned the music down.

'That used to be your favourite,' Brian said, puzzled, as Led Zepplin's 'Whole Lotta Love' receded from thumping anthem into background music.

'It still is, but I'm not sure how much the residents of Polcarrow will appreciate it,' Effie replied, secretly hoping they could just slip into the flat unnoticed by the neighbours. She didn't want to draw too much attention to herself just yet. What if the locals weren't the welcoming kind?

Wide eyed, Effie took in the charming traditional, whitewashed fisherman's cottages, which almost tumbled down the narrow streets towards the sea. Hanging baskets swung in the breeze, waiting to be filled with spring blooms. Front doors were painted cheerful, primary colours and the tiny gardens were filled with an assortment of miniature palm trees, fishing buoys and weathered benches. The closeness of the buildings gave Effie an image of a community that was nestled all together. How would she fit in?

As they wound their way down the sloping streets towards the harbour, Effie caught tantalising glimpses of the sea glinting like a mirror through the gaps in the houses. The church tower stood proud like a beacon, its clock ticking away the quiet afternoon. There was a sense of slowness to the village, of a place tucked away from the modern world. Effie saw very few people. Was Clive mad having a go at opening a bookshop somewhere so tiny, so off the beaten track?

However, she couldn't deny that the village was delightful, and Effie couldn't help but fall in love at first sight. It was everything anyone would imagine a Cornish fishing village to be, like somewhere straight from a romance novel. In her mind, she cast herself as the heroine forced to flee her staid city life, running headlong towards the sea in search of romance and adventure. She'd devoured numerous books filled with these stories and never grew tired of them.

Once they'd passed the church, Brian turned the car onto the harbour road, slowing down as they passed a row of ice-cream-coloured fisherman's cottages. Pink, yellow, blue, white and green. Effie instantly fell in love with the pale pink one, it was perfect for a romance lover. She imagined living there, transforming the house into a perfect refuge from the world, filling it with brightly coloured furnishings and rows of bookshelves. With her scant budget, Effie knew that dream would have to remain firmly tucked inside her heart.

They trundled along the seafront, the satnav taking them towards an adorable looking vintage-style café, which was sadly closed for the day. 'Lola's' read the sign above the door. Effie couldn't wait to try it. She was pleased when they pulled to a stop at the building next door where a shiny red sports car was parked at an obnoxious angle.

Pushing open the car door, Effie stepped out. Hands on hips, she surveyed the quaint harbour, excitement flickering in her belly that she was going to be living so close to the sea, in a cute Cornish village. A smile spread across her face. People dreamed of this. Crossing the road, Effie peered down onto the beach. The sea was out, and a young couple was walking a dog along the shallows whilst some children played football. There was something untouched about Polcarrow, which reassured her.

'Excuse me.' A voice broke into her reverie.

Effie turned around to see that a smart-suited young man had emerged from the red car. 'Yes?' She crossed back over the road towards him.

'Are you Effie Lovell?'

Taken aback that he knew her name, she stammered, 'Yes, who are you?'

'Greg Davey, estate agent, here to give you the keys. Was expecting you twenty minutes ago, I nearly drove off.' He gave a shallow laugh and made a big show of checking his chunky, designer watch.

Effie narrowed her eyes at him. 'We got held up,' was all she said.

Greg glanced from her to Brian. 'Right, well, shall I give you the keys and let you in? Follow me.'

Effie and Brian exchanged a look before following him around the back of the property, only half listening as Greg explained that the stairs were private, only she'd be using them, and they only led up to the flat. Effie studied the nondescript white door as Greg fumbled with the keys. It was plastic, so she wouldn't be able to paint it in a more exciting colour.

Greg eventually found the right key to unlock the flat, pushing open the door and going, 'Ta-da,' like he was some sort of magician.

Brian rolled his eyes as he signalled for Effie to go inside. Glancing between the two men, she took a breath. This was it, the start of her new life. She stepped over the threshold and glanced around. Her earlier excitement fizzled. Effie didn't know what she'd been expecting but the photos she'd seen in Clive's paperwork had clearly been taken at a complimentary angle. They had implied a beautiful flat, neatly finished and flooded with sunlight.

What she found was . . . fine. Serviceable, unloved. Effie swallowed back her disappointment as she took it in. Blank white walls, still bearing the shadows of the paintings that had been up previously. A tired-looking red sofa was pushed against the wall in front of the window. Effie went over to it. When she knelt on it to push the window open, the springs creaked in protest. At least the sea view was a bonus.

From her position on the sofa, she glanced around the living space, taking it all in. A tiny, dated kitchen, a table with two mismatched chairs, an empty plastic fruit bowl. It was OK. It would have to be. Reminding herself that Clive was footing the bill, she bit her tongue against voicing any complaints, not wanting to sound ungrateful.

Hauling herself up, Effie made her way towards the back of the flat. She heard her dad opening and closing cupboards, the impatient sound of Greg tossing his keys and tapping his foot. She pushed open the bedroom door to find a stark white wooden bed frame and matching wardrobe. At least the bed looked brand new, and the mattress was still in its plastic wrapper, but the bookshelf was wonky and the room, like the rest of the flat, looked like it hadn't been cared for in a very long time.

Steeling herself she headed towards the bathroom. It was stark, white and blue, functional, but it needed a really good scrub. As Effie caught her reflection in the mirror, she tried to replace the shocked look with a smile. It wobbled across her lips. This was fine, she told herself, it was far better than she'd ever be able to afford by herself. A sea view was basically gold dust unless you had a small fortune to spend. Plus, she had her cleaning equipment and all her soft furnishings, she'd have it looking homely in no time.

When she emerged from the bathroom she caught her dad's concerned eye. He'd known her long enough to realise her silence was her way of processing her feelings, hiding her disappointment. Greg was loudly chewing gum and tapping away at his phone, clearly desperate to get away. Part of her couldn't blame him.

'And the shop?' Effie asked hopefully.

Greg glanced up. 'Oh, it's the red fob. I'd show you in but, you know, you were late and I have places to go, people to see.'

Brian threw him a withering look. Effie actually couldn't wait to have him out of her sight. Crossing over to him, she held out her hand for the keys.

'All OK?' he asked but was obviously hoping she wasn't going to raise any concerns.

Tight lipped, Effie nodded. 'What was the shop before?'

He shrugged and reached for his notes. 'Oh, it's been all sorts. A souvenir shop mostly. Buckets and spades, you know. Anything else?' he asked. Effie shook her head. 'Right, I'll leave you to it,' he said and without a backward glance, retreated down the stairs.

Once he'd gone, Brian turned to Effie. 'Are you sure this is OK?'

She nodded and replied rather too brightly, 'Of course! A bit of a clean and once I have my own things in here it'll be perfect.'

Brian didn't look convinced. 'Shall we go and look at the shop?'

Part of Effie wanted to put it off until the morning, but she knew that if it was in as bad condition as the flat, she'd appreciate having her dad there for moral support.

They traipsed back downstairs. The flaking red door they stood in front of did not inspire confidence. Effie exchanged a concerned look with her dad before unlocking the premises. The bell chimed delightfully as she pushed the door open. Effie paused on the threshold, sending up a prayer that the shop had been more loved than the flat. Kicking aside a faded pile of junk mail, she stepped into the small space and glanced around, taking it all in.

A counter was situated at the back with an old till standing on it. The walls boasted floor-to-ceiling shelves, varnished and darkened with age. Effie knew they would need to be updated to fit in with the signature white and blue theme of Books by the Sea. Spinning around she came face to face with the sea view, which must have been the selling point, even if it was obscured behind very dirty windows. Her heart sank. The whole property was stale and slightly grubby, completely different from the photos Clive had. It clearly hadn't been used in a while.

Effie made her way across the dusty floorboards, past the counter and around a box of abandoned till receipts and discovered a small office and kitchen area hidden in a backroom. Two mugs were upturned on the draining board and although there was a kettle and microwave, neither looked safe to use.

Anger momentarily flashed though her. What on earth had Clive been thinking? Had he even viewed the shop? Effie knew he wasn't very practical; the photos had shown a shop that needed some TLC, but this was beyond what she'd been expecting. Getting the bookshop up and running was going to take a lot more than just arranging books on the shelves. It didn't just need a clean, it needed a good scrub and full redecoration.

Effie's face crumbled as she emerged back into the shop.

'Come here, love.' Her dad held his arms out.

'It's awful.' She tried not to sob.

'I wouldn't go that far,' he said diplomatically. 'Yes, it needs a clean and a refresh, but you'll work your charms on it in no time. Ring Clive in the morning and get him to send across some cleaning products, or a cleaner and some new paint. Or even a decorator.'

Effie wiped her eyes. 'Thanks, Dad.' It was reassuring to think she could get someone in to help with the mess. Surely Clive would understand?

'You can do this; I have every faith in you. It'll be all right.'

Effie nodded, glancing around at the tired interior. It was a mess, but she could see the potential rising from the gloom, especially with the sea view. It was a good space. Once the windows were cleaned it would be bright and airy. Wiping away her tears, Effie reasoned there was no point in crying, it wouldn't solve anything. What she needed was a to-do list. She'd call Clive in the morning, double-check that in his haste to expand his literary empire, he hadn't overlooked the state of the property. Effie just hoped that Clive had a brilliant plan up his sleeve to help her transform this tired old shop.

Chapter Six

With a brave face, Effie waved her dad off, having reassured him for the hundredth time that she was going to be fine. As his car disappeared around the corner, Effie sagged against the peeling red shop door and sighed, another job for the never-ending list, she thought, as she peeled off some of the flakes. She pulled the keys out of her pocket and locked the shop. Sorting that out could wait until the morning.

Trudging upstairs to the flat, Effie stood, hands on hips, surveying the mess. Her belongings were piled up in the middle of the living room waiting to be distributed into her new home. But would this slightly sorry-looking flat ever feel like home? she wondered, as she glanced around. Well, there was only one way to find out. Effie pulled her phone out of her pocket, selected her favourite Taylor Swift playlist, rolled up her sleeves and set about giving the flat a thorough clean.

She found an ancient vacuum cleaner stashed in a cupboard full of odds and ends, which wheezed its way across the floor but at least it seemed to make the carpets look slightly better. Effie started in the bedroom, moving from the sad, slightly threadbare grey carpet to the wardrobe and windowsill. The room looked much brighter once she'd cleaned the window, which only had a view of the back of the shop and the café next door.

She quickly moved on to making up her bed, cheered by the brightly coloured floral bedding she'd bought new. Smoothing down the pillows, the excitement of making the flat her own returned. That was the difference between here and her university halls of residence. They'd been tiny, uniform, grey and no matter how much she'd tried to make it look homely with posters, books and cute cushions, her room had always felt like a temporary location for her.

Once all her clothes were hung in the wardrobe, some of her books stacked on the shelves in the corner, she studied the end result. Seeing the empty room transformed into a pretty bedroom made her smile. A little bounce on the bed to test the mattress and she was ready to turn her attention to the bathroom.

At least there was a bath, she consoled herself as she pulled on her rubber gloves and began to spray the surfaces liberally with bathroom cleaner. She loved lounging in the tub, candles flickering, an audiobook on the go. Effie had banned herself from reading paperbacks in the bath after one too many had met a soggy end. Once she'd got the bathroom gleaming, she took pleasure in lining up her lotions and potions and made a note to buy a new shower curtain and some fresh candles.

A wave of tiredness caused her enthusiasm to ebb then. Perched on the edge of the bath, she removed her rubber gloves and pushed her hair out of her face. The notion of leaving the rest of the flat until tomorrow was tempting but with the shop also being uninhabitable, she resolved to get her living space put right that evening. At least then she'd feel like she'd tackled half the problem.

Pausing to make a cup of tea and crack open a packet of custard creams, Effie surveyed the rest of the mess. More bags of books, her knitting supplies and some kitchen equipment. However, opening the cupboards revealed that a few saucepans and a mismatched set of crockery had been left behind. Finishing her tea, Effie wiped out the cupboards and began to stack her collection of novelty mugs and put away the food supplies and equipment she'd brought with her.

With the kitchen gleaming, Effie faced the saggy red sofa, her eyes snagging on the sea view that would make all this work feel worth it. The sun was lowering in the sky and golden rays were streaming into the flat. Effie quickly snapped a photo to post on social media. As the photo uploaded, she resolved to try and make the best out of a situation that was teetering on being very bad. Effie sent the photo to her parents. Rosemary had sent numerous messages checking in on her, fretting, worrying. To reassure her, Effie took photos of her bedroom as proof she was settling in, then turned her attention to making the little living space feel cosy.

Once she'd vacuumed the sofa, turning out a selection of coins and a plastic keyring from its depths, Effie plumped up her cushions and draped her heart print blanket over one of the arms. There wasn't much space for her books, but she did the best she could with the bookshelf in the living room, cramming it tightly. Her knitting, however, would have to remain in the jute bag she'd carried it in. Effie added buying a basket to store her knitting to her mental list.

As the sun began to lower towards the horizon, she took in the transformation. The flat might not be perfect, the paintwork scuffed and faded, but with her belongings filling out the spaces it was transformed. Giving herself a satisfied round of applause, Effie suddenly felt less daunted by the prospect of sorting out the shop. She could do it. All it would take was a little bit of elbow grease and determination.

Flopping down onto the sofa, Effie wasn't sure what to do with herself next. Turning her face towards the window, the evening sun streaming through, she decided to go and have a look around the village. After pulling on her shoes and jacket, Effie stuffed her keys in her pocket and made her way down towards the beach. The tide was slowly coming in, trickling lazily across the glistening sand. Effie inhaled the fresh sea air, obliterating the scent of the cleaning products she'd used. The flat might have needed an overhaul and the shop was practically a disaster zone, but this, this view, the wide horizon, was enough to fill Effie up.

Turning around she took in the sorry-looking exterior of the shop. Clive had been right about one thing, it was in a prime location. The café next to it was all closed up for the night but its folded back awning and sign reading 'Lola's' gave Effie hope. A bookshop and a cute café, it was exactly what readers wanted. But was it enough? Polcarrow was tiny. Effie could take in its entirety with one sweep of her eyes. The church tower, a large art deco house perched at the top of the hill, the pub at the other end of the bay. Would people come here? Could she make it a success?

Making her way off the beach, Effie wandered along the harbour road, past the ice-cream-coloured fisherman's cottages, wondering who was lucky enough to be tucked up in them on a Sunday evening. She made her way up the main street, past the tiny local shop and the chippy to the church. Effie found churches fascinating. She wasn't religious herself, but the fact that the buildings had been the centre of the community for hundreds of years amazed her.

Effie tried the door but it was locked. A vague memory surfaced, an article about a mural, had it been in Polcarrow? Clive had mentioned *Cornish Life* magazine and she seemed to remember her mum talking about it. She ran her fingers over the seashells pressed into the mortar around the door. They almost shimmered in the evening light. She took a photo before making her way out of the churchyard and up the winding streets, passing the cottages they'd driven past, wondering how the locals would feel about a bookshop opening. Would they like it? Who didn't like a bookshop? Would they welcome her? Or see her as an incomer to the village?

Stomach rumbling, Effie made her way back to her flat. *Her flat!* She'd never had somewhere to call her own before. It would all be fine. She'd meet new people, she'd make a success of the shop, everyone would envy the life she'd set up by the sea.

However, that first night, with the flat scrubbed clean, dinner eaten and night descending over the beautiful seascape she'd admired during the golden hour, Polcarrow felt bleak and dark, miles from civilisation. But Effie knew she had two choices: sink or swim.

Chapter Seven

'Did you actually view the shop before you signed the lease?' Effie asked with more annoyance than she'd intended when she called Clive at half past nine the following morning.

'Erm, er . . . Well . . . Of course I did!' he spluttered before deflecting. 'The location, Effie! The location! It's perfect. Look, I know what you're going to say, it needs some work, but trust me, it will be perfect.'

'Some work,' she muttered as she wiped dust off the windowsill.

Effie glanced out of the window where the spring sunshine was glinting off the waves in the harbour. Yes, it was perfect, but she wasn't going to be won over so easily.

'The view is spectacular,' she conceded, 'but the shop is a mess. It's going to take a lot more than a once-over with some cleaning products. The walls need repainting, the shelves are varnished wood, it's not in keeping with the main shop aesthetic. I sent some photos.' She paused, heart pounding. She wasn't used to being so assertive. It felt good. Terrifying, but good.

The silence down the phone was heavy. What if Clive was reassessing whether or not Effie was suitable for the role. Just as she opened her mouth to try and back-pedal, tell him it was fine, she'd find a way, Clive sighed down the line.

'I saw those,' Clive said. 'I did view the shop, the estate agent said loads of people were interested and I just had a hunch, you know? Didn't want anyone else to get it. Maybe I didn't think through how much work just a lick of paint actually would be. I got a bit carried away. Effie, but this really is the perfect location though. I feel it in my bones. Do you see that?'

'Well, yes,' she admitted, 'it is beautiful but—'

'There's three weeks until opening. I'll hold off sending the stock, but you let me know what you need to get the place looking shipshape, all right? I'll send anything you need.'

Effie could sense he was trying to get off the phone. Clive didn't like confrontation. She glanced around the tired interior and told him, 'I'm going to need to redecorate. So, I'll need to order painting materials and equipment.'

'That's fine, Effie, honestly, send me a list and I'll order it in and let you know when it'll be delivered. See, this is why you're perfect to open the new shop, you think outside the box.'

'But I've never decorated before,' she told him, glancing around at the walls, trying to convince herself that a couple of coats of paint would be enough. 'Could you send someone to do it?'

'Ah, well, I don't really have the budget for that, I'm afraid, one of the reasons I sent you down early. You're a capable woman, Effie, but if it's too much I can send Zach to help?'

Effie's blood ran cold. 'Erm, no, I'm sure I can manage by myself.' Zach would love to know she was struggling, so there was no way he was going to find out. 'It's just some paint.'

'That's the spirit!' The relief in Clive's voice almost convinced her she could do this. 'Right, send that list, got to go, keep me posted. That view, Effie! That view! The book bloggers will love it!'

Having ended the call with Clive, Effie surveyed the shop. With the morning sunlight streaming in she could see its potential emerging from the shadows. It was a good space. A comfy chair in the bay window for customers to sit and peruse their purchases whilst admiring the sea view would be a social media win.

Grabbing her notebook, Effie perched on the windowsill and began to make her list. White paint, brushes, rollers . . . anything else? She wasn't sure. How hard could painting be? She picked up her phone and opened her message app, her finger hovering over her dad's number. He'd know what to do. Effie hesitated. She'd been here less than twenty-four hours; she couldn't contact her parents already. Also, it wasn't their problem to fix. This was an opportunity to stand on her own two feet.

Instead, she fired off a list of what she needed to Clive, instructing him to have it delivered as soon as possible, otherwise, she'd have to delay the opening. As the new shop had been already announced on their social media pages, Effie knew threatening to put back the opening would put the fear of God into Clive, and the equipment would likely arrive via express delivery.

Rolling up her sleeves, Effie filled a bucket with hot water and grabbed some cleaning products, switched on an empowering rock music playlist and set about scrubbing the shelves so that they'd be clean enough for her to start painting. She was halfway through her second bucket of water and 'Bat Out of Hell' when the door was pushed open. So engrossed in what she was doing, the tinkling bell made her heart leap.

Effie spun around, dropping her cleaning cloth and silencing her phone. 'We're not open yet,' she called out, panicked, taking in the glamorous woman who stood in the doorway. Her fiery red hair was rolled into an elaborate vintage style, an old-fashioned apron pulled across her blue floral dress. She cast her eyes around the shop, as if checking it out for size.

'Oh, I know that, I've just come to say hello—' the woman bustled in '—and I won't be the first to pop by,' she advised, stepping forward and holding out her hand to Effie. 'I'm Lola, by the way, I run the café next door. We've all been dying to know what's going on in here since the sign went up.' Her eyes left Effie's and skittered around the empty shop.

Effie shook Lola's hand. 'It's going to be a bookshop.'

'A bookshop! How delightful! No one had book-shop on their sweepstake. We were all dreading it being another souvenir shop.'

'Well, we do sell souvenirs,' Effie said, 'but tasteful ones.' Tasteful ones? What on earth? New people, out of context, always made her anxious, especially confident glamorous ones. Effie watched as Lola made her way around the little shop, running her fingers along the shelves and disappearing into the small office where Effie heard the sound of cupboards being opened and closed.

'This reminds me of when I took over the café,' she called, 'a ghastly mess. But I had it shipshape within two weeks. Repainted everything. Have you been in?' Lola asked as she emerged from the back room.

Effie shook her head. 'I only arrived yesterday. I've been busy getting settled in.'

Lola checked her watch. 'It's almost half ten, you've definitely earned a break.'

Effie, who'd been up since six fretting, supposed she had. Her stomach rumbled in support of taking a break. 'I guess that settles it,' she laughed, grabbing her phone and bag and following Lola out of the shop. The morning air was warm with spring promise and Effie took in a deep breath of fresh sea air. She could do this.

Lola pushed open the café door. Effie followed her inside and stopped in her tracks. The café was gorgeous. The walls were painted the palest grey with lemon accents, creating a calming yet cosy vibe. Effie took it all in, from the beautiful assortment of vintage teapots on a shelf above the counter, to the delicious-looking cakes and bakes stacked temptingly in glass domes to the floral bunting strung along the ceiling. The aroma of coffee and chocolate made Effie's mouth water. It was adorable.

'Wow, this is . . .' Effie trailed off as a large sheepdog bounded playfully over to her, almost knocking her off her feet.

'Scruff! What have I told you? You can't just barge into people.'

Effie followed the voice and saw an elderly gentleman sitting at the window seat, stooped and wizened by the years, yet his eyes twinkled with mischief.

'You OK with dogs? He's friendly. Too friendly where the ladies are concerned.'

Effie nodded. 'Yes, I'm fine with dogs. Hello. Scruff.' Gingerly, she held her hand out and watched as Scruff sniffed her palm, then her feet before satisfied, returning to his master.

'Passed the initiation test,' the old man laughed. 'I'm Alf and what I don't know about Polcarrow isn't worth mentioning. Are you just going to stand there?'

'Erm, no, erm . . .' flustered Effie as she took the vacant seat across from him. 'I'm Effie, I'm in charge of opening the bookshop next door.'

'Ah yes, didn't think much of the lad who turned up with that flashy car. What sort of books?'

'All sorts, but we try to specialise in ones set in Cornwall or about Cornwall.' Effie explained the ethos surrounding Books by the Sea: 'We like to stock local authors and promote literature about Cornwall.' Alf nodded approvingly. 'Maps, walking guides, ghost stories, romances. As well as the usual bestsellers and children's books.'

'That sounds marvellous.' Lola appeared at her elbow. 'What would you like?'

Effie glanced at the selection. 'It's got to be a cream tea, hasn't it? Those scones look divine.'

'They are!' Alf confirmed, patting his middle.

'Perfect choice.' Lola winked. 'Freya, one cream tea please.'

'Sure!' the girl behind the counter, her dark hair piled into a messy bun, called.

'So, what brings you here other than the bookshop?' Lola asked, taking the spare seat.

'Just the bookshop,' Effie explained. 'My boss wanted to open a new branch and decided I'm the best person for it so here we are. Except, his keenness to acquire the property has meant I've been thrown into a minor renovation project.'

Alf and Lola both made sympathetic noises.

'What's it like here? I mean, do you need a bookshop?'

'I think everywhere probably needs a bookshop,' Alf said diplomatically. 'I'm not going to lie, we're only a small village, but people are starting to visit again. It might be nice for them to have a bookshop to look around. If you're asking about Polcarrow itself, well, we get by. I mean, look at that view, how could you complain?'

Effie glanced out of the window and agreed, 'It is gorgeous.' Her stomach tightened. Had Clive really done the right thing investing in a shop somewhere so small?

Lola gave her a long look that made Effie squirm. 'Hmmm. I think you're here for more reasons than that,' she said as Freya placed a tray laden with scones and a strawberry-print teapot on the table.

'Lola, no,' Freya cautioned with a roll of her eyes.

Effie glanced between them. 'What?'

Delight shining on her face, Lola reached into her pocket and pulled out a pack of tarot cards.

Alf spotted them and rolled his eyes. 'My cue to leave. I don't believe in all that hokum. I'll be round though to see how that shop is turning out. Have a good morning, ladies. Nice to meet you, Effie.'

A chorus of goodbyes followed Alf out of the shop as he tugged Scruff away from the baked goods. Effie reached for a scone and began to slice through it.

'No, Lola, seriously,' Freya groaned as she poured the tea, passing Effie a cup. 'You don't have to indulge her, you know.'

'Don't listen to her.' Lola pulled the cards out of the box. 'My cards never lie, Freya herself knows that. A year ago she was trapped in a miserable relationship in London, slaving away over an art degree that she completely flunked. I knew a new life awaited her here. Could feel it in my bones, and here she is, gorgeous boyfriend, new house and making money from her paintings.'

Wide eyed, Effie glanced between them. 'Is that true?'

'Yes,' Freya sighed, 'it's all true and I'm very, very happy, which, of course, Lola likes to take credit for. But you don't have to have your cards read.'

'Of course you don't,' Lola echoed, placing the cards on the table, 'but humour me, please, it's just a bit of fun. No one comes to Polcarrow just to open a café or a shop; there's always something else.'

Effie glanced at the cards sitting on the table between them, then up at Lola. With her twinkling eyes and soothing voice, she was impossible to resist. Effie had had her cards read years ago and had secretly been disappointed when the generic prediction had failed to materialise. However, now she was here in Polcarrow, and she couldn't deny she felt a little bit of magic in the air. Effie was almost thirty and despite being given the opportunity by Clive, deep down she was horrendously lost and feeling left behind in life. A little bit of tarot wouldn't do any harm, would it?

After stirring milk into her tea, Effie took a sip. 'OK, why not?'

'Excellent.' Lola clapped her hands together in glee. 'Shuffle them, make three piles. Think about what you want guidance in, what you want most from your future.'

Effie closed her eyes and shuffled, her mind whirring to get her intentions correct, ask the right questions. What was the right amount of shuffles? She only stopped when she thought she'd been going a bit too long. Opening her eyes, as instructed, she made three piles.

'Which one are you most drawn to?'

'Erm, this one.' Effie signalled to the one on her right.

'Perfect!' Lola picked up the two other piles and stuck them back into her pocket and began to lay out the cards from the one Effie had chosen.

Anticipation prickled along Effie's spine as she leaned forward. Even Freya was wide eyed as she waited to see what fate the cards would reveal.

'These are good,' Lola began hesitantly, 'you've been sent here to get away from something, or someone. Yes, someone. You are safe from that person for now, but they will rear their ugly head. Oh, don't worry, you'll be fine, because this card indicates you're going through a huge moment of growth. You've come here, Effie, to really step into your power.'

Relief washed over Effie as she exchanged smiles with Freya and Lola, something shifting inside her. She felt that these two women were going to become new friends, mostly because they looked the sort who'd bundle you into their arms without you asking. Coming into her own power sounded really positive.

'You have been very lost.' Lola tapped one of the cards. 'This is telling you to go back to things you love, reconnect with that part of the soul you've missed.'

Effie almost gasped as Lola held the card to her. It showed a mermaid swimming in the sea. She glanced out of the window towards the swell of the waves, an ache in her chest to plunge her body into the cold water, allow it to rush up her limbs, revive her.

'That's caught your attention,' Lola said.

'I used to swim a lot, my dad always called me a mermaid.'

'I can see why.' Lola indicated the long blonde braid that was currently wrapped around Effie's head like a crown.

Effie touched it. When it was loose, it fell to her elbows in unruly waves. She'd always been conscious of how much hair she had, had always tamed it. Maybe now was the time to let go a bit?

'And this, I love this card, it's my favourite. True love! Love is coming into your life! A big romance.' Lola almost swooned. 'But where from? It says he's already here in the village.' She hurriedly turned over a few more cards. 'Effie! This is exciting! I wonder who it will be?' Lola mused to herself and laid out a few more cards.

Romance? Effie hadn't had romance on her mind since an excruciatingly bad Tinder date two years previously. She'd decided she much preferred her men to be from the eighteenth century and stuck firmly in the pages of a book. The idea of true love in real life, although a wonderful notion, seemed slightly, well, preposterous.

Freya buried her face in her hands before turning to Effie. 'Consider this your warning. Lola will now be sending any man who walks into this café next door in an effort to matchmake. She just can't help herself.'

'Oi, I don't see you complaining, worked out perfectly for you and Angelo.'

Angelo? Effie recognised the name and something tugged at her memory. Freya and Angelo. Artists. 'Hang on, you're not the couple who painted the mural last summer, are you? I remember reading about it. I went to the church last night to have a look but it was closed.'

Freya nodded proudly. 'Yes, that was us. Shall I show you, once we've finished this?'

'Erm,' Effie began, knowing that she was meant to be getting on with preparing the shop, but what could she actually do now without the supplies, other than vacuum the carpet and wipe down the shelves? That could wait. Lola and Freya were looking at her so expectantly, so warmly, that Effie caved. 'That would be really, really lovely.'

Lola topped up their tea. 'Wonderful, welcome to Polcarrow, Effie, where I'm sure all your dreams will come true.'

With a smile on her face, Effie picked up her cup in a toast. The way Lola was smiling made Effie believe everything she'd said was true. Were all her fortunes about to change?

Chapter Eight

A loud thump, like a something being dropped from a height, woke Effie with a start. Oh gosh, was someone breaking in? Heart hammering, she bolted upright ears pricked for any more sounds. No, the noise was outside in the street. Huddling under the duvet, she tried to slow her heart rate back down with steady breaths. Glancing at the clock, she saw it was nearly two in the morning. It was probably nothing, she told herself, as she tried to drift back off, only to be woken again by another loud thump. This one was accompanied by an angry voice outside her bedroom window.

'I've come back home, you know where, ugh, don't, I don't want to go through this again.' A man's voice, fraught with tired emotion carried through the night.

Effie turned over. Waited. Silence. Just as her body began to relax, the voice came again, more urgent, winding up to a full-blown argument. With gritted teeth, Effie waited, hoping the man would move away. Effie listened for another ten minutes as the conversation went round and round in circles, making her blood boil, spoiling the fuzzy, slumbery vibes she'd managed to hang on to.

'Ugh.' Effie pushed the duvet off and staggered out of bed towards the window. Pushing it open with more force than intended, she leaned out and shouted, 'Could you please take your call somewhere private, some of us are trying to sleep!'

The man glanced up, horror flashing across his face as Effie glared down at him. She caught a hint of thick blond hair, a grey hoodie and a look of remorse in his eyes.

'Sorry, sorry.' He gave Effie a dismissive wave before turning back to whoever was on the end of the line. 'Look, let's talk again in the morning, I'm disturbing the neighbours.'

Effie glowered at him as he ended the call, slipped his phone into his pocket and continued to bump his case up the stairs that led to the flat behind the café. The man glanced back as he reached the door. Caught watching him, Effie retreated, slamming her window to further convey her displeasure, sleep a distant memory.

The following morning Effie stood by the front window, drinking her tea whilst watching the sun come up over the sea. Yawning, she put her mug down and rubbed her tired eyes. Effie had lain awake, alert and annoyed after angrily confronting the man who'd disturbed her sleep. After he'd apologised there'd been the sound of more cases being hefted up the next-door stairs until the door finally closed and silence seeped back through Polcarrow.

Unable to get back to sleep, Effie's mind had alternated between her ever-growing to-do list and thoughts about banging on her neighbour's door bright and early, treating him to a taste of his own medicine by giving him a piece of her mind. She'd even begun to plan out what she'd say to him, which didn't help her already riled up mind calm down.

However, she must have fallen back to sleep because her alarm had bleeped through her dreams, dragging her back into the reality of Tuesday morning. She'd pulled herself out of bed and flicked on the kettle before realising that with the paint not due to arrive until the following morning, she had nothing much to get up for. Effie started to make a proper list of what needed to be done. She loved to tick things off a list, loved the satisfaction that came with completing a job.

As she sat on the sofa compiling her to-do list, her eyes kept straying to the sea. It lapped onto the shore, beckoning her in. The siren call of the swoosh of the waves echoed in her ears. She tried to ignore it, tried to focus her mind on how she'd tackle righting all the wrongs she'd stepped foot into. The unloved flat, the sad-looking shop, the overwhelming task of redecorating.

Her eyes strayed back to where the sun glinted off the waves. Why not go for a swim? Effie loved the embrace of water around her limbs, the cold shock from that first plunge, which always made her gasp. Back home, she had swum occasionally, but had been put off by lugging her stuff to the beach and home, but there was no excuse here, she could cross the street barefoot and within moments be in up to her knees. The temptation was so strong, so why was she trying to resist it?

Effie curled into herself. She was shy, worried what everyone else might think of her, not that anyone else in Polcarrow seemed to have the same qualms. She'd spotted many faces pressed up to the shop window the previous afternoon, trying to peek through the grubby glass to see what she was doing. People had lingered in the café when she'd gone in for her mid-afternoon mocha. Effie could feel their ears straining for gossip, as she ordered a fruity flapjack.

Part of her loved this, knew it was good that the locals were craving the big reveal, knew it would be vital for the business's success. Clive had confirmed the new sign was to be delivered at the end of the following week. Effie sucked in a breath at that. So much to do and only her hands to do it. She knew she should ask for more help but she really didn't want Clive to think she was incapable or risk anything getting back to Zach, who'd revel in her not coping.

Effie studied the sea. Smooth, good conditions, the sun had risen gently over the horizon, promising a glorious spring day. She stretched her arms above her. Gosh, she ached from cleaning all the shelves the previous day in an attempt to get them ready to paint. A swim would do her the world of good, it'd ease her muscles, it'd invigorate her.

Without giving it another thought, she put her mug in the sink and headed into her bedroom, where she wiggled into her wetsuit, dug out her flip-flops and threw on her dry robe. Effie was crossing the road, cramming her wild hair into her swim cap before she fully realised what she was doing.

Before she lost her nerve, Effie made her way down the stone steps. Pulling off her flip-flops, she sank her toes into the cool golden sand, this part of the beach not yet warmed by the sun. It oozed between her toes like the memory of childhood holidays. Making her way towards the sea, she paused at the halfway point and turned around to survey Polcarrow. From the beach she could see it was even quainter than she'd first realised. Effie felt that if she stretched her arms out wide enough, she could gather the whole village to her in an embrace.

With her back to the sea, the village stretched from the headland on her right to the pub, perched on the edge of the harbour, on her left. The rest of Polcarrow was charmingly stacked up the hill, watching over her, windows glinting like eyes waiting to see what her next step would be.

Effie made her way across the damp sand, the briny early-morning aroma of the sea awakening her senses. The waves lapped against the shore with a beckoning swish that she was unable to ignore. The March sun wasn't at its full potency, but she knew that on a hot summer's day, the beach would be a haven for families.

Standing toe to toe with the sea, the waves lapped at Effie's feet as if pleased to welcome her home. She breathed in and out, dragging the clean sea air deep into her lungs, feeling it buzz through her body. Effie shrugged off her dry robe, dumped it on the sand, confident that no one in Polcarrow would pinch her stuff, and strode into the waves. She winced as the cold sea rushed over her toes, her feet, up her ankles, as if to swallow her up.

As the surf engulfed her, all her worries started to ebb away. Swimming had always been how she processed complicated feelings. As an anxious teenager, she'd splashed around trying to calm her nerves before her exams. At university, finding the local pool had been a much-needed balm, an escape from the student life she didn't naturally fit into. She was much happier doing lengths than downing shots. She'd swum every day, early mornings, late nights, turning over in her head the complicated essay questions she needed to answer about *King Lear*, or ruminating over whether the guy in the student union coffee shop was flirting with her. There had never been a problem she couldn't solve with a swim.

Effie waded deeper into the waves until she was far enough out to bob down beneath them. The shock chill of the water alighted down her spine, the thrill sparking along her nerves. She began to swim, slowly at first, finding her way through an unfamiliar sea, wondering how far she should go. Probably not too far. After all, there was no one about to help if she got into trouble.

As Effie swam, she mulled over the realities of what opening a new shop entailed. Had she been blinded by the excitement of being as close to her own bookshop dream as she'd likely get? Should she have viewed the shop before accepting the role? Had Clive really considered the amount of work that was needed to get it up and running? Effie realised hindsight really was a beautiful thing and would've stopped her from getting lumbered with a project she was completely unprepared for. She knew if she called her dad he'd be straight down at the weekend with a set of paint-brushes and a classic rock playlist, but, although this was a fun, comforting thought, she knew this wasn't Brian's problem to solve.

Effie had to make the bookshop work. Clive trusted her, she didn't want to let him down either. Painting shelves and walls might be a long, boring task, but how hard could it be? She had her audiobooks to help her through.

Plus, there was a steady stream of delicious baked goods next door at Lola's to reward herself with. Her mouth watered at the thought of the scones and triple choco-late brownies. Effie could never resist anything chocolate based. She thought about grabbing a hot chocolate with marshmallows, her favourite post-swim treat, once she was out of the sea.

Realising she'd swum a lot further than she'd planned, Effie turned and made her way back towards the shore. Her limbs ached in a good way, her soul invigorated from having challenged her body, and her mind clearer. Everything felt much more manageable. The sea always put everything into perspective. As she reached the point where she could stand up, Effie scanned the beach, shock reverberating through her when she saw a man standing watching, a professional camera trained on her.

All the good vibes the sea had given her fizzled away at the sight of him. How dare he take photos of her? Grabbing her discarded robe and flip-flops, Effie marched up the beach towards him.

'What on earth are you doing?' she demanded, signalling to the camera.

Shocked, the man lowered the camera, horror flashing across his face. 'I thought . . . I thought . . . you were . . . a . . .' he spluttered, embarrassed.

'A what?' Effie growled, tugging off her swim cap, blonde waves flying everywhere. There was something familiar about him.

'A mermaid,' he gasped before catching her thunderous look.

Effie glared at him, realisation dawning on her that this was the same man who'd disturbed her sleep the night before. Up close he was attractive in a tousled, unshaven, rugged way, as if he'd just leapt out of bed to catch her. His pyjama bottoms and bare feet gave this away.

'Look, I'm sorry, really I am, I didn't mean to cause offence. I thought you were a seal,' he explained, turning his camera around to show Effie the screen.

Effie looked at the photos. They were a bit blurry. If she squinted, she could see how he might mistake the grey blob for a seal. 'Did you not see my robe?' She held it up, almost shoving the neon pink interior in his face. A very good-looking face she realised as her heart skipped an inconvenient beat. He smelled of sandalwood and interrupted sleep. Effie pulled herself back from leaning in.

Flummoxed, the man glanced from the robe to the camera and then to Effie. Even though she was glowering at him, even though anger flashed through her body at having her peace interrupted, she couldn't help but take in his sandy curls, pushed back from a kind, tanned face, bright eyes sparkling as blue as the Cornish sea. The intrusion was worse because he was so good looking: tall, broad and blond, like a Viking warrior. Effie huffed internally, crossing her arms, suddenly aware of the wetsuit clinging to the curves of her body.

'I'll delete them,' he offered, showing her as he erased the images, 'is that better? I didn't mean to be weird, I honestly didn't think I was photographing a person.'

Effie shrugged, still rattled by the situation and his good looks, by the way he'd ruined her sleep. 'Yes, thanks.' Her voice was clipped. 'First you wake me up in the middle of the night, and now you disturb my swim.'

'I didn't . . . I wasn't,' he began as it dawned on him that Effie was the same person who'd shouted at him for waking her up. 'I explained. I'm sorry, I apologised, and last night too. I didn't realise anyone lived in the flat.' He grappled for something. 'Is this the wrong time to say nice to meet you and introduce myself?'

Effie huffed in response as she shoved her feet into her flip-flops. Hugging her robe to her she strode past him. 'It's fine,' she called, her voice tense, 'just don't do it again.' She needed some time to process what had happened. He'd made a genuine mistake, he'd apologised and still she found herself aflame with anger towards him.

Effie strode across the road and pushed open the café door. It was early, but Lola was busy setting out the day's wares. The scent of freshly baked scones hung temptingly in the air.

'Good morning, my lovely, what can I get you? Oh, are you OK?' Lola's brow furrowed as she took in Effie's wet, slightly distressed state.

'I don't know,' Effie said. 'I went for a swim and when I got out, that man was taking photos of me.'

Lola darted out from behind the counter and peered through the blinds. 'Jake?' There was a suspicious hint of delight in her voice as she threw Effie a glance to gauge her response.

So that was his name. Effie nodded. Jake was rooted to the spot, eyes flicking between the sea and the café, as if wondering whether or not he should follow her. Effie saw Lola give a quick shake of her head and Jake slinked off.

'You know him?'

'Of course, he lives in the flat above the café, has done for a couple of months since he moved back home. He's a photographer, out and about a lot, used to be big on social media. His mum, Jan, is a part of the village committee.'

Effie's fists balled with anger. 'He woke me up in the middle of the night having a phone call between our flats, now he's taken some photos of me,' she said through gritted teeth as she followed Lola back to the counter.

'Oh dear, looks like you've got off to a bad start, which is a shame. Jake is a sweetie, honestly, I'm a very good judge of character.' Lola smiled encouragingly as if she knew something Effie didn't. 'I'm not one to gossip but I will say he's been through a bit of a tough time according to his mum.'

'Hmm,' was Effie's response. She didn't feel in the mood to grant him any graces due to a so-called 'bad time' after her encounters with him. Glancing down, she saw she'd trailed sand all over the floor. 'I'm so sorry, I've made a mess.'

'Oh, don't fret about that, you're not the first or last to walk sand in here. What can I get you?'

'Hot chocolate, please, marshmallows but no cream. It's always my post-swim treat.' Effie managed a smile. 'It was the only thing the sports centre vending machine did that was half decent.'

With a smile, Lola turned towards the coffee machine and the sound of milk being frothed filled the air. Effie basked like a contented cat in the morning sun that streamed into the café, whilst Lola whipped up her drink.

'Any more?' Lola asked.

Effie turned her attention back to Lola to see her hovering over her hot chocolate with the bag of marshmallows. A generous amount of the pink and white sweets had already dropped onto the foamy top, oozing the drink over the edge of the cup.

'Thanks, but that's probably enough,' she said smiling, as she paid with loose change from her pocket.

Effie picked up the cup and moved to the table by the window. She was just settling down to enjoy her drink when the café door opened, and Jake walked in, his pyjama bottoms swapped for jeans and desert boots. Their eyes met but Effie pulled hers away before she could be drawn any further into his swirling blue depths.

Chapter Nine

Indignation fuelled Effie for the rest of the day as she channelled the complicated feelings Jake has arisen in her into angrily sanding down the dark shelves that lined the shop walls. By the time the sun dipped towards the horizon, she was exhausted and aching, but in a good, productive way.

Hands on hips, catching her breath after whipping the vacuum cleaner round, pride swelled in Effie's chest as she took in what she had achieved. Once everything had been cleaned down, the shop would be ready for painting. With the paint arriving the following morning Effie was pleased that not only was she on track, but that she'd managed to do it all by herself.

After a bath and a quick dinner, Effie fell into bed, drifting off before she could finish the chapter of her book. She woke with the dawn, her muscles stiff as she stretched and yawned. Another clear day. She peered out of the window at the sea glinting in the sun and hesitated. She didn't want to draw any more attention to herself. But as the kettle boiled and her eyes skimmed over the pages of her book, she knew the best thing to properly wake her up would be a swim. Plus, there was no way Jake would dare make the same mistake twice.

Effie went for her swim. As she pulled herself through the waves she tried, but failed, to keep her eyes from being tugged towards the window above Lola's café. The blind was up and Effie thought she saw someone linger, but on second glance, she decided it was a trick of the light. The idea of Jake watching her did strange things to her insides. She didn't like the scrutiny, the invasion of her privacy, but part of her craved that bright blue gaze, wished their meeting had happened on more auspicious terms.

Breaking through the surf, Effie made her way out of the sea. Throwing on her dry robe she noticed that the café wasn't open yet, so made her way back across the street, up the stairs into her flat where she jumped in the shower, washing away the briny scent of the sea. The doorbell buzzed.

'Shit,' Effie hissed as she frantically wrapped towels around herself as the buzzer went again, this time sounding impatient.

Skidding out of the bathroom, Effie fumbled to open the flat door, but there was no one there. The buzzer went again. Effie darted back inside, pushed open the window. Standing on the pavement, hands on his hips, looking unimpressed was a delivery driver. In front of the shop door was a pallet of paints and decorating equipment.

'Sorry, I wasn't expecting you this early,' Effie called, 'give me two minutes and I'll be down to let you in.'

'Don't worry, love, can't stay any longer, I'll just leave it there.'

'But—' Effie glanced at the delivery and then back to the driver '—I can't carry all that.'

He shrugged and waved the paperwork. 'My instructions are only to deliver to the door.'

'Can't you . . .' Effie trailed off as he shoved the paperwork into his back pocket, headed back to his van and slid open the driver's door. She watched in disbelief as he pulled away, speeding along the harbour front, beating a hasty retreat. First the estate agent, now the paint delivery driver, what was it with all these men desperate to get away so fast?

Drying herself and getting dressed in record-breaking time, Effie rushed down the stairs, braiding her hair as she went. She had to get the stuff off the pavement before someone complained. Effie opened the shop door and stared at the pile of paint pots, rollers and paintbrushes. How much paint did Clive think she needed? Why had he ordered four gigantic tubs? It was all wrapped in protective plastic. Effie was scrabbling around in the counter drawers trying to find some scissors when she heard a voice asking, 'Do you need a hand?'

Effie's heart leapt in panic at the sound of the voice. Turning towards the doorway, smoothing down her hair and clothes, she saw Jake standing the other side of the delivery, takeaway cup in his hand, hair pushed back from his forehead in a way that made Effie's fingers itch to ruffle it. *Hang on, where had that come from?* She narrowed her eyes at the thought, reminding herself that even if Jake was sort of the enemy, it was OK to find him attractive, especially that morning when he was wearing jeans and a white T-shirt, leather bracelets on his wrists and a smattering of tattoos up his arm. She tried not to stare at them.

Effie swallowed, about to tell him that she was fine, but she knew she couldn't easily lift all the pots of paint.

'Here.' He pulled a set of keys out of his pocket, including a penknife, which he used to slash through the plastic wrapping.

'I didn't know people still had penknives,' Effie said, the whole thing happening too quickly for her brain to catch up.

Jake slipped it back into his pocket. 'I was obsessed with the idea of them as a kid. My grandad got me it when I was ten and I'm never without it. You never know when you may need one.'

'And have you needed one much?' Effie asked, curious.

'Not as much as I imagined,' he said with a laugh.

'Thank you.'

'I also got you this.' He placed the takeaway cup on top of the pile. 'Lola said you have a hot chocolate after a swim, extra marshmallows. I saw you go out – please don't think I was spying – I saw you when I was opening my blinds. Ugh. I'm sorry. I bought this as a peace offering, to say sorry for yesterday. I'm really embarrassed. When I was deleting the photos I couldn't believe how silly I was to think you were a seal! Mortified.'

Effie took the cup, pulled off the lid and studied the pink marshmallows bobbing on the surface. They looked like little melted hearts. She took a sip. 'Thank you. I'm sorry I snapped at you, but—'

'It's fine, you had every right to. I don't usually take phone calls out in the street in the middle of the night. I didn't mean to make you uncomfortable with the photo either.' Jake scratched his ear. 'I wanted to start again seeing as we're going to be neighbours. My name's Jake, I was born and raised here but have only just moved back. I've been living above the café for a few weeks. Turns out whilst I was, erm, travelling, my dad commandeered my old bedroom for his train set. It's impressive but . . .' Jake exhaled as if he wasn't sure what to make of his dad's hobby taking precedence over him.

'Replaced by a train set?' She couldn't help but smile.

'Uh-huh,' Jake laughed and held out his hand.

Effie took it, making sure her handshake was just on the right side of firm. However, as Jake's warm fingers closed around hers, a jolt flew through her, making her forget who or where she was.

'Erm, I'm Effie,' she stuttered, 'I moved here on Sunday. I'm getting the shop ready for my boss.'

Jake peered in through the doorway, taking in the sad sanded-down shelves, the tired blue carpet. 'What, all by yourself?'

Effie pulled herself up. 'Yes, all by myself,' she said as if it were a challenge.

'When are you opening?'

'Easter weekend.'

Jake sucked in a breath.

'What?' she asked, irritated. The breath seemed to signify he knew more than she did. 'It's just some paint,' she pointed out, her voice more defensive than she'd intended. 'You think I can't do it?'

'What? No!' He gave her a once-over, as if appraising his opponent. 'I'm pretty sure you can do anything, but Easter is only three weeks away. Why didn't your boss get it ready for you?'

Effie opened her mouth to speak but nothing came out. She had no words to defend Clive. 'I don't know,' she admitted, wondering why she'd never asked this question herself, 'he's not the practical sort and I like a challenge.' Did she? Well, yes, perhaps now she did. 'He chose me to set up and open his new branch.'

'Wow, he must really trust you.' Jake looked impressed.

'Yes, I guess he does.' She glanced around the shop, the enormity of transforming it overwhelming her. She turned to Jake with false positivity. 'Look, it's fine, it's just a bit of paint, I don't have anything else to do.' She plastered a smile on her face to hide the creeping panic that it was a lot of work.

'At least let me give you a hand carrying this stuff in.' Jake ripped at the plastic and started to unload the paint pots.

Effie watched as he carried them inside, as if they weighed nothing. Jake lined them up against the wall below the window. Finishing her hot chocolate, she grabbed the paintbrushes and stacked them on the counter.

Once everything was inside, Jake's eyes roamed over the shop and back to Effie as if he knew she'd bitten off more than she could chew. He hesitated before volunteering, 'Do you want some help with the painting?'

Effie's resolve almost crumbled under his kindness, but she was determined to prove she could do this herself. Shaking her head, she said, 'It's fine, thanks, honestly. I mean, how hard can it be?' She smiled and gave a little shrug.

Jake's narrow-eyed silence unnerved her. It made her think he knew something she didn't, which only irked her.

Chapter Ten

'Ugh.' Effie sank back against the counter. It turned out that painting a whole shop wasn't hard, but it was deathly boring. She checked the time. 'What? I've only been doing this for an hour and a half?'

She glanced from the paintbrush to the shelves. They weren't turning out as she'd expected. Despite her sanding the varnish off, the wood underneath was still lumpy. They looked more like an enthusiastic school project than the beginnings of a sophisticated shop.

Effie put the brush down and reached for her phone, ready to call Clive and tell him she didn't care about her promotion, or the threat of him sending Zach, setting up the shop on her own was impossible. Maybe she could convince him to send in professionals. Just as she was about to press 'call' the bark of a dog almost made her leap out of her skin.

'Oh gosh, it's you.' Effie spun round to find Alf and Scruff lingering in the open doorway.

'Sorry, love, didn't mean to give you a fright—' Alf's eyes twinkled '—just wanted to see how you're getting on.'

Effie signalled with the brush towards the shelves. 'Not very well,' she admitted, her cheeks colouring as she recalled brushing off Jake's help. How foolish she'd been. 'I think Jake was offering to help but I turned him down.'

'Jake, ah, he's a good lad, known him since he was a babe in arms. He's done well for himself,' Alf said proudly.

Effie made a non-committal noise in response.

'Would you like his help?'

Effie sighed. 'I'd take Scruff's help if it meant it was done quicker.'

'Oh, I wouldn't trust him with a paintbrush,' Alf said, 'he's the messy sort. He prefers a more supervisory role.'

Despite her internal gloom, Alf's kindness brought a smile to her face. 'He's welcome to stay and supervise,' Effie said.

Although she usually preferred her own company, spending all her days and evenings alone was starting to wear on her. All the conversations she'd had in the café had been pleasant, friendly, but she still felt like an outsider, like she didn't know how to properly insert herself into the cosy Polcarrow life she'd seen playing out around her. *Give it a few more weeks*, she reminded herself, *you've only just arrived*.

'Why don't you come next door and take a break? Lola's made some fresh scones,' Alf tempted.

'I'd wondered what that divine smell was.' She sighed. 'I'd love to Alf, but if I keep stopping, I'll never get this done. But thank you.'

Alf nodded. 'I'll bring you round a cuppa.'

'Alf, you don't have to do that,' Effie said. 'That's very kind.'

'Come on, Scruff.' Alf gave the dog's lead a tug.

Effie watched them amble past the window before picking up her paint tray and brush and heading back to the shelves. Lemony sunlight streamed in through the window, it was the most perfect day and she was stuck inside.

'Come on, Eff, if you get these done, you can go out and enjoy the weather,' she muttered to herself as she climbed back onto the stepladder.

A gentle knock at the door made her turn around. Rather than Alf and Scruff, Jake stood there, a tray with two takeaway cups and a scone in his hands.

'Delivery.' He held up the treats. 'Alf said you were struggling.'

Effie narrowed her eyes at him. 'You haven't come to gloat, have you?'

'No, why?'

'After I asked how hard could painting be?' She signalled to the shelves. 'It's bloody hard. And boring.'

Jake cracked a smile. 'Well, I did kind of know that. But you were so determined to do it yourself.'

Effie harumphed as she made her way down the ladder steps.

'Have you done anything like this before?'

Effie shook her head and sighed. 'No and I didn't think it'd be hard. I mean, it's just paint but those shelves look, well, rubbish.'

Jake handed her the tray, which Effie carried over to the counter. Famished, she took a large bite of the scone, letting out a happy sigh as the soft, buttery and fruity flavours burst on her tongue.

Jake gave her an amused look. 'Good?'

Mouth full, Effie gave him a thumbs up. As she ate, Effie watched Jake inspect her work and tried to quell the irritation he ignited in her. Too good looking, too kind, too much like the boys she'd unrequitedly lusted after. She took a sip of her drink. She would not be lusting after Jake, despite the fact he was constantly showing up in crisp white T-shirts that highlighted his nicely tanned and toned arms.

'Do you own any T-shirts that aren't white?' It was out of her mouth before she could stop herself. 'I mean, it can't be the same one worn three times, it's spotless.'

Jake tugged the T-shirt away from his body, 'I have a few. I thought you were too busy glowering at me to notice what I'm wearing.'

'Oi,' Effie spluttered, startled by the flirtatious gleam in his eyes. Cramming the last bit of the scone into her mouth, she wandered over to him. Dared herself to stand as close as possible. Side by side, they surveyed the shelves before turning at the same time towards each other. Effie's breath caught as his blue eyes roamed over her face, raising colour in her cheeks. She opened her mouth, but nothing came out.

'You have paint here.' He reached towards her face as if he was going to wipe the paint away before withdrawing his hand.

Effie froze. The few seconds they stared at each other stretched out longer than was comfortable. Effie broke his gaze and wiped at the paint. It was dried on. 'Ugh, I'll sort it later,' she said with a sigh.

'Effie, let me help. My dad is a painter and decorator. I used to help him in the school holidays. I actually quite enjoy painting. Instant results, the subject doesn't complain if they don't like the lighting.'

'You'd help me? Why?'

'I still feel so awful about taking your photo, plus, I'm at a bit of a loose end. I'm trying to start a photography business but it's still very early days,' he explained. 'I hate not having anything to do. Also, Effie, I hate to say this—' he tapped the shelf she'd started on '—but with all the will in the world, I don't think you know enough about decorating to get this to a properly professional standard.'

Effie knew she should be insulted, that she should protest, but Jake was right, not only did she not have the ability, but she also lacked the will. Usually she hated asking for help, felt it flagged up a weakness in her, but as she looked at Jake, so openly offering a hand, she knew she'd be a fool to refuse.

'OK, Jake, if you want to help, that would be great.' More than great, she thought as she smiled shyly at him, but she didn't want him to think she needed him that much.

Chapter Eleven

Effie was transfixed. She hadn't realised anyone could take so much time, so much care, over painting some shelves. As soon as she'd relinquished her paintbrush into Jake's capable hands, he'd taken over, not in a boorish way, but in a soothing, knowing exactly what he was doing way. He showed her, without mansplaining, how to make sure the paint went on smoothly.

'You need to use thinner coats and more of them, rather than slapping it on so it goes blobby,' he explained as he dragged the paintbrush along the shelf.

Effie had to force her attention away from the way his arm muscles flexed as he slowly painted the shelf. The time and care he was taking. The focus. Her mind couldn't help but wonder what else his inner patience might be good at. Her face flushed at the turn her thoughts had taken and she shoved them away. She couldn't, wouldn't think of Jake like that. He'd thought she was a seal for God's sake!

'Think you've got it?'

'Uh-huh,' Effie spluttered as she fumbled around for another brush, all other words tangled in her throat.

They painted in silence for a few moments. At first it was companionable, allowing Effie's heart to stop racing and her mind to settle. It was sort of therapeutic, painting slowly and carefully, trying to achieve a high finish rather than slapping the paint on and hoping for the best. She snuck a glance at Jake, feeling guilty that she'd dragged him into this mess, but he looked anything other than bothered by it. Did he even look like he was enjoying himself?

'What?' Jake asked with a smile, as if reading her thoughts.

'Nothing.' Effie quickly batted away. She didn't like to draw attention to herself, therefore usually didn't like to probe into other people's lives, but she could sense Jake hanging on, wondering. 'What do you prefer? Photography or painting?'

Jake tipped a bit more paint into his tray. Effie noticed he didn't have any splatters on him, whereas she was glad she'd worn her oldest clothes. There was a smear up her arm and a blob of paint on her left knee.

Jake exhaled. 'That's a tricky question. I'm a photographer now, so maybe that's what I prefer. I used to help my dad decorating during school and university holidays. He never thought photography was a viable job. It started as a hobby when I was at university studying marketing, of all things. I found out I was good at it. Here.' He put his brush down and pulling his phone out of his pocket, beckoned Effie over.

Not wanting to stand too close, Effie craned her neck over the gallery Jake had opened on his phone. 'Wow,' she breathed as she watched him scroll through stunning landscapes and beautifully lit portraits. His phone contained a whole atlas of places Effie had only ever dreamed of visiting. New Zealand, Thailand and the Great Barrier Reef all zipped past her eyes. 'They're beautiful. You've been to so many places!'

'Thanks, yeah, I have, I guess.' He laughed nervously before continuing, his body language slightly uncomfortable, as if he didn't really want to admit the next bit. 'My ex, Tara, is an influencer. Well, she wasn't when I met her, but we decided to go travelling together and basically with her style and my photos we managed to create a lifestyle we could live off. It was fun at first, but always trying to get the perfect social media shot eventually drove me mad. It became no fun. Taking three hundred photos of her posing with a cocktail in a hammock. I prefer capturing the rawness of life. Real people, real moments, you know?' Jake swiped open his phone and before Effie knew what had happened the sound of a camera click snapped into the room.

'Hey! I'm a mess, don't!' Effie protested.

'You're not a mess, you're . . . you're . . . natural,' he said as he scanned through what he'd taken.

Their eyes met and they both knew he had been about to say something else. Effie felt her heart tug her towards him, to that possibility. Had he been about to say 'beautiful'? She was almost embarrassed to admit how much she was hoping he had.

'Here, look.' He held the phone out again.

Effie studied it, at first only picking out her imperfections: her wild hair, the old lime-green T-shirt, the paint on her cheek. However, the more she looked, the more she began to feel that Jake had somehow captured the real her. 'I look a bit startled,' was all she managed.

'Well, yeah, I did take you by surprise, but I'd rather take those sorts of photos than the influencer ones. I'm trying to build up my brand. Landscape, events, particularly weddings.'

'What about book shop openings?' she asked. 'I've been trying to start the social media pages for this place and well, it's not going great.' It was her turn to put the brush down and pick up her phone. So far all she had were a few pictures of the view.

'To be fair you've not got much to work with,' Jake said kindly. 'Once the shop is finished and dressed it'll be so much easier to create the right balance.' He glanced around him. 'It's also about spotting opportunities.'

She watched as Jake clocked the open door, clicked open the camera on his phone, played around with his positioning and snapped away.

'See, look.' Getting up, he turned the screen towards Effie. 'It's like an opening, a beginning.'

Effie followed his gaze towards the half-open door, sunlight streamed in creating a pathway across the floor. Through the gap she could see a hint of blue sky and sea.

There was magic in the photograph, the light was bright, welcoming, like a pause in time, an invite.

'Wow, Jake, I'd never have thought of taking something like that! It's awesome!'

'Give me your number and I'll send it to you; you can use it to create intrigue.'

Effie repeated her number to him and within a couple of seconds her phone pinged with the incoming message. Effie was quick to post the photo and was thrilled to see how it lifted the social media page she'd set up for the new branch.

'Thanks, Jake, for all of this. I mean, you don't have to, it's not your responsibility.'

Jake shrugged. 'I need something practical to do other than wandering around taking pictures of the sea. I enjoy a bit of physical work, makes me feel useful. But I can leave you to it if you'd prefer,' he said with a cheeky wink.

'No!' Effie gasped. 'I hate decorating! You're a lot better company than . . . Ah, it doesn't matter.'

'Than who? You can't leave it like that.'

Effie felt her face warm. 'Than my audiobook,' she told him, her voice rather prim as if she didn't want him to ask what she was listening to. Cowboy romance. Or cowboy smut, as Maddie gleefully called it.

'Audiobooks? I've never tried one. I think I'd fall asleep.'

'Audiobooks are great,' Effie enthused. 'Of course I love paperbacks the most, but they take up so much space and I get physically attached to my copies. But audio is great for when I'm driving or doing the cleaning or in the bath. That way I am never without a book.'

'What sort of books do you like?' he asked as he turned his attention back to the painting.

It was a very normal question to ask. Effie was asked it all the time, but she always felt like she should bring out the latest literary tome rather than see the flicker of judgement that came when she admitted she mainlined happy-ever-afters. She sensed Jake was interested, was waiting for the truth.

'Romance,' she said. 'I like the historical ones the best. Earls, Vikings, knights. Sometimes cowboys.'

Jake nodded. 'Nothing wrong with a bit of romance. My nanna loved Mills & Boon. I think the house was propped up by them.' Then he turned to her and with a heart melting smile, asked, 'Are you a romantic?'

'Yes, of course I am!' Effie spluttered, even though she wasn't sure how much of a romantic she really was underneath it all. She'd never been bought flowers, or been taken on fancy dates, all her romances had taken place between the covers of the paperbacks she adored. Brad hadn't exactly had a romantic bone in his body, more keen on chugging beers with his mates than wining and dining her. Effie was embarrassed about the rose-tinted glasses she'd viewed their future through at the time. There was no way she was going to admit that to Jake. However, the idea of candlelight and roses was something she craved and part of her wanted Jake to know she was a romantic.

'What about you?' she asked.

'Hopeless romantic,' he admitted. 'I know it's all a bit cheesy, but life is tough so why not add some romance. Just got to find the right girl.' He gave Effie a wink.

'I've just got to find the right boy,' she quipped back, her heart hammering as she wondered if she was flirting. She never flirted, usually just got herself tongue tied.

Awkwardly she turned back to her painting and tried to ignore the glances Jake was throwing her way. The idea of him turning up at her door, nice shirt, a bouquet of roses and that heart-skipping smile was an image she couldn't help but indulge in.

Chapter Twelve

Lola's eyes almost popped out of her head when she brought the sandwiches out to Effie and Jake. They'd decided to take advantage of the midday sun and sit at one of the outside tables. Effie pulled her cardigan tighter around herself, secretly thinking it was a bit on the chilly side. Still, the March sunshine was a warm promise of summer when she turned her face towards it. She allowed herself a few moments to imagine how lovely it'd be to sit here with an ice cream, the seafront busy with families, the bookshop a roaring success. Effie's mind began to fill with images of the shop thriving under her management. Sunlight flowing in through the window, an armchair and a little table piled with books, customers she knew by name, sharing recommendations, decorating seasonally.

'BLT?' Lola asked, rousing her from her daydream.

'That's me.' Effie sat up from where she'd been lounging as Lola placed the plate in front of her.

'So, you must be the toastie.' Lola placed an oozing ham and cheese toastie before Jake.

'Yep.' He patted his stomach. 'Melted cheese is my biggest weakness.' He took a bite which resulted in him waving his hand in front of his mouth and wincing. 'Too hot.'

Starving, Effie went to pick up her sandwich, the thick granary bread was bursting with plump tomatoes and the tantalising scent of freshly cooked bacon made her stomach rumble. However, Lola had other ideas.

'So nice to see you becoming friends,' she said as she pulled out the spare seat and sat down. 'Especially after the swimming incident.'

Effie blushed, recalling the specifics of Lola's tarot card prediction. New love. She snuck a glance at Jake, who was itching for his sandwich to cool down enough to eat. Could he be it? Effie threw a glance at Lola. It seemed far too obvious. Effie caught Lola trying to communicate something with her raised eyebrows and encouraging smile, finished off with a subtle nod in Jake's direction. Thankfully he was too engrossed in his sandwich to notice the silent exchange. Effie shook her head. Jake had dated a travel influencer – they were always glamourous, perfectly turned out and every time he'd seen her, Effie had been wearing a baggy T-shirt or a wetsuit. She didn't think she was his type.

'I'm helping Effie paint the shop,' he told Lola.

'Are you?' Effie didn't think it was possible, but Lola's eyebrows raised even further.

'I hate painting,' Effie explained as she took a bite of her sandwich, almost swooning as the delicious flavours popped on her tongue. Salty, hot bacon, fresh tomatoes and crisp lettuce, the perfect combination in her opinion.

'Oh gosh, this might be one of the best BLTs I've ever had,' she groaned, hastily taking another bite. Lola brimmed with pride at the compliment. 'I've got until Good Friday to get the shop shipshape. With Jake's help I think I might do it.'

'We must talk about the opening!' Lola gushed. 'Easter weekend, it'll be perfect. What do you have planned?'

Caught off guard, Effie froze with her sandwich halfway to her mouth. 'Erm, nothing yet. I'm just trying to get it ready to open. I've not spoken to Clive about it. He did say something about trying to arrange a local author to come and cut the ribbon, sign some books, but I've not had time to follow that up.'

'If I'm helping you, it'll free up some time for you to concentrate on the other parts of the opening,' Jake said, popping the last bite of his sandwich into his mouth, before swooning. 'Lola, that was stunning.' He used his finger to wipe a stray smear of cheese off the plate.

'Thank you,' Lola said before changing the subject back to the bookshop. 'Easter Saturday is less than three weeks away! You'll need catering. Hot cross buns and Easter bunny cakes, book-shaped biscuits,' she reeled off, a vision forming in her head that didn't quite transfer into Effie's.

'I hadn't even thought of all that,' Effie said. 'I've been too busy panicking about getting the shop looking presentable. I hadn't even considered guests might want some treats. But of course they would.'

'I make my own hot cross buns,' Lola pointed out proudly. 'I could do some mini ones. What if I make a selection of treats and you can try them and let me know what you think?'

Effie sat back in her seat as if trying to put some physical space between herself and Lola's ideas. 'I'll have to check with Clive if there's budget for that sort of thing. We've always just popped to the supermarket for refreshments,' she admitted.

'That won't do!!' Lola gasped in horror.

With the bookshop situated next door to a café peddling stunning bakes, Effie had to agree. 'You're right. It'd be great if you could bake some buns and biscuits for the opening. If Clive isn't happy, I'll pay for it.'

'I'll offer a discount, especially as being next door to each other is definitely going to help both our businesses. Leave it with me, I love planning a party, although I always get a bit carried away. Are you coming to Alf's birthday on Saturday? It's his ninetieth. I'm making a three-tier cake.'

'No, I hardly know him,' Effie pointed out. Jake shifted uncomfortably in his seat.

'Oh, I'm sure he won't mind. It'll be the most perfect way for you to meet the rest of the village. Jake, why haven't you invited Effie? Your mum has been busy making all the bunting.'

'It sounds lovely, but I can't just crash the party,' Effie protested.

'You won't be crashing it,' Lola said, getting up and taking their empty plates, 'I'll let him know I've suggested it. Do you want anything else?'

Both Effie and Jake shook their heads. Once Lola had bustled back inside the café, their eyes met and they both began to laugh, shaking their heads in disbelief. Lola was a very difficult woman to say no to.

'I'm sure you'll be fine to come along,' Jake told her. 'Alf has always enjoyed a fuss. He pretends he doesn't, but secretly he loves it.'

'Thanks, but I'm not sure it's my thing. I wouldn't feel comfortable just turning up,' Effie said, memories of lingering awkwardly at far too many parties flashing through her mind. One of the joys of getting older and having a smaller, more understanding friendship group meant that it had been a relief for Effie to realise she could decline an invite or simply leave an event early. No judgement. Polcarrow was somewhere new and everyone was exceptionally sociable and friendly, maybe they wouldn't understand.

'I'd like you to be there and Lola's right, it's a perfect way to meet everyone. It'll be weirder if you're the only one not there.'

'What if I wait and see if Alf invites me?' Effie compromised, still unsure about just turning up.

Jake considered this before nodding his agreement. 'If he doesn't, I'll just sneak you in.'

Later that afternoon Effie was busy packing up their decorating equipment and Jake was in the small kitchen cleaning down the brushes, singing along to Queen on the radio, making her chuckle with his Freddie Mercury impression, when there was a knock at the door. Stretching her aching back, the thought of plunging into a steaming hot bath the only thing that was keeping her going, Effie crossed the shop and pulled open the door. Alf stood there, Scruff by his side.

'Hello,' Effie said, bending to give Scruff a scratch behind his ears, which set his tail wagging happily. 'How can I help you, Alf?'

'Is your young man about?'

'He's not my young man, Alf,' Effie rushed to remind him.

Alf gave her a look that seemed to say, *You'll see*.

'Jake,' she called, 'Alf's here.'

Jake emerged from the kitchen, drying his hands on a towel. He draped it casually over his shoulder before running his hands through his hair, pushing it back off his face. Effie's breath caught at the sight of him as the blond waves fell back into place, framing his face.

'Hey, hey, buddy,' he greeted Scruff. 'How can we help you?'

'I hear Lola's been dishing out invites to my birthday party. She shouldn't do that, but she can't help herself.' He rolled his eyes.

'It's OK, I wasn't expecting an invite,' Effie assured him.

'Don't be daft. Of course you're welcome! What I'm saying is, she shouldn't be dishing out invites on my behalf. I was going to toddle over tomorrow morning and ask you – properly, that is. So here I am. What are you doing on Saturday afternoon?'

Effie threw Jake a glance and he gave her an encouraging nod. 'Nothing,' she said.

'In that case, consider this your formal invite to my ninetieth birthday party.' Alf beamed. 'I can hardly believe it, you know, ninety. I'm already planning on getting to one hundred, so this is just a warm-up. Dress nice but not too fancy if you don't want. But please come, it'll mean everyone will be able to get a look at you in one go. Nosey lot they are. Like to meddle. Harmless though.'

'Ah, OK, sure, why not,' Effie said with a cautious glance at Jake. She wasn't sure she liked the idea of being on display to the entire village.

'You've really sold it,' Jake laughed. 'Mind if I bring my camera? I'd love to take some photos.'

Alf gave him a look whilst considering the offer. 'That would be splendid. Now, I'll leave you two young'uns to whatever you have planned this evening.' With a wave, Alf shuffled off, practically dragging Scruff with him.

Effie turned to Jake and exhaled. 'Should be fun,' she said, but Jake's focus was still on Alf as he crossed the road and made his way onto the beach.

'That man is a legend,' Jake said as he turned back to her. 'He seemed ancient when I was a kid but he just keeps going. I hope I'm that sprightly at ninety. Hey, if you're nervous about going alone, I can meet you beforehand and we can go together?'

'You sure?'

Jake nodded. 'I wouldn't have offered otherwise.'

'OK, that's kind, thank you,' Effie said, her nerves about attending a social function starting to settle.

'Cool. Let's pack up for the day. I've washed everything. Are you ready to go?'

Effie nodded. She'd tidied everything up whilst he'd been in the kitchen. She picked up her bag and headed towards the door, holding it open whilst Jake switched the radio and lights off. Once outside, with the door locked, Effie suddenly felt nervous around him. Should she offer to buy him a drink? Would he want to spend any more time with her? Jake was smiling at her in a way that discombobulated her normally ordered mind.

Before she could broach the subject, Jake's mobile rang. He pulled it out of his back pocket. Effie noticed the name Tara flash up on the screen. His ex. It was a sobering reminder of the type of woman he usually spent time with.

'Sorry, Effie, I've got to take this.' He gave an apologetic wince. 'See you tomorrow.'

Before she could say anything, he was already walking away, leaving her paint-stained, exhausted and feeling forgotten in the doorway.

Chapter Thirteen

'Which one do you prefer?' Effie held up a blue floral and a pink striped dress to her laptop. Maddie was on the other end of a video call, eating a large tub of strawberry yoghurt and casting a critical eye over all the outfits Effie had chosen. 'Or maybe I should just go for jeans?'

'Uh-uh, nope.' Maddie shook her head. 'It's a lovely spring day, it's a birthday party in a church hall, you can't rock up in jeans.'

Effie sank onto her bed. 'Yes, I can. I have a nice top I can wear with them,' she said half-heartedly. She was embarrassed to admit to herself that she wanted to make an effort for Jake, show him she scrubbed up well. The call he'd taken from his ex had been a reality check. He dated influencers, not bookshop assistants. Ugh. Why was she even thinking about dating him? She shouldn't be so easily won over by a charming smile and paint-brush-wielding expertise.

Effie reached for a pretty floral blouse with a lace collar. It was cute. It was more her style. The dresses had sat in her wardrobe since last spring. She'd packed them thinking they might be useful for the shop opening, not expecting a party invite.

'I'd feel better in jeans,' Effie said, more to convince herself than Maddie. 'I don't want to draw attention to myself.'

'Any more than you already have with your morning swims, opening a new shop and getting one of the locals to help you decorate. Tell me, is this guy who's been helping you going to the party?'

Effie's face flamed. 'Maybe, but it's not like that. He's just bored and likes decorating. What? Why are you shaking your head.'

'You wouldn't be ringing me for clothing advice if this guy meant nothing.'

Effie opened her mouth to protest but quickly closed it. Maybe she did fancy Jake a bit? The thought made her even more flustered. A glance at the clock revealed she had twenty minutes before they were meant to meet. 'Shit, Maddie, I have to go, I'm running out of time. Have a good afternoon.'

Maddie peered at the time on her laptop. 'Shucks, me too, lunchbreak nearly over. Wear the dress. I prefer the pink one. Love you.'

Effie watched as the screen went blank before flopping back against her pillows clutching the two dresses. They were both really pretty but the only way she was going to feel comfortable was in her jeans and the blouse. It felt far too early in the year for a cute summer dress. Anyway, she was only planning on popping along for half an hour. Parties, especially ones full of people she didn't know, put the fear in her.

Once her makeup was done, her hair plaited in a coronet around her head, a few wispy tendrils escaping around her face, Effie pulled on her jeans and the blouse. It looked cute. It felt safe. Her eyes strayed to the dresses. No, it was too late to get changed and her nerves were already jangling. Instead, Effie hung the dresses back up and checked the contents of her bag for the fourth time. Lipstick, phone, purse, could she slip in a book? No, that would be rude. Carrying a book with her had always been her comfort, so she compromised and tucked her Kindle inside.

After closing her bedroom door, Effie made her way into the living room, slipping her feet into a pair of bright yellow Converse. Her heart raced as she thought about walking into the church hall, all the locals turning to stare at her, questions in their eyes. Questions they'd no doubt find a way of asking. In the bookshop she felt safe. If anyone turned up to see what was going on, they were on her turf. They never lingered long either when they saw she was busy. But a party, oh gosh, there'd be no way out. People would try and twist her arm and get her to stay.

Panic began to rise in her chest at the thought of everyone turning to gawp at her as she stepped foot in the hall. Effie tried to calm her breathing, but it felt as if her heart was trying to clamour its way out through her throat. She froze as a battle raged inside her between picking up her bag and leaving the flat and just cancelling. She could claim she was sick. The air around her was thick, suffocating, and somewhere through the smog of it, a loud knock came at the door.

It sounded again. Effie caught the time on the kitchen clock. Ten past three. The plan had been to meet Jake outside at three. Swallowing down her fear, she crossed over to the door and with shaking fingers unlocked it.

'Effie, are you OK?' Concern flashed across Jake's face.

'I can't go,' she said desperately, 'I can't do this.'

'What?'

'The party,' her voice came out high pitched, panicked. 'I can't go and see all those people.'

Jake took her in, realised what was happening. 'Effie, listen to me. Look at me.' When she did, he placed his hands on her shoulders and calm instantly descended through her. He made her feel tethered. 'Deep breath. In for four, hold, out for four. And again.'

Effie did as instructed. Jake matched her shaky breaths with his own smooth ones. His eyes never left hers. Slowly, she felt the panic in her limbs begin to dissipate, felt herself drawn back into the room, into the present.

'What's up, Effie?'

She squirmed slightly before admitting, 'I don't like big crowds or parties or clubbing. I get anxious at social gatherings. I tend to avoid them. I know that makes me sound boring.' People had always called her boring at university and it had stuck, wedged itself in the gaps where her confidence had been chipped away. 'I'm much happier with my books.'

'Effie, that is perfectly OK, you don't need to like parties. Or clubbing. I couldn't say for sure, but I don't think Alf is the clubbing type. Scruff, however . . .'

Effie laughed. It felt good. She felt . . . safe. Jake wasn't judging her.

'Just remember it's a ninetieth birthday party in a church hall. You don't have to stay for more than half an hour if you don't want. You can leave at any time. I'll bring you home. You don't even need to make an excuse.'

'Are you sure?'

Jake nodded firmly. 'I'm sure and I promise, if you feel like you've had enough, I'll walk you home. I've got you, Effie. You've got this.'

Effie thought her reaction would be to not believe him, but as she stood in her living room, Jake's firm hands on her shoulders, holding her in place, she realised he really did have her back.

'You ready?' he asked gently.

Effie nodded. When he removed his hands, she felt as if she'd float away. 'Let me grab my cardigan.' Effie picked it up from the sofa. It was oversized, blue with daisies on it.

'Very cute.'

'I made it myself,' she said proudly, giving him a twirl. When she stopped, he was looking at her as if trying to process something.

'You look lovely,' he managed, his voice thick as he shifted from foot to foot, his eyes suddenly darting around the room before falling back on her.'

'Thank you.' A smile spread across her face. A true smile because Jake had really seen her, in a way no one else had for a long time. Jeans and a nice blouse, her social anxiety, he'd taken all this in and was still there, holding open the flat door for her. A little bit of trust began to creep in. Jake was a good guy. Maybe Maddie was right and there were some complicated, but also, extremely simple, feelings swirling around inside her for Jake.

Effie exhaled as she locked the door behind her. Once they'd made their way down the steps, Jake paused and offered Effie his arm, like a gentleman in a Regency romance. She tried not to swoon as she took it. Their eyes met. Next to Jake, Effie felt safe, special. It was unusual, something that would take getting used to, but also, she knew not to get carried away. Maybe he was just being friendly. She still had that question mark drawn over Tara after the call. Was she really just an ex?

'You really made this yourself?' He gave her sleeve a little tug as they walked along beside the beach.

'Yes, knitting and books, it's like I'm an old granny,' she joked.

'Not at all! It's comforting to meet someone who knows what they enjoy. Most of the women I've met, well, for starters, they're nothing like you. They want the flashy lifestyle. You're gentler,' Jake said, 'it's refreshing. I like it.'

His praise warmed her. 'Thank you. When I was younger I always thought I was a bit boring. Old fashioned. It's been easier to accept myself as I've got older and people have got more into crafting and quiet pursuits, but I always expect people to be judgy.'

'You're clearly not meeting the right people,' Jake said. 'I really don't think anyone who plunges into the freezing cold sea every morning could possibly be called boring. I tried dipping my toe in and nope! That was enough.'

'It's really not that bad once you get in,' she said, 'and then when you get out you feel like you could conquer the world. Did you not swim when you were a kid here?'

'Of course! But not in the winter. I'll go in in the summer when it's warmer.'

'Cold water is so invigorating though! Can't I convince you to give it a go?'

Jake gave it a few seconds thought. 'Maybe. But only up to my knees. Start me off slowly.'

Effie shook her head. 'Far better to take a full plunge, get it over with.'

Jake shuddered. 'I'll need some convincing on that. I admire you, Effie, not just the mad sea swimming but coming here alone, organising setting up the shop, which your boss should have done. You should give yourself more credit. Not everyone could do this.'

'Thanks, it was my choice though. I could've said no. I've always wanted to run my own bookshop though, it was my childhood dream. Well, still is my dream. This was the best way of achieving it.'

'That's so cool, Eff!'

She beamed at him. 'Thanks, that's why I want to prove to myself I can do it. If it was my own shop, I wouldn't have any help. Not that I'm not grateful for you, you've been a lifesaver.'

Jake shrugged this off. 'It's nothing, honestly. So, what was life back home like?'

'Really cosy. I lived with my parents, but we got on really well. You know how hard it is with property prices. I've worked in the shop since I came home from uni. I loved it. I had no plans to leave but when Clive offered this to me, suddenly I was curious about what was over the horizon. I did go away to university. Hated it. Bad experience. I was so unhappy. Swore I'd never leave. But, Polcarrow isn't far from home and it's small and safe.'

'There you go. Where did you go to uni?'

'London. It was a big dream. I thought I'd be intellectually stimulated, that I'd find the place I'd thrive in, but no, if anything it crushed me so I was even smaller than I already felt. I never told my parents until after I graduated. How silly was I to think London was everything when I have this on my doorstep?' Effie signalled to the sea.

Jake regarded the rolling waves thoughtfully. 'I've been all over the world but since I've come back to Polcarrow I've realised home is actually a lot more beautiful, with a lot more to discover than I originally thought.

It's making it hard to decide what to do next.' Before Effie could ask him about this, he changed the subject back to her. 'I'm sorry university wasn't a good experience. I think there's way too much pressure put on it being the best time of our lives. How do you feel about it now, looking back?'

'Still not good.' Effie turned to him. 'I try really hard to put it to the back of my mind. Really hard. But I feel like that failure is tied up in who I am today, like it's shaped me.'

'Do you still feel like a failure?'

Effie cast her mind back to the moments in her flat before Jake knocked on the door, the desperation to cancel. She knew if she had done so then she would've felt like she'd let everyone down. Most importantly, she'd have let herself down.

'Not right now I don't,' she admitted, giving him a shy smile.

'Good.' He patted her hand. 'I think we better get going. We're way past three o'clock.'

If going to a party was hard enough, the thought of walking into one late was even worse. Effie allowed Jake to lead her away from the seafront and up the narrow streets that closed around them like a secret, towards the church and its hall. Effie could hear music and there were balloons swaying in the breeze. She batted one away, giggling as it swung back towards her. When she caught Jake's eye, she realised he was watching her as if he'd never seen anything quite like her before.

'What? I like balloons,' She explained with a shrug. 'They're so joyful and remind me of being a child.'

'I'll see if I can get you one to take home.'

'Oi! Don't laugh at me!' Effie was giggling herself.

'I'm not. It's adorable,' Jake managed as he reached for the door handle, pushing it open slightly. 'Shall we?'

Effie froze. This was it. Her eyes skittered over the door before resting on him. Jake waited patiently for her cue. Effie took a deep breath, plastered a fake-it-until-you-make-it smile across her face and nodded.

'You first.' Her stomach clenched slightly as she watched Jake confidently step into the hall. Taking a deep breath, eyes half closed, she followed him in.

Chapter Fourteen

Effie had expected everyone to turn and stare, especially as they were thirty minutes late, however, to her relief, everyone just carried on with what they were doing. Children kicked balloons like they were footballs, adults stood in huddles, glasses of fizz in hand, chatting. Effie took in the beautifully decorated hall. Bunting hung from the rafters, photographs of Alf at various stages of his life were dotted around the hall and a sea shanty band was putting their own twist on hits from the past sixty years. A group of women was enjoying themselves dancing and even Effie found herself tapping her feet to the beat.

'See, not so bad,' Jake whispered as they made their way over to where generous platters of food had been laid out.

Effie followed him, taking the paper plate he handed her. 'No, not so bad.' She turned to him. 'Thank you, Jake. If you hadn't shown up, I would probably still be sitting in my flat.'

Jake piled some sandwiches onto his plate. 'It's nothing, Effie, honestly, and if you really hadn't wanted to come, I wouldn't have forced you.'

'Really?'

'Of course not. Not everyone enjoys socialising. Especially if it means meeting a whole village. I know what this village is like.' He raised an eyebrow. 'You're definitely stronger than you give yourself credit for.'

Effie watched as Jake made his way along the buffet table, loading his plate with sandwiches, sausage rolls and crudités. Effie selected a couple of egg and cress sandwiches and followed him. 'Usually, people see me not wanting to go somewhere as a negotiation point.'

'That's not right. If you don't fancy something, then a no should be a no,' Jake said with a shrug, as if it were a no-brainer.

Effie hadn't thought it was possible, but she swooned a little more. What on earth was happening to her? This was Jake, the annoying man who'd taken some dodgy photos of her swimming. A man who called her a mermaid, then a seal. It must've been her desperation to get the shop painted that had addled her brain. There was no other explanation for it. Her inconvenient crush was down to him being attractive, kind, helpful. Oh gosh, Maddie had been right, she *was* developing a crush.

Grabbing some potato wedges, Effie tried to put having a crush on Jake out of her mind, but her eyes homed in on him, as if she was attuned to his every movement. He was waiting for her at the end of the savoury section. She grabbed a mini quiche and followed him over to where Alf was sitting on a large chair that looked like a throne, Scruff at his feet.

'You came!' Alf beamed at them.

Jake broke a potato wedge in half and snuck it to Scruff.

'Oi, he's been spoiled today, thinks it's *his* birthday.'

'Happy birthday.' Jake seized Alf's hand and gave it a shake, before leaning in for a quick hug.

Not quite as at ease with physical affection towards people she didn't know well, Effie waved awkwardly. 'Happy birthday, I hope you're enjoying your day.'

'I am! I can't wait to see what Lola has whipped up for the cake. I asked for three tiers. Lemon, chocolate and Victoria sponge. I'm going to have a slice of each.'

'That sounds like a very good plan,' Jake agreed.

'You two should circulate, introduce yourselves to people, especially you, young lady. Everyone is really excited about the bookshop.'

Effie gave him a nervous smile. 'That's great, hopefully we'll get lots of business.' She knew she had to network, but glancing around the busy church hall, she knew she'd need a glass of fizz to take the edge off her nerves.

'We better find somewhere to perch and eat this.' Jake gestured to his plate. 'See you later, Alf.'

Alf gave them both a salute and Effie followed Jake over to a couple of spare chairs. Jake waved at a woman with wild curly hair who was holding a chubby baby on her hip.

'My mum,' he explained. 'And that's Cara, my brother's daughter. They've popped down from Newquay for the weekend. I stayed with them for a few weeks before coming back here. It was like I was building up to coming home.'

'Where did you live before?'

'Bristol. It's where I went to uni. Where I met Tara, my ex, and where we planned to get married and grow old together,' Jake explained with a hollow laugh.

'Oh. What happened?' Effie asked, alarm bells ringing but noticing he still referred to her as an ex. Maybe the phone call meant nothing. Anyway, it wasn't like there was anything going on between her and Jake.

Jake sighed. 'I don't want to spoil today by getting into all that. It's in the past. Or at least I'm trying to leave it there. I reckon everyone in here is dying to ask as well.'

Her mind swirling with questions she couldn't ask, they finished their food in silence, Effie taking in the people of Polcarrow, her new neighbours. Effie knew she had to bite the bullet and get on with introducing herself to everyone.

'Shall we get a drink and circulate?' Effie asked.

'Are you sure?'

Effie nodded. 'Yes, I feel a better now I'm here.'

'Sure, why not, sounds like a good idea.' Jake took her empty plate, and they made their way over to the drinks table. 'What do you fancy?'

Effie looked over the selection. Fizz was celebratory but always gave her a headache. There were soft drinks, beer and bottles of local cider. 'Cider, please,' she said to the man behind the table.

'You must be the bookshop lady,' he said as he passed her a bottle. 'I'm Steve, pub landlord, not seen you in yet.'

'Erm, sorry, no, I've been busy,' Effie flustered as she took her drink from him. She wasn't comfortable enough to go into pubs alone.

'Any time, love, any time. How you doing? Not seen you for a while.' Steve turned to Jake.

'One of those beers, please. I've been away, just got back earlier this week. Been helping Effie with her shop.'

'Ah, I see.' Steve raised his eyebrows. 'Well, off you go, enjoy yourselves, there's plenty of food. I think Lola's catered for the whole of Cornwall.'

Jake steered Effie away. 'See that wasn't so bad, was it? And we should definitely go to the pub. It's got gorgeous views of the bay, especially at sunset. What do you think?'

'Yes, that'd be nice,' Effie said shyly, whilst trying to shush her brain for leaping to conclusions about it being anything other than a friendly drink. She always did this, fell for men who showed her the tiniest bits of kindness. She'd got it wrong before and was determined not to make the same error of judgement somewhere everyone knew everyone else's business. Lola spotted them and waved them over.

'How wonderful to see you, my lovelies,' Lola cooed as she gave them both a kiss on the cheek. 'I know it can be a lot to face the whole village, but this is the perfect opportunity for you to meet everyone in one go,' she said to Effie before tugging on the arm of a handsome blond man, pulling him over to her side. 'This is Tristan, local vicar and my fiancé.' Lola shimmered with happiness as she glanced up at her beloved, who was beaming down at her as if she was the most precious thing on earth. 'We're getting married in May. So much to do!'

'But you have it all in hand, don't you, my dear,' Tristan said before turning to Effie and Jake. 'Pleased to meet you.' Tristan shook Effie's hand. 'Lola has been telling me a lot about you.'

'Has she?' Effie wondered what it was that Lola had been saying.

'You're our swimmer, aren't you? I'm not brave enough to take a dip this early in the year,' Tristan winced. 'So full respect to you.'

Effie laughed self-consciously. 'Does everyone know?'

'Nothing stays private in Polcarrow for long,' Lola warned.

Jake let out a knowing laugh at this observation. 'Too true.'

Effie sucked in a breath, feeling suddenly very exposed. They chatted for a few more minutes about the party, Lola gushing about how she couldn't wait to see Alf's face when she brought out the cake. Effie filled them in on her plans for the bookshop, Jake discussed his photography plans, including making sure Alf had a record of his party as a keepsake.

'Ah! I've forgotten my camera!' Jake exclaimed. 'Effie, are you OK if I leave you? I just need to go home and get it. I'll be two ticks.'

Feeling a bit more at ease from the cider and from talking to Lola and Tristan, she nodded her head. 'I think I'm going to be all right.'

'Thank you, I won't be long, promise.' He gave her arm a quick pat as he made his way towards the exit.

'Oh my!' Lola exclaimed as her eyes followed Jake out of the hall.

'Not matchmaking again are you, my love?' Tristan warned.

'Would I?'

Tristan turned to Effie. 'She can't help herself, but, I would say Lola's got a pretty good track record. Freya and Angelo. Then, there was us, but I was smitten from the moment I saw her, just took her a few months to catch up.'

'I'm so glad I did.' Lola smiled up at him.

Their love for each other was so strong that Effie almost felt as if she was intruding.

'How are you finding Polcarrow?' Tristan asked.

'It's lovely, but I've not seen much of it, been so busy with trying to sort the shop out,' she explained.

Lola slipped her hand out of Tristan's arm. 'In that case, let me introduce you to everyone.'

'Everyone?' Effie gulped, glancing around the room.

'Yes, then I can fill you in on all the little bits and pieces you need to know as an incomer,' Lola whispered as she slipped her arm through Effie's and started to lead her around the hall.

First, Lola introduced her to Sue and Cathy, prominent members, and friendly rivals, in charge of the village committee. Cathy narrowed her eyes suspiciously at the idea of a bookshop opening, whereas Sue almost combusted with excitement on the spot.

'A bookshop? In Polcarrow? That is amazing! You will be able to order things in, won't you?'

Effie nodded. 'Of course! Anything you like. We're opening on Easter Saturday.'

'Two weeks!' Sue exclaimed. 'That's not long, but I've been hearing you've had some help.' Sue signalled towards the curly-haired woman Jake had pointed out as his mum.

Joining them, she gave Effie a quick once-over before holding out her hand and pulling Effie into a hug. 'I'm Jan, you must be Effie. I'm so pleased to put a face to the name Jake keeps mentioning. He's such a good lad, so happy he's home. So, tell us more about this bookshop? How's it all going?'

As Effie chatted to her captive audience, she grew more and more at ease. She enjoyed seeing people's reactions to the bookshop, which were, thankfully, mostly excited and positive, peppered with questions about if she'd be running a book club, or what sort of books they'd be stocking, and wasn't it nice that the village would have a bookshop rather than having to order from big business off the internet.

As Effie answered questions and discovered things about the village and its inhabitants, she began to relax, to feel herself start to gently ebb into the flow of village life. Coming to Polcarrow didn't seem quite the disaster it had on Monday morning.

Chapter Fifteen

Effie was busy chatting to Lola's friend and barista, Freya, when Jake returned. She was enjoying connecting with someone her own age, someone who'd also moved to Polcarrow after a disastrous end to her life in London.

'That's absolutely amazing,' Effie gasped in response to Freya telling her how she'd fled down to Cornwall to escape a failed relationship and how Polcarrow, and a little help from Lola and Angelo, had helped her resurrect a completely dead artistic career.

'I know! Sometimes I pinch myself.' Freya took a sip of her drink. 'I had been selling my work in a gallery in St Ives but I want more creative control. Angelo and I are planning on opening a mini gallery. There's some space behind Lola's café. No idea how successful it'll be, but I need to try.'

'I'm sure it'll work out. It makes me feel better about the bookshop if there's other businesses for people to visit. Polcarrow is lovely, so I can see why Clive wanted to open a shop here, but . . .'

'It's the arse end of nowhere,' Freya quipped.

Effie couldn't help but laugh. 'I might have put it a bit more eloquently.'

Freya shrugged. 'But it's true. However, there's some magic here. People seem to be drawn here. Lola came because of a note in her grandmother's recipe book, Tristan because he was burned out, Angelo because he was fleeing his entire life. I think this is a place people come to heal,' Freya said philosophically. 'Things here have a habit of working out. Hey, has Lola been all smug about your friendship with Jake?'

Effie blushed. 'Maybe a little.'

'Don't mind her, she loves to matchmake, although it took her and Tristan forever to realise they were meant to be together.' Freya rolled her eyes. 'Do you like him?'

'Jake?' Effie startled.

'Umm hmm. Sorry, you don't need to answer that, it's none of my business.'

'That's OK . . . I . . . he took photos of me swimming because he thought I was a seal,' Effie said, 'and I shouted at him. He was very annoying but . . . also apologetic and he's been helping with the shop. I don't know,' she admitted, knowing full well that her head had been whipping around every time the door opened, her heart plummeting when she didn't see Jake.

Freya accepted this as an answer. 'But here's a warning, the villagers love a good gossip. Be careful. He's back.' She winked and gave Effie a little nudge.

Effie's heart leapt as Jake slipped into the hall, a rather expensive-looking camera hanging around his neck.

She swallowed a gulp of warm cider as she watched him scan the crowd, his brow a little furrowed until the sight of her smoothed it out. With a smile cracking like dawn across his face, Jake made his way across the hall towards Effie.

'I'll leave you to it.' Freya gave her arm a squeeze. 'Pop up to Bayview any time, I'll show you my work. Or we can go to the pub or something.'

'That would be lovely,' Effie said, knowing she meant it. The gentle way all the social invitations had been extended to her had felt genuine. The idea of putting down roots in the village was becoming less daunting.

'All set?' she asked Jake as he pulled up beside her.

'Yep, let me just take a few test shots. Say cheese.'

'I'm not saying cheese!' Effie laughed as he snapped away.

Jake peered into the screen, flicked through the photos. 'Looking good. Do you want to see?' He held the camera out to her. 'I can delete them if you like.'

Effie flicked through them. She never usually liked photos other people took of her. They always managed to make her face look wonky but somehow Jake made her look ethereal and beautiful. 'Definitely won't mistake me for a seal in those,' she said as she stepped back, draining her glass of cider.

Jake grinned. 'You're never going to let me forget that, are you?'

'Nope, because it's the most ridiculous thing I've ever heard. A seal!'

'I was half asleep from travelling!'

Effie raised an eyebrow at him. 'No excuse.'

Before Jake could protest any more. Tristan stepped onto the small stage and leaned into the microphone. 'Erm, can we have a moment please?' The hubbub of the hall died down as the crowd turned towards him. 'Thank you, everyone, for coming today, it's a pleasure to celebrate such a milestone in Alf's life. Ninety years old, or should that be young?' Tristan paused as whoops, cheers and applause thundered around the hall. 'I think it's a marvellous age to reach and it's safe to say that, Alf, you are the heart and soul of this community. Polcarrow would not be the place it is without you at the helm.'

Alf bowed his head in acknowledgement of the accolade. More applause sounded. Scruff barked in agreement.

'Now, we all know you're waiting for the cake but before we get to that, we have something else for you, Alf. Now, we all wracked our brains because what do you buy the man who has everything and wants for nothing?'

The crowd murmured in excitement. Effie caught sight of Freya standing at the corner of the stage next to a tall man with long, wild dark hair. Between them they were carrying a large rectangular object which they brought over to Alf and placed on an easel.

'Is that for me?' Alf gasped.

'It's been a long time since I've done portraiture. I did consider a sculpture,' the man, who Effie realised was Angelo Borelli, renowned artist and Freya's partner, explained, 'but I didn't know how you'd feel about being turned into abstract art.'

Alf gave a shrug. 'It would make a change from a pair of socks.'

Everyone laughed.

'Shall I do the honours, or do you want to?' Angelo asked.

'You do it, I'm too comfy here,' Alf said giving the arm of his chair a pat.

Angelo tugged at the sheet covering the object. It fell away to reveal a vibrant painting of the old fisherman, sitting regally beside the fishing boat Angelo had helped him restore the previous summer, Scruff at his feet, Polcarrow stretched out behind him. Timeless and beautiful, it captured the twinkle in the old fisherman's eye and the essence of Polcarrow, all wrapped up in a golden hour glow.

'I'm very rarely speechless,' Alf said after a moment, 'but this, well, can you believe it? An Angelo Borelli original of me! What do you make of that, boy, hey?' He scratched Scruff's ears, his voice thick with emotion.

'Do you like it?' Angelo asked, uncertainty flashing across his face.

'Like it? I love it! Although I think I might need to take some time to really give it a good look.' Alf beckoned Angelo over and pulled him in for a tight hug. Effie's eyes welled at the sight of the old man and the artist, the strength of the bonds that kept the community together.

Angelo pulled himself up, and glancing around caught Tristan's eye, who leapt to the rescue by saying, 'Isn't that the most wonderful painting? We can all admire it later because now I think it's time for the cake.'

Alf's face lit up. 'Just what I've been waiting for.'

Effie watched as Lola emerged from the hall kitchen carefully carrying a three-tier cake. Iced in white fondant, it was decorated with edible lifebuoys, fishing nets and on the top sat a beautifully recreated fishing boat with sugar paste figures of Alf and Scruff seated in it. Jake slipped forward with his camera, taking photos without getting in anyone's way or stealing the limelight from Alf, who beamed as everyone launched into a rousing rendition of 'Happy Birthday'. A round of cheers and hip, hip, hoorays followed, which set Scruff off barking.

'Speech!' someone called.

'All right, all right.' Alf pulled himself to his feet as Tristan handed him a microphone. The hall fell silent as everyone waited to hear what the old fisherman would say.

'Well, ninety, can you believe it? I can't. Well, I can, but you know what I mean. Time isn't guaranteed to any of us, but I am truly blessed to still be here, still in my own home in Polcarrow, still waking up to the sight and sound of the sea every day. People dream of life over the horizon. That was never for me. What more do you need other than love and friendship. I am honoured to be part of such a thriving, caring, kind community. Now, I don't have any secrets about how to get to this ripe old age, other than living well, never dwell on anything, enjoy the simple things because really, that is what life is about. Now, I don't know about you, but I'm quite keen to have a piece of this cake! And I'm sure Lola is very keen to put it down.'

'Oh Alf, you read my mind!' Lola said as she carried the cake over to the table.

Alf followed her. He took the knife she offered and sliced into the cake, cutting a large chunk. 'This is for me—' he winked at the gathering '—and doesn't it look splendid. Now, I'll leave it to Lola to serve, she knows more about cutting up cakes than I ever will!'

A round of applause went up and as Effie caught Jake's eyes, she saw her own emotions reflected back in them. Jake smiled at her, warm and reassuring. Along with Alf's words, it took her breath away. Polcarrow, it seemed, a place where lost souls found safe harbours, was becoming more and more like home every day.

Chapter Sixteen

Effie woke the following morning with a slightly sore head. Rolling over in bed, the previous evening fell into place like a disjointed jigsaw puzzle. The party had wound up in the church hall once all the cake had been eaten and then many of the guests headed over to the pub. Normally, Effie would've made her excuses and gone home at that point, but it had been so easy to be swept along with her new friends. She'd enjoyed herself immensely. Nerves dulled by another pint of local cider, Effie had found herself doing the rounds, exchanging information about her life, listening to everyone's hopes for the bookshop, and garnering their interest for it.

The enthusiasm and excitement from the villagers had made Effie determined to make it the best bookshop she could. Although she knew it was Clive's shop, Effie didn't think he'd mind if she took some matters into her own hands and gave Polcarrow the bookshop its residents craved. After all, he wanted it to be a success. The most popular request had been for a book club. Sue had already been trying to form one and had made enquiries about holding it at Lola's café on a Thursday evening.

Effie saw no reason not to join forces with her and set one up.

By the time she'd left the pub, wandering home alone, the sun long gone, Effie was brimming with ideas and swaying slightly from a third pint she knew she'd regret in the morning. Jake had been busy talking to Angelo and Effie hadn't wanted to disturb him, so she'd left alone.

Now the morning was here, she was glad to only have a slight headache, one that she knew would be soothed by a swim in the sea. Yawning, Effie climbed out of bed and pulled on her wetsuit. The sky was slightly overcast but that was no excuse not to take a dip. She left the flat, crossed the road and padded down the steps onto the beach, shrugging off her dry robe and flip-flops before making her way into the sea.

The first wave was cold and instantly woke her up. Slowly, she made her limbs move through the water, her head clearing with each stroke. She was just wondering if she'd earned a day off from all the decorating, it was Sunday after all, and figuring out what she could do, when she remembered her parents were due to visit. They'd texted the previous evening whilst Effie had been on the way to the pub, and she'd agreed. She couldn't wait to show them the progress she'd made. On finishing her swim, feeling revived, Effie lingered on the beach, lying to herself that she wasn't searching for Jake.

After a few minutes, when he didn't show, Effie pushed him and the complicated feelings he rose in her, from her mind. Back in her flat, she jumped in the shower and rinsed the sea salt from her hair. Two cups of tea and a bacon sandwich later, she felt completely human again. She was giving the flat a quick tidy when a knock on the door sounded. Rushing over, Effie pulled it open, thrilled to see her parents standing there, her mum holding a bunch of early spring flowers.

'Hello, love.' Rosemary passed Effie the flowers before bundling her into a hug. 'I've missed you so much!'

'It's only been a week,' Effie reminded her, as she squeezed her mum back as best she could whilst also holding the bouquet. 'I've missed you too.'

'How's it going?' her dad asked, glancing around the flat. 'It looks a lot better in here than when I left last week.'

'I got to work on it straightaway.' Effie gestured to the room. 'Let me take your things and I'll give you the not so grand tour.'

Effie took her parents' coats and bags and hung them on the hooks on the back of the door. She then showed them around the tiny flat, pointing out the sea view, opening cupboards to show them how she'd stored things. Seeing it through their eyes made Effie proudly realise how much she had achieved in a week.

'What about the shop?' Brian asked with a grimace.

'It's coming on slowly; I've had some help.'

'Did Clive send someone, like he should've done?'

Effie shook her head. 'No, my neighbour, Jake, has been helping me paint. His dad's a decorator.'

Her parents exchanged a look at the mention of Jake. Effie blushed, not knowing whether or not to protest that he was just a friend or to ignore the look. She chose the latter. Her mum had started to drop hints that it'd be nice for Effie to find a real young man, not a fictional one.

'Would you like to see it?' Effie said to deflect attention away from her love life.

'Yes please!'

Grabbing her keys, she slipped on her shoes and opened the flat door. 'Follow me.'

They made their way back downstairs where Effie unlocked the shop, her mum commenting that it was in a prime location and gushing over the sea view. Effie pushed open the door and could see how far the transformation of the space had gone. It looked much brighter painted white, like a fresh start. It even looked bigger than it had when she'd started.

'Wow!' Brian exclaimed. 'It's like a whole different place. I felt awful leaving you here last week. That estate agent was a right pillock. You've done really well, this looks great. Can't wait to see it when it's all finished.'

'Neither can I actually,' Effie said proudly. 'The books should be arriving next week and then the other stock. I'm really looking forward to dressing the space. Clive said I could buy a couple of armchairs for the window, create a sort of homely vibe. What do you think?'

'If I was sitting there, I don't think I'd ever want to leave,' Rosemary said as she crossed over to the window. 'What a view! He definitely chose the location well.'

Effie followed her. 'I know, despite everything, Clive got that right!'

'What's everyone in Polcarrow like?' Rosemary asked with concern.

'Oh, they are lovely! So lovely! I've been made very welcome. I went to a birthday party yesterday.'

Her parents exchanged another glance at this. Effie wasn't known for being a social butterfly.

'It was ninetieth one, so nothing too wild,' she explained, 'but it was nice to be invited. I met so many people and they're all very excited about the shop.'

'That's wonderful, I'm so relieved,' Rosemary said. 'I've been worrying all week, haven't I, Brian?'

'Yes, you're lucky I kept her away this long, Effie. Especially after she found out you're based next to that café.' He nodded in the direction of next door.

'I've been drooling over the online reviews. Apparently the scones are to die for.'

'Lola's? It's amazing, shall we go? She's usually open by now.'

'I thought you'd never ask!'

Effie ran back upstairs to grab her purse before leading her parents next door. The café was indeed open. Alf and Tristan were sitting in the window seat, a toast rack between them and a heated debate going on about what type of tea was the best to drink. A newspaper was open on the table but any attempt to do the crossword had been abandoned. Scruff was eyeing a spaniel that was out with some dog walkers, as they queued for takeaway coffees, with a bit of curiosity and suspicion. The buttery aroma of fresh scones hung in the air. Rosemary almost swooned at the quaint vintage vibe.

Lola glanced up as Effie and her parents made it to the front of the queue. 'Good morning, did you have a nice time yesterday?'

'I did!' Effie beamed before introducing her parents to Lola.

'Lovely to meet you. We're all really excited about the bookshop. I have so many ideas for the opening, which we still need to discuss properly,' Lola reminded Effie.

'Oh yes, of course. Can we have one hot chocolate and two flat whites. Do you want any cakes?'

Rosemary peered into the counter. 'Oh my! I don't know what to choose! They all look divine. Chocolate chip shortbread, millionaire brownies, the scones! Look at them! Your dad wants to go to a seafood place he's seen a bit further along the coast for lunch, so I don't want to be too full. Ooh, look at those raspberry blondies. Nope, it's got to be a traditional Cornish cream tea.'

'Perfect choice, fresh out the oven.' Lola smiled as she selected one of the biggest scones and placed it on a plate, before, glancing at Brian, waiting for his choice.

'The booking's for two thirty so as it's only eleven I'm pretty sure one of those scones won't ruin my appetite too much,' Brian said, pointing to the scones. 'They look delicious.'

'I can assure you they are.' Lola winked as she plated up another cream tea before turning expectantly to Effie.

Effie took in the sheer size of the scones and scanned along the other baked offerings. 'I'll have a blondie,' she said, the tart red berries oozing against the white chocolate made her mouth water. She was still quite full from her bacon sandwich and didn't want to risk ruining her lunch, not if there was fresh seafood involved.

'That would've been my second choice,' Rosemary said.

'Wonderful, take a seat and I'll bring them over,' Lola said once they'd paid.

'How do you stay away from here with all those cakes?' Rosemary asked as they sat down.

'The truth? I don't. The cakes have helped get me through the last week.'

Lola brought the tray over to them, unloaded it, told them to let her know if they needed anything else and left them to their elevenses. They all tucked in, Rosemary enviously pinching a bit of Effie's blondie. Conversation ranged from Effie's daily swims, the new extension the neighbours were trying to get built back in Penzance and a catch-up on all Rosemary's regular patients, who had all been filled in on Effie's grand adventure and were waiting for the next instalment.

'Mum, you make it sound like I've gone to the other side of the world, not a few miles down the road!'

'It feels like the other side of the world,' Rosemary remarked, 'what with all those little roads we had to drive down.'

Just as Effie was about to say something about the state of the roads, the café door opened, and she caught her breath at the sight of Jake. Hair damp from the shower, wearing his signature white T-shirt and blue jeans, he looked absolutely gorgeous.

'Morning, Effie . . .' He trailed off as he saw her parents, unsure how to greet them.

'Hi, Jake. This is my mum, Rosemary, and my dad, Brian,' she said. 'This is Jake, he's been helping in the shop.' She really hoped her blush wasn't too obvious.

Handshakes were exchanged along with greetings. Lola brought Jake over a coffee and Brian insisted he join them. Effie squirmed a bit inside, but Jake was wonderful, asking questions, telling her parents all about his photography, showing them some of the photos on his phone. By the time the coffees had been drunk, Rosemary had managed to twist his arm into coming out for lunch with them.

'So that's Jake,' her mum said with an encouraging smile as they headed to the car.

'Yes, that's Jake,' Effie confirmed without elaborating further. It was bad enough that she was wrestling with her own suspicions that she had a crush on him, without everyone else muscling in on the match-making. Jake was kind, but he was fresh from a break-up, and Effie didn't want to get her own hopes up, let alone anyone else's. Yes, he was gorgeous, but she could still be getting carried away and reading the signs wrong.

'He's been a really good friend, he's helped me out no end with the café, but he's had a recent break-up so I think it's best to just be friends,' she reiterated, hoping her mum would leave it at that, although she couldn't help wondering if they'd ever be more than just friends.

Chapter Seventeen

'Effie, take a seat.' Lola accosted her the moment she pushed open the café door following her Tuesday morning swim. 'I've got something for you. The usual?'

'Yes please.' Effie pulled her dry robe around her. It was a damp, cold morning, so the warmth of the café was a welcome reprieve.

Alf patted the spare seat beside him. 'Been for a swim, love? You're a brave lass.'

'Not as brave as you were, I bet,' Effie said, 'at least I can stay in the bay and not go all the way out to the ocean.'

Alf shrugged. 'That was a long time ago. I miss it. But you have to respect the sea. It can turn in an instant. I used to swim in my youth. Sometimes I wonder why I ever gave up. The sea is a good place to calm the brain. Puts things into perspective.'

Effie nodded her agreement. 'That's why I do it. Sets me up for the day. It's easier to swim here every day now the sea is just across the road. It beats a swimming pool any day.'

'There you go.' Lola placed a large mug of hot chocolate in front of Effie followed by a plate of bite-sized hot cross buns. Alf's eyes widened at the sight of them. Sensing the baked goods, Scruff sat up.

'I didn't order any buns,' Effie said, 'but they're adorable.'

'I said I could cater for the shop opening, here's my first offering. Mini hot cross buns. Try them, see what you think.'

Effie picked one of the buns up and bit into it. The dough was pillowy and soft, the fragrant spices hitting her palate as the fruit burst on her tongue. 'Oh my gosh, that's one of the best hot cross buns I've ever had!'

Lola beamed with pride. 'Freshly baked this morning.'

Effie helped herself to a second one, ravenous from her swim. Alf picked one up and took a bite.

'Why aren't these already on the menu?' Alf asked. 'It's two weeks until Easter. At Christmas we had mince pies coming out of our ears.'

'Don't fret, Alf. I'll be rolling out my Easter treats this week. Buns, bunny biscuits, mini simnel cakes. I'll decorate the café for spring later. Found some gorgeous bunting. It'll be like an Easter grotto, if that's even a thing.' Lola laughed before admitting, 'I've just been tied up trying to get my wedding plans sorted. Tristan and I thought it'd be fun to do it as soon as possible, but I didn't expect the past few months to go quite so quickly.' She sighed as she sat down between them.

'When are you getting married?' Effie asked.

'Late May bank holiday weekend. I know! I know! It's not even two months away. I must be mad.'

'Don't believe the panic,' Alf told Effie. 'She's got it all planned out, I'm sure.'

'Everything other than a photographer,' Lola sighed, 'they're all fully booked. Have been for months.'

Effie's mind turned to Jake. However, the most she'd seen of his photos was of the interior of the shop and some stunning landscapes. But wasn't he trying to build up a business doing weddings and events? She fished a gooey marshmallow out of her mug and contemplated putting his name forward.

'Anyway, enough of my woes. Effie, would you like me to make some buns for the opening? I can also do chocolate nest cakes and oh, what about book-shaped biscuits?'

'That would be wonderful, let me just clear it all with Clive. We're having a chat later about the shop progress. Apparently, he's arranged for someone to come and open it, but he won't tell me who!'

'A celebrity?' Lola gushed.

'Probably a local author,' Effie told her. 'No idea who though. We are a little bit out of the way.' She'd spent the previous night searching all her favourite authors online, trying to figure out who might want to make the journey. Effie was secretly hoping for a romance author. She'd made a list and sent it to Clive, placing her favourites at the top. He'd replied with 'We'll see what the budget looks like.'

Effie's thoughts were interrupted by the café door opening. Jake stepped inside, holding a small folder in his hands. She hadn't seen him since he'd joined her parents for Sunday lunch. He'd been brilliant company, chatting to her dad about his music taste and her mum about her job. When Effie had kissed her parents' good-bye that evening, she'd been rather concerned that her mum was about to start issuing wedding invitations.

Jake had had some business to attend to the previous day, and Effie hadn't known what to do with the feelings of missing him that had risen as she'd spent a rather boring morning giving the walls what she hoped would be a final coat of paint. Even her trusty Viking warriors couldn't lift her spirits.

'Morning.' Jake beamed at them 'Was hoping to find you all here. I've got something to show you.' He dropped the folder onto the table and slipped into the spare seat.

'Coffee, Jake?' Lola asked.

'Yeah, sure, thanks, extra shot this morning, please.' Jake drummed his fingers on the table as he waited for Lola to return.

'What have you got for us?' Alf asked when Lola was back.

'Remember I took some photos at the party. Yesterday I went to get them developed properly and I wanted to show them to you.' He pulled the glossy prints from the folder and passed them to Alf.

As Alf slowly went through them, Effie was surprised to see nerves come over the normally confident Jake. From the corner of her eye she watched as he dragged his hands through his hair, tapped sugar packets against his cup and took a hurried sip of too hot coffee.

'Well, young man, these are splendid,' Alf said.

Jake sat forward. 'You think so?'

Alf nodded and signalled for Lola to come over. 'Here, have a look.'

Lola sat down and took the photos from Alf then slowly leafed through the prints before passing them on to Effie. Even from the first few it was obvious that Jake had a natural talent for capturing the moment. He'd managed to get the joy on Alf's face as Lola presented the birthday cake to him, Scruff's eagerness to get in on the action, the delighted surprise when Angelo revealed his portrait. Even the photos Jake had taken of unsuspecting Polcarrow residents were flattering. Effie's face coloured as she reached the last one. It was one of the test shots he'd taken of her when he returned to the hall.

Effie went to pass the photos back to him, but Lola took them for a second glance.

'What do you think? Are you happy with them?' Jake asked.

'They're amazing, Jake,' Effie said, 'you've really captured everything. You're so talented.'

'Splendid, boy, absolutely splendid, I could be a model!' Alf quipped and struck a pose. 'You've really flattered Scruff here.' The dog barked in agreement.

Jake exhaled with relief. 'Thanks, that means a lot. Honestly. You see, I'm thinking of starting a business doing event photography, but I've not got very far with it yet. Yeah, my landscapes have been popular online, but photographing people is a whole different business. They fascinate me. The stories their faces tell, you know. I loved taking these photos. Your comments have given my confidence a boost. Thanks, guys.'

An epiphany passed across Lola's face as she handed the photos back to him. 'Jake, these are wonderful. I'm wondering if I can ask you something.'

'Go on.' Jake took the package back from her.

'Tristan and I are getting married the last weekend in May. Everything is sorted other than a photographer; there's just no one available. I had no idea finding one would be so hard. But these photos are amazing. Really natural, I love them. Would you be interested in photographing our wedding?'

Jake contemplated this. 'Really? I'd love to but a wedding is different from a birthday party.'

'Yes, I do mean it, and not just because we're desperate,' Lola insisted. 'Those photos are truly something special. We don't want anything too formal, and you've clearly got an eye for detail.'

Effie watched as Jake considered the offer, her own heart racing with expectation. Surely this would be the best way for him to get his new venture off the ground.

'Gosh, Lola, that's quite the honour, but could I do a few test shots first, check you're happy. You know, like an engagement shoot?'

'An engagement shoot?' Lola's face lit up. 'Of course! I have the perfect dress!'

Alf rolled his eyes. 'Of course you do.'

'I want to make sure you're completely happy with the photos before we agree to anything. Dreaming of taking event photos is one thing, being entrusted with someone's wedding is another.' Jake gulped.

'I have every faith in you. Honestly, Jake, I do.' Lola's voice was soothing and sure. Effie couldn't imagine anyone ever saying no to her.

Jake caught Effie's eye and gave a nervous laugh as he raised his cup to his lips. 'No pressure,' he said before draining the coffee and catching Effie's encouraging gaze, disbelief shining in his blue eyes. Part wonder, part terror at what he'd agreed to.

No pressure at all, Effie thought, for either of them setting up their new lives in Polcarrow. It seemed the village really did have a way of sprinkling magic onto the roots of its residents' new beginnings.

Chapter Eighteen

Although she'd been anxious about attending Alf's party, it turned out that Effie putting in an appearance had been the best type of publicity for the bookshop. On Thursday morning, Sue knocked on the door and waved to catch Effie's attention. She switched off the vacuum cleaner and headed over to unlock the door.

'Morning,' she greeted as she pulled the shop door open to let Sue in.

'Thought I'd pop by and see how you're getting on. Everything all right?' Sue stepped inside and cast her eyes over the freshly painted shelves and walls.

'Yes, it's going as well as I could hope, still quite a bit to do though,' Effie said, as she watched Sue glance over the interior as if measuring it up to see how it'd fit with her own committee plans. She'd quickly learned that Sue was the driving force behind a lot of happenings in Polcarrow, so having her on side could only be a bonus.

'Oh, doesn't it look wonderful?' Sue sighed as she made her way over to the window with the sea view. 'I'm so glad to see the space being used. Such a waste to keep it closed. It looks so much bigger now it's all white. Used to be dreadfully dark.'

'Definitely,' Effie agreed before admitting, 'I had wondered what I'd taken on when I arrived here and if I'd get it done on time, but I'm pleased with how it's turned out.' As she said the words, Effie realised it was true. She felt an immense sense of pride that she had managed to turn the shop from drab to dazzling in such a short space of time.

Of course Jake had been invaluable help, and the Easter Saturday launch didn't feel quite as daunting now. All Effie was waiting for was the boxes of books to arrive and to add her own finishing touches. She wanted the shop to look both spectacular and cosy, especially as it was situated next door to Lola's café. Effie planned for them to be in perfect harmony with each other, to create the ideal place for book lovers to flock to. What more could anyone want than books, tea and cake?

Jake was out for the day catching up with to two old schoolfriends who were expecting a baby and wanted to book him for a pregnancy photoshoot, so Effie was glad of some company and the chance to take a break. 'How long had it been empty?'

'Oh years. It sold all sorts really, stuff for tourists, odds and ends for locals. I don't think we'd ever thought of it opening up again. People have been interested in it, but nothing ever came of it. Too much work, never the right time, you know the sort, a shame to leave it empty,' Sue explained. 'I'm glad it's going to be a bookshop. Feels very wholesome.'

'Me too. But I'm still a bit worried it's too out of the way,' Effie confessed.

Sue took a sip of her drink and shook her head. 'Not at all. Not with social media. A bookshop with a sea view next to a vintage café, I think your business is going to be fine.'

'I'm glad you think so but it's not actually mine, although I wish it was,' Effie said. 'My boss took a chance on the location so I feel pressure to make sure it works out.'

'Hmm, maybe, but you can only do your best and see what happens. Lola took a chance and look how that's worked out,' Sue reminded her. 'Are you just selling books or other bits and pieces? I do like a knick-knack.'

Effie smiled. 'Mostly books, but not just novels, we'll be stocking photo books, local history, greetings cards, maps for walkers. There'll also be a small shelf for quality second-hand books. I'm going to have a section at the back for kids' books, too.' She pointed to the far corner. She'd ordered a brightly coloured rug and was waiting for its delivery. It was the area of the shop she was most looking forward to transforming.

'Oh Effie! That sounds so lovely! Very exciting! Are you going to do story time? My kids loved story time when they were little.'

It hadn't occurred to Effie to offer anything of the sort, but now Sue had mentioned it, it seemed like a good way of getting people involved in the shop. 'That's a great idea, I don't see why not.'

'I'm sure the parents would love it. If you need any excitement drumming up, let me know. People keep telling me they're looking forward to the opening.' Her phone pinged. 'Oh, is that the time, I better get going, nice to see it coming along well. Looking forward to the launch. I could contact local press if you want? And we must talk about the book club; I've been trying to organise one for ages.'

'Sure! That would be great,' Effie said as she waved Sue off.

If the rest of the day was anything to go by, Effie wouldn't need to drum up support via the village committee or local press because almost everyone in Polcarrow popped by to have a look at the shop, see how she was getting on and chat about their favourite books. Steve liked ghost stories, the scarier, the better, so he could try and spook the punters. Tristan was interested in local history and several teenage girls asked if there would be a romantasy section, their eyes wide as they swooned over fairy princes. Effie found herself in a long conversation with the woman who cleaned the holiday lets about romance, both of them deciding that Vikings beat brooding dukes every time.

As she was about to close up for the evening, her phone rang. 'Hello?'

'Effie, how's it going? Just wanted to touch base on a few things. Are you ready for the books to be brought down? Surely the paint's dry by now,' Clive fired away. 'I've got the till to be installed, you ready for that too?'

Effie perched on the windowsill. 'Yes, I'm ready for the books and the till.'

'Excellent, the photos are looking fantastic. I knew you'd manage to transform the space. How's it going with the locals? Are they keen? Or obstructive?'

'Oh definitely keen,' Effie replied, 'they're full of suggestions for what they want to see. I've been asked about running a story time for kids and one of them wants me to help with a book club.'

'A book club, why didn't I think of that? That's an excellent idea. Maybe we could extend it to this branch? Glad they're keen,' he said, 'just do what you need to make it a success. Not so sure about story time though, I don't want us running a crèche, we're a shop. But you know, I trust you, Effie, just do what you can to get the public through the door.'

Before Effie could respond she heard the sound of Clive clicking his computer mouse. 'What's this about an order for two armchairs? Yellow? Our colour is blue.'

Worried her plans might be thwarted, she made her case. 'For the window. Yellow is nice and bright. Perfect for a spring launch. Trust me. It'll complement the décor really well. Blue looks great in Penzance but Polcarrow is a much more gentle place, I really think the yellow will be perfect. There's a view over the sea. It'll be nice for readers to sit and look through what they want to buy.'

Clive gave a dissatisfied grunt. 'Are you sure? I get that it's a good space, but we want people buying books, not just lounging around.'

Effie steeled herself. She was not going to back down where the chairs were concerned. 'What we need is customers. Polcarrow is a little out of the way but the shop is next door to an adorable café. If we create a cosy atmosphere with a sea view the shop will end up all over social media and that'll draw the customers in.'

'Hadn't thought of that, good thing you're setting this up, not me. You've clearly got your finger on the pulse. Do what you need, Effie, but I want books sold not just girls posing on armchairs with them, all right? Gotta go, keep me posted, send some more photos. I'll let you know when I'm popping down with the till.'

Effie hung up and glanced around the shop. She snapped a few pictures then fired them off to Clive. Sometimes she wondered why on earth he ran a bookshop, as he wasn't much of a reader. He'd inherited the shop from his father, who had been a bookworm, the business having been started by Clive's grandfather. Clive was keeping it running through a sense of sentimentality, which was admirable.

However, Clive didn't seem to understand that book lovers liked to linger among the shelves, pulling off books, inspecting the covers, reading the blurbs, flicking through the pages, sometimes giving them a surreptitious sniff. Clive wanted sales. Effie, who loved a wander around a cute characteristic bookshop, who followed lots of them on social media, understood what readers wanted. Books were a safe haven, an escape and the shops that sold them needed to reflect this. She wanted this shop to provide a place of comfort and wonder to readers, to have them step through the door and feel as if they'd been gathered into a gentle, bookish hug.

Effie closed up and let herself out into the cool evening air, twilight already starting to draw in over the bay. Locking the door, she wished the shop goodnight. As she pulled away, her hand ran down the door. Stepping back, she took in the dull, flaking red paint, which gave off the unkempt, unloved vibe of an abandoned shop. Effie picked off some more of the paint, exposing the wood beneath. Painting the door was next on her list of jobs.

Taking a few steps backwards, the ethereal evening light softening the village around her, Effie took in the shop, the vacant window, the empty shelves, a locked-up shell of potential. She thought of the two yellow armchairs, as bright as the spring sun, as joyful as a daffodil. Her mind fell to the tin of navy door paint she'd ordered, which remained unopened in the kitchen. Nothing about the heavy night-time shade felt right. Could she extend her yellow theme out here? A door the colour of the sun to greet the dawn? Clive said he trusted her. Would this be step too far? Yellow was warm, welcoming and hopeful, everything she wanted the shop to be.

Chapter Nineteen

'Do you need a hand?'

Effie glanced up from where she was kneeling on the doorstep, scraping the old flaking paint off the door. Her heart leapt at the sight of Jake hovering; his checked shirt pushed up over his tanned forearms, his golden hair glinting in the sunlight. Effie swallowed as she dragged her eyes up his body to meet his.

'I'm actually quite enjoying it,' she said as she sat back, 'it's very cathartic to be scraping off this old paint.'

'I can see. Going well?'

'Yes, I spoke to Clive.' Effie stood up and wiped her brow. 'Sue popped by yesterday and we had a chat about what I'm going to be doing in the shop. She is full of ideas! Story time for the kids, why didn't I think of that? Although Clive was less enthusiastic about the idea but he told me to carry on with whatever I've been planning. I know the door is meant to be blue but I was feeling defiant and yellow is just so much brighter.'

Jake gasped, 'You rebel!'

Effie laughed, 'I can always paint it blue later if he's not happy, but I thought yellow would be so nice and bright what with it being springtime. How were your friends?'

'Good, good. It seems mad that Mags and Ewan are having a baby. It doesn't feel like five minutes ago we were all sneaking cans of cider down to the cove. They liked what I'm offering. They booked me in for next week.'

'Oh Jake, that's amazing!'

'Thanks. Still daunting though. Now, do you fancy a hot chocolate and you can tell me about these plans you've hatched?'

'I've already had my daily hot chocolate, but a cup of tea would be lovely.'

'I'm sure you're allowed more than one hot chocolate,' Jake told her.

Effie shook her head. 'I like my little rules. Plus, it wouldn't be a treat if I was drinking them all the time.'

'Fair enough. I'll grab us some lunch. I'm starving and it looks like you've earned a break.'

Effie watched Jake head into Lola's. Effie had missed him, a feeling she hadn't wanted to inspect too closely, even though he had only been away overnight. It had, however, been good to throw herself into the shop without the distraction of Jake's sunny, disarming smile.

The previous evening, following her chat with Clive, Effie had sat down with a notebook and made copious lists of things she needed to do to make the shop look inviting, events she could host and stuff she needed to buy. She'd then gone on a mini online shopping spree buying Easter- and book-themed accessories for the opening. The gorgeous rainbow-coloured rug for the children's area had arrived first thing and it looked delightful.

Jake came out of Lola's carrying two takeaway cups and a couple of paper bags. 'Fresh pasties,' he said. 'I've not had a single pasty since I've been back in Cornwall.'

'What? How long have you been back?' Effie asked as she downed her tools and followed him over to the harbour wall and perched on it, scanning the sky for seagulls.

'About a month. Six weeks-ish.'

'A month! No pasties? Have you had a cream tea?'

'Erm, not yet . . . Confession, I'm not actually a huge fan of them.'

Effie gasped in mock horror. 'That is outrageous! I might have to revoke your citizenship,'Effie took her pasty from him. 'How can you not like a cream tea? How have you resisted all of Lola's baking?' She bit into the pasty. It was good, the filling piping hot and the pastry flaked perfectly. 'Ummm, this is an exceptional pasty,' she sighed through a second mouthful, only just realising how ravenous she was after her morning's work. 'What?' she caught Jake looking at her.

'Nothing.' He shook his head, smiling, 'it's just . . . no, it doesn't matter.'

'It does now! I hate it when people start to say something and then backtrack,' she said, clutching her pasty to her as a seagull swooped in, a memory of the sausage roll stealer surfacing.

Jake scanned the sky for seagulls and when he deemed it safe, unwrapped his pasty and took a bite, his eyes widening as the flavours hit his tongue. 'Wow, that is one of the best pasties I've ever had! Please don't tell my mum, she prides herself on her pasty-making.' He chewed thoughtfully for a bit before saying, 'Coming home felt comforting but alien at the same time. I didn't know how to feel about it all but one really good thing about my return to Cornwall is meeting you, Effie.'

Effie swallowed her mouthful. 'I'm very pleased to have met you too, Jake. You've been a huge help and a great friend.'

'Thanks.' He smiled almost shyly. 'I liked your feistiness on the beach that morning.'

Effie laughed. 'No one has ever called me feisty before. Quiet maybe, boring definitely.'

'How many times do we need to go over this? You're not quiet or boring, Effie,' Jake said. 'I always feel like I need to be on my toes with you.'

Effie gave him a questioning look. It was a curious thing to hear herself described by someone else, someone who was using completely different adjectives to those she was used to. 'Why do you feel like you need to be on your toes with me?'

Jake shrugged. 'I don't know, maybe because I never know when you're going to call me out. Tell me off for not liking cream teas or something.'

'I wasn't telling you off, just shocked, which is a perfectly reasonable response to such an outrageous confession.' Effie shook her head in disbelief. 'I don't get it. What? Why are you looking at me like that?' she asked before taking another bite of her pasty.

Jake studied her for a few moments before saying, 'This is going to sound so trite but you're really not like any of the girls I usually meet.'

Effie rolled her eyes but couldn't help her heart hoping he was talking romantically. 'I can't believe you said that. What sort of girls do you normally meet – actually, don't answer that. Ones who own hair straighteners, I guess.' She gestured to her messy topknot.

Jake laughed. 'Don't forget the curling tongs. No, Effie, you're doing your own thing. The swimming. The wild hair. The shop. Knitting. It's nice.'

'I thought that was normal girl stuff,' Effie said as she scrunched up her pasty bag and took a sip of her tea.

'Not where I'm from. My ex was an influencer, remember,' he said quietly.

'How could I forget?' Effie mumbled, staring down at her grubby leggings and old T-shirt. The mention of Tara was like a cloud across her sun.

'It was all fake, Effie,' Jake said in a low voice. 'All her friends were influencers. Or trying to be. I was their photographer. The amount of shots I had to take before there'd even be one semi passable one. The outfit changes. The posing. Yeah, it was fun at first, I enjoyed the freebies, but in the end . . .' He trailed off. 'I like that you're not like that.'

Effie gave him a look. 'How do you know I don't change my outfit multiple times or take hundreds of selfies?'

Jake spluttered around for a reply.

'It's OK. I get what you're saying. It's a bit clumsy, but it's nice. Thank you. I don't get many compliments like that. I usually get ignored.' Effie tucked Jake's compliments away, reminding herself that he was just being kind, friendly, not to read too much into it. 'You've turned out to be completely different from what I expected too.'

'Go on,' Jake encouraged.

Effie sensed him hanging on to whatever she was going to say next. She sipped her tea before explaining. 'I thought you were rude and inconsiderate. That late night phone call, ugh, disturbing my sleep. The photo taking, nope, not cool but, as I've got to know you, I've realised you're a really decent, genuine guy. I don't think I've ever met anyone who'd have volunteered to help paint a shop for no payment. Although I still think I should ask Clive to pay you.'

'Effie, I didn't help you because I need money.' His voice was tight as he found the words. 'I helped you because I wanted to. I actually enjoy decorating, and no offence, but you needed some help. I still can't believe your boss didn't get anyone in to do it properly. Anyway, I was just kicking around at a loose end. Do you have any idea how hard it was for me to come back here after living the so-called high life?'

Effie shook her head.

Jake finished his pasty, tossing the end of the crust to a waiting gull. They watched in fascination as it swallowed it down whole in record-breaking time.

'It was hard. Really hard. I have to start everything again. From scratch. All my mates are settled down, nice jobs, on the property ladder, having blooming babies for goodness' sake, and me, well, yeah—' Jake held out his hands '—so helping you gave me something to focus on.' Jake's voice softened as he admitted, 'I also helped because I was intrigued by this woman who emerged from the waves, put me firmly in my place about my photos and snapped at me about my telephone habits. You seemed fearless. Lola told me you were opening the shop and, yeah, I wanted to get to know you better. Is that OK?'

Effie swallowed, not quite sure what to make of his words. Did he mean as friends or in a romantic sense? Knowing she couldn't ask him that, she just nodded. 'Yes, that's fine, more than fine, actually. Thank you. I don't know what I would've done without you to be honest. Probably still be painting blobby shelves or something.' She laughed nervously as their gazes caught and held for a few seconds longer than necessary.

Both a little unsure what to say or do next, they picked up their teas and turned their attention back to watching the gulls flying overhead. The birds occasionally dipped down into the waves before soaring back up high again. Effie snuck a glance at Jake. She felt something had shifted, but she didn't know what, other than that she liked it. But could she trust it?

Chapter Twenty

Ever since Effie had been a little girl, she'd imagined owning a bookshop. She'd played bookshops at school whilst the other children were busy running around the playground playing tag. She'd made her teddies and dolls sit in a neat circle on her bedroom floor whilst she read stories to them from the lofty position on her bed. Effie couldn't remember a time when she hadn't been accompanied by the safety blanket that was a well-thumbed book. She'd clutched on to them at dentist appointments, burrowed into them on long car journeys or snuck them into parties, just in case she needed to escape the games. No gift was more exciting to Effie than a book token.

Effie had owned as many books as her parents could afford to buy. Most of them acquired from charity shops, the pages scarred from previous readers, the corners tatty and preloved. The idea that books could be shared, passed along between readers had amazed a young Effie, who now, at the age of twenty-nine, could still remember how her jaw had dropped open on her first visit to the library when she was told she could borrow fifteen books. She couldn't recall a time when her library card hadn't been maxed to the limit.

Such was her love of books that Effie had volunteered to help in the school library, a room tucked away in the large authoritarian building, attached because having a library seemed to be the sort of thing a school needed. Effie had loved reshelving the few books that were borrowed. The librarian, a life-weary woman called Mrs Lloyd, who seemed to find children who loved books slightly bothersome, tolerated Effie, who had remained undeterred from her stoic duties.

University had been full of dry, prescribed texts, classics Effie had already read, Shakespeare she spent hours trying to get her head around. The dissection of the stories had sat heavily on Effie. She might have loved the written word, but was of the opinion no one knew what the author really meant. She'd even tried, but failed to write her own sweeping historical romance, frustrated that all the novels she'd consumed hadn't triggered a dormant talent for storytelling.

Landing the job at Books by the Sea had been perfect, even if from the outside, it didn't appear very aspirational. Effie got to stack shelves, open up boxes of brand-new novels, be the first to inhale that glorious scent of ink and paper. She spent hours chatting to customers, dishing out recommendations, swapping notes on what to read next. She loved to help organise the few author events they had hosted, hanging on to every magical word the writer would say about the craft of storytelling. Effie hadn't believed she could ever be happier.

Until now.

OK, so it wasn't her own bookshop by the sea, like she'd dreamed of owning, but it was the next best thing. Now she'd got the miserable business of decorating the shop out of the way, a distraction she hadn't enjoyed, despite Jake's help, Effie could finally, *finally* start the process of turning the empty shell of a shop into a cosy, welcoming book haven.

The first shipment of books arrived on the Tuesday, four days before opening. The delivery driver had been much more helpful than the last one and had wheeled the heavy boxes into the shop. The armchairs were due to arrive on Thursday. A burst of confidence flashed through Effie about getting it all finished on time for the Easter Saturday opening. She had the bunting, bouquets of fake flowers and the door was a stunning, cheerful daffodil yellow. She was so proud of it. Every time she unlocked the door, a beaming smile spread across her face.

Effie sliced through the wrapping on the first box, tugging out the reams of bubble wrap to reveal a stack of books by local authors. There were ghost stories, local history and two full sets of the cosy mysteries by Christie Kernow, who was the local author Clive had arranged to give a talk on opening day. Effie picked up her latest book and set it aside, knowing she had better read it before Saturday so she could ask engaged questions. Cosy mysteries weren't normally her cup of tea, but she'd been charmed by Christie's writing style and devoured them all the previous summer. Effie knew how important it was to keep ahead of what was being published and set locally. Holidaymakers always told her reading about Cornwall was like a holiday in book form.

Effie made a cup of tea, perched on the windowsill and opened the first page of the book. She'd been eagerly awaiting the next instalment in the series and couldn't resist dipping in. She was ten pages in, turning the pages reverently so as not to damage them, when the door opened. Effie glanced up and saw Jake standing there, taking in the half-filled shelves.

'Wow, it finally looks like a bookshop,' he said. 'Reading on the job?'

Effie closed the book. 'No, just getting prepped for Saturday.'

'Ah, is it good?'

Effie shrugged. 'It's a very nice, easy read, I could spend all afternoon here with it. I think Christie's going to be a popular choice.'

Jake rifled through the pile of Christie's books. 'They have very nice covers.'

Effie rolled her eyes. 'You can't judge a book by its cover. You can borrow one if you want, as long as you don't spoil it.'

Jake placed the book he was holding back on the pile. 'I wouldn't trust myself. I'd definitely bend it or something.'

'Books are to be read,' Effie reminded him, 'I don't like all this keeping them pristine. I like a book that looks like it's been enjoyed, dug into. How's your day been?'

'I've been trying to find a nice location for Lola and Tristan's engagement shoot. I'm feeling the pressure.'

'But Mags and Ewan were happy, right?' Effie said as she slipped off the windowsill and began to break down the cardboard box she'd emptied.

Jake took it from her and folded it up. 'Yeah, they were, just waiting to get the prints back. It was a good start, I was happy, so were they but a wedding feels like extra pressure. Capturing someone's special day. You can't redo the church shots if they go wrong. Shall I take this out the back?' He held up the flattened box.

Effie nodded. Jake gathered up the wrapping and empty boxes and carried them outside to the communal commercial bins. Effie had opened the next box and was busy organising some coffee table books on a shelf when Jake returned. She watched as he flicked through one that contained absolutely stunning photos of Cornwall, a thoughtful expression on his face. She could see his mind whirring as he studied how the shots had been captured, the lighting, the composition and the sheer luck on the day.

'I don't know why I'm so worried,' he said as he passed the book to her, 'Cornwall itself is a right old poser!'

'And I'm sure Lola will tell you exactly what she wants. She's a woman who knows her own mind,' Effie reminded him. 'I wish I could be a bit more like that.'

Jake tilted his head to study her. 'Really?'

Effie nodded as she swapped a couple of books around so that the height order was more pleasing to the eye. 'Yes.' But she sensed some doubt in her voice.

'The thing is, Effie, I'd love to have words with whoever knocked your confidence,' Jake said as he passed more books to her, 'because I think you're perfect just as you are.'

Effie's fingers collided with his so that she almost dropped the books. Lunging to save them, she knocked into Jake. His hands clasped around her arms to stop her from toppling over, their eyes meeting like a pause in time. Jake's eyes darkened, Effie's heart quickened. Was this what romance novels called 'having a moment'? If so, Effie found it thrilling and discombobulating.

Not wanting to give herself any mixed signals about Jake, knowing how prone her imagination was to wild flights of fancy, Effie stepped back and slid the books onto the shelf. She didn't need to complicate the friendship by acting impulsively. Plus, Effie sensed something jittery about Jake, as if he was about to take flight. When she turned to pick up the next few books, Jake was still standing there, transfixed, as if he'd never seen anything quite like Effie and didn't know what to do about it either.

Shelve books. That's what she told her wildly beating heart. *Just keep shelving.*

Chapter Twenty-One

Effie let herself into the shop early on Easter Saturday morning. Opening day. Sipping a cup of herbal tea, a burst of pride shot through her as she took in what she'd achieved.

Shadows hung over the shop from where the blinds were still down. Through the grey stillness, the spines of the books burst in a rainbow of colours from the shelves. Effie ran her fingers along them, imagining people picking them up, flicking through pages, devouring blurbs as they chose what book to buy. Who would like the ghost stories? The romances? The historical volumes? Effie couldn't wait to see where Polcarrow's reading tastes would lie, what it would reveal about the people.

The two yellow chairs had arrived the previous afternoon, their delivery cutting it fine and doing little for Effie's already jangling nerves as she waited to add the finishing flourishes. However, they had been worth the wait. Situated in the large bay window, with book-shaped cushions placed onto them, they provided the perfect spot for customers to sit and peruse their purchases whilst contemplating the sea view. She'd stacked some photography books on the table between them, to entice readers to pick them up, flick through them.

Beanbags and baskets of soft toys completed the kids' area tucked away at the back of the shop. Effie had placed a sign on the counter that listed the story times that were available and had chosen the most enchanting picture books to entice both children and parents. The teen section was well stocked with a variety of different genres and storylines. She'd selected titles written by less well-known authors in order to encourage younger readers to branch out and explore literature they wouldn't normally encounter.

Effie ceremonially raised the blinds, allowing fresh morning light to flood the space. She watched as it came alive, the muted colours bursting bright before her eyes, the bunting she'd hung and the vases of fake spring flowers added additional pops of colour. Effie gave herself a little round of applause. The shop was everything she'd dreamed a bookshop could be. OK, so it was more in line with her own personal vision than the Books by the Sea brand, but since Clive hadn't put up much real resistance to her vision, she'd decided it was worth just going for it. She could always change it back.

Checking her watch, she saw it was only 8 a.m. The sun glinting off the sea caught Effie's eyes. Could she? A swim would definitely calm her nerves, centre her. But there was still so much to do before the grand opening at ten. She didn't think she'd have enough time for a swim and a shower, plus she'd washed her hair the previous night and didn't fancy having to tackle that task again.

Effie was just about to head upstairs when a knock on the door caught her attention. Her face burst into a smile as bright as the morning sun when she saw Jake standing there, in his trademark white T-shirt, making her wonder how he really did keep them so spotless. She unlocked the door and let him in.

'I couldn't sleep,' he confessed, 'I'm so nervous and excited.'

'Why are you nervous and excited?' Effie laughed.

'For you, silly, you've put so much into this shop, I want it to go well.'

His concern for the shop touched her heart, making it melt in a way she wasn't ready for. Not sure what to say, she reached out and touched his arm, enjoying the fuzzy flow of electricity that passed between their bodies.

'Thanks, Jake, and for everything you've done.'

'I enjoyed it, honestly, maybe I'll get back in with my dad and his decorating business if the photography thing doesn't work out.'

'It will work out. Your photos are brilliant. Could you take some today if it's not too much hassle?' she asked shyly. 'I'm sure Clive will be able to cover any expenses.'

'For you, Effie, I'll do it for free.'

'Are you sure?'

'I could do with a bit of exposure. Are you all set?'

Effie nodded. 'Think so. If I've forgotten anything, it's too late now. I just need to set out the refreshments table. Pop the corks on the fizz and we'll be all done.'

'What time is the guest speaker?'

'Christie is due to arrive just after half twelve ready for her reading at one. I hope it's going to be popular. In fact, I hope the whole shop will be popular, I'm starting to feel the pressure.'

'You've done an amazing job, Effie, done everything you can. Your boss chose the location, if it doesn't work out, then it's really down to him.'

'Of course, it might sound silly, but the entire time I've been down here setting the shop up, it's felt like it's my own. I'm a little worried I've made it too much my own and about what Clive might think.' She signalled to the chairs and the bunting.

'It looks fantastic, Effie, honestly. I'm sure he'll love it.'

Effie gave him a small smile and exhaled. 'Don't mind me, I'm just nervous.' She signalled down to where she was still wearing her floral pyjamas. 'Look, I need to pop upstairs and get changed. Shall I meet you in Lola's in a few minutes?'

'Of course! I'll order some breakfast. I'll try and get the best seat. Even if I have to fight Scruff for it. See you in a bit.' Jake paused, leaned in momentarily as if he was about to kiss her on the cheek, before awkwardly pulling back and making a hasty retreat from the shop.

Effie watched him go, her cheek blazing with the almost kiss.

'Don't you look smashing?' Alf said as Effie pushed open the café door and stepped inside. 'Doesn't she look lovely, Jake?' Alf gave the younger man an elbow that caused him to almost choke on his coffee.

Effie smoothed down the skirt of her yellow and white gingham midi-dress. It was slightly lower cut than she was normally comfortable wearing, but the little puffed sleeves had been too cute to resist. She'd plaited her hair into a coronet and wound spring flowers into it like a crown. She gave her audience a twirl. Scruff barked his appreciation. Alf gave a whistle. Effie's eyes caught on Jake's. He was speechless, as if he'd never seen her before. Self-conscious, Effie nervously patted her hair.

'Wow, Effie, you look . . . beautiful. But you always look beautiful,' he fumbled, before turning back to his breakfast, his ears flaming red.

Jake thought she always looked beautiful. The comment froze Effie to the spot. No one had ever told her she was beautiful before, well, other than her parents and sometimes Maddie. 'Thanks,' she said as she slipped into one of the spare chairs and gave Scruff a fuss. The tension between herself and Jake was so high that she thought it'd smother her.

Thankfully, Lola emerged from the kitchen at that moment, carrying a tray of scrambled eggs and avocado on toast and attention was back on breakfast.

'Morning, my lovelies. Jake's ordered the works today, got to keep you going.' She placed the tray on the table, followed by a couple of empty plates. 'There's toast, eggs, avocado and some bacon, help yourselves. What a pretty dress.' Lola reached out and gave the sleeve a stroke. 'Are you all ready? What can I get you to drink?'

'Tea please and yes, I think I'm ready. Or ready as I'll ever be,' Effie replied as she helped herself to a couple of poached eggs and a slice of avocado on toast.

'Excellent. I've been up since five getting your hot cross buns ready, the book biscuits look amazing, but I drew the line at the chocolate nest cakes in the end. Decided kids, chocolate, sticky fingers and books would be a bad combination.'

'Thanks, Lola, that hadn't even occurred to me!'

'I'll have enough chocolate-based treats in here for anyone who needs a fix though,' Lola told Effie. 'I'm braced for a very busy day. Are you coming to the Easter egg hunt tomorrow?'

This was the first Effie had heard of it. 'I didn't realise there was one. I've been too busy with the shop to notice anything else happening.' She'd actually been planning on putting her feet up following the imagined intensity of the opening day as well as preparing for the upcoming school holiday trade.

'Jake, did you not mention it? Your mum has been organising it,' Lola called over her shoulder as she headed to the counter to make Effie's tea.

'I've been so busy helping Effie with the shop that I forgot,' he said before turning to Effie, 'it could be fun. I loved it so much as a kid that I got banned because I always found the most eggs! People thought it was rigged because Mum ran it.'

'Has the ban been lifted?' Effie asked as she tucked into her breakfast.

'No idea,' Jake laughed as he helped himself to some bacon. 'You're not banned, so we could team up?'

'That sounds like fun,' Effie said. 'I've not been on an Easter egg hunt since I was a kid, but you need to know something – I wasn't very good. I never found many eggs. My parents always bought me a conciliatory chocolate bunny at the end.'

'Maybe we can change your egg-hunting fortunes tomorrow?'

Effie smiled at him. 'That sounds like a challenge. But for now, let's concentrate on getting the shop opened without any drama.'

Chapter Twenty-Two

Effie paused, hand on the key, eyes on the clock, watching as the seconds ticked by until 10 a.m. The hour was confirmed by a ring of the church bell. Effie glanced through the window at the eagerly waiting crowd. Her parents were front of the queue, chatting to Jake who was just behind them. A few of Polcarrow's other residents made up the numbers but Effie couldn't see Clive. He'd promised to be there when the shop opened. She flicked her gaze at the clock then checked her phone. Nothing. Where was he?

Just as Effie decided she couldn't wait any longer for him, not when there was a crowd gathered and a tasty pile of hot cross buns waiting to be eaten, she heard the words, 'Sorry, excuse me,' as someone pushed their way through the crowd, which parted to reveal a rather frazzled-looking Clive. He exhaled before giving Effie a nod. She paused to savour the moment before turning the sign from 'closed' to 'open' and pulled the door back.

'Wow, you're all keen, aren't you? I see Effie here has done a sterling job,' Clive remarked, glancing from the crowd to Effie and back again. 'I'd like to officially declare the Polcarrow branch of Books by the Sea open!' Clive stepped back as Effie pulled the door open wide.

A round of applause went up led by her parents and Jake. Effie stepped back to let the customers in, greeting them all individually and chatting to some of the kids who bundled in, dressed as their favourite book characters. A smile spread across her face as she watched the kids run over to the book corner and start to pull picture books off the shelves with a wild abandon that warmed her heart. Clive hovered by the door, greeting the villagers, shaking their hands and deflecting any praise onto Effie.

'You've done a marvellous job, love,' her mum said as she gave Effie a hug, 'it's gorgeous. I don't think you'll move your dad from those chairs.'

Effie glanced over to where her dad had quickly ensconced himself in one of the armchairs, already engrossed in a Cornish wildlife book. 'I hope he's going to buy that,' she laughed.

Jake was busy taking photos and the villagers were making short work of the hot cross buns. Effie noticed Sue lingering at the counter. 'I'll be back in a minute, Mum, my first sale!'

Effie darted around behind the counter where Sue had placed a pile of books, including Christie Kernow's latest. 'You're the first person to buy something,' she said as she started to scan the books, taking extra time to glance at the titles.

'Am I?' Sue beamed proudly.

'And all excellent choices,' Effie confirmed as she rang up the total.

Sue swiped her card. 'Wonderful, glad you approve. Right, I need to dash off for a bit, pick the kids up from football, stick them in the shower, but I will absolutely be back in time for Christie.' Sue checked her watch. 'Hmm, it'll be tight, but she's my favourite and I can't wait to meet her and have her sign her new book. Been looking forward to it coming out. I've read every one of her books.'

'So have I!' Effie enthused. 'Which one was your favourite?'

'Oh, I forget the title, but the one about the lost necklace. I read it twice.'

'*Links to the Past*,' Effie told her. 'That was one of my favourites too.'

'Yes! That's the one! Do you think she would sign all my copies?'

Effie finished placing the books in a Books by the Sea bag and held it out to Sue. 'I'm sure she would be delighted to.'

Sue took her books. 'Thank you. It's looking wonderful in here, Effie, well done. I'll see you later.'

Effie watched as Sue grabbed a hot cross bun, exchanged quick greetings with other customers and headed off into the bright April morning. Clive extracted himself from an intense-looking conversation with Alf and Tristan and made his way over to the till.

'Effie! This is marvellous! Look at all these people!' he enthused as he started to help her bag up the next customer's purchases. 'Sorry I was late, mad traffic. Got stuck behind a herd of cows, of all things.' Clive passed the bag to the customer as Effie took the payment. Taking a step back to catch his breath, he took in the bustling shop, a look of amazement across his face. 'Is the whole village really here?'

'Pretty much,' she told him, 'Everyone has been so excited about the opening and looking forward to Christie's reading.'

'Oh Effie, that's great, wonderful to hear.' He turned and studied her for a few seconds before admitting, 'I know you had to leave everything behind to come here, but I'm really glad you decided to take it on. I can see it's been great for you. And for the shop. I know you liked to melt into the background before but no one else in the team could've set a shop up like this. I don't even think Zach would've managed it. I'm really proud of what you've achieved. I'm sorry the shop was in a right state, I didn't realise it was quite that bad. Turned it around though, like I knew you would. I actually love the yellow, might have to think of a refresh for the whole brand. Right, I'd better circulate. I'm famished, those buns look good.'

Before Effie could get another word in, Clive was off, grabbing a couple of buns before introducing himself to customers. She watched as he shook hands and engaged people in conversation, chatting about the shop and their book choices. He might have turned up late to his own shop opening, but Effie had to give it to him, he was very good at doing the schmoozing required to make customers feel special.

'Smile!'

Effie glanced up, a grin spreading across her face as Jake snapped a few photos of her behind the till.

'It's brilliant lighting. I've made use of your dad hogging that chair by taking some photos of him looking like a very engrossed reader.'

Effie laughed as Jake showed her the pictures. 'They're great.'

'I'll send them to you and you can use them on the social media pages. You've got a queue, I'll let you get on.'

Jake darted out of the way, heading to the back of the shop where she could hear him engaging a child in a dinosaur costume in conversation about her favourite reptiles. Clive occasionally joined her behind the till to help serve if the queue became too long, but mostly he was on the floor talking to the customers. Effie smiled, served, chatted about books and answered questions about story time and the book club.

'Rather than having one prescribed read a month, I'm planning on offering a few in different genres to keep everyone happy. Romance, crime, non-fiction, then we can all meet up and discuss why we like the book we did and hopefully be inspired to try some of the different genres,' she explained to a couple of the local mums.

'I don't want it to be stuffy; I just want to encourage people to read more.'

'Sounds right up our street. I don't like all those worthier than thou books, I like a good bonkbuster. Hot man doing filthy things,' one of them admitted, causing the other to laugh.

A spark lit in Effie's head. 'I love a romance too. Especially the Viking and cowboy ones. Maybe we could have a special romance book club night one time?'

'Now that I like the sound of. Ah, I better go and rescue Jake before Amelie bores him to death with all the facts she knows about crocodiles. Keep us posted on the book events. I'll definitely bring my kids along to story time.'

Effie was buoyed up by the business she was doing and the enthusiasm for the events she had planned. She may have had her doubts but Clive had been right about Polcarrow being the perfect place to open a bookshop. She was just about to tell him this when the sound of his phone ringing shrilly broke through the gentle hubbub of the shop. Everyone turned to watch him fumble his phone out of his pocket.

'Sorry, sorry, I need to take this.' His face paled as he excused himself from where he'd been chatting with Alf and headed outside to take the call. Distracted by the look on his face, Effie watched him pace up and down the pavement before he headed back inside, his expression grave.

'Effie, I need a word,' he said, summoning her to the back of the shop and into the small kitchen area where Jake was going through his photos. 'Who's this?'

'Jake, local photographer and he gave me a hand with the painting.'

'Oh right, that's nice,' Clive said, distracted, before turning his back on Jake to focus on Effie. 'We have a problem. Christie is stuck further up the train line. Signal issues. We're going to have to cancel. She's not going to make it on time.'

Chapter Twenty-Three

Effie stared at Clive in disbelief. 'What? Surely there's something we can do? Can we pay for a taxi?'

'A taxi would cost a small fortune.' Clive winced.

'But she's our main attraction!' Effie cried, thinking of Sue gathering up all her books to be signed. 'There must be something we can do.' Effie cast her eyes around the small space from Clive to Jake and back again.

'Where is she?' Jake asked.

'About half an hour away. Forty minutes maybe. As long as there's no cows blocking the road.'

Jaked looked at the clock. It was quarter to twelve. 'I'll go and pick her up. Just delay the start.'

'What? Jake, seriously? We can't ask you to do this.' Effie threw a glance at Clive.

Never good in a crisis, Clive looked at him dumbfounded.

'Call her, tell her I'll pick her up. Get her to wait. If this is important to you, Effie, then it's important to me.'

Momentarily lost for words as Jake fixed her with a long look, a look that told her he'd never, ever let her down, Effie considered the options. 'We can't ask you to drive all that way and back again.'

Jake pulled his keys out of his pocket. 'Consider it done,' he said as he headed to the door. 'Call her, tell her to expect a young man in a white Corsa.'

Clive stared after him, phone still in hand. Effie grabbed it from him and dialled the last number in the call log. 'Hello, is that Christie, my name's Effie, I'm running the Polcarrow branch of Books by the Sea. Well, yes, hello, lovely to speak to you too, I know, I know, Clive's explained, but we have someone coming to collect you. Look out for a white Corsa. He's on his way.'

Effie chatted for a few moments, then finished the call and handed the phone back to Clive, barely masking her irritation about how useless he'd been. 'There's a queue, I need to go,' she said, her mind full of Jake leaping into the breach. How could she ever have thought he was annoying?

Effie tried not to cast too many concerned glances at the clock as she continued serving customers. Jake had texted to say he'd collected Christie and that, thankfully, despite all the travel palaver, she was in good spirits. However, he didn't think he'd make it back in time for her one o'clock slot. Clive was being completely useless, lingering in the corner, helping himself to book biscuits and avoiding her eye. He'd been having a very long conversation with Steve about a book on haunted local pubs. Effie had overheard the landlord's bold claims that his pub was haunted by a one-legged smuggler that had put the complete collywobbles into her boss.

During a lull in custom and with a small gathering of people arriving to meet Christie, including Sue with an overflowing tote bag of books, Effie cornered her boss and hissed, 'You have to make the announcement.'

'Me?'

'Yes, you, it's your business,' she reminded him. Now that she was here in Polcarrow Effie was beginning to realise just how much Clive had delegated to his staff.

He glanced around at the assembled crowd and then at his watch. 'Shall I give it a few more minutes?'

Effie shook her head. 'No, go and tell them now.' She gave him a little shove towards where the chairs had been set out for Christie's talk.

Clive cleared his throat as he made his way over to Sue and her friends. 'We've got a bit of a problem,' he told them, 'Christie has been delayed so we'll be starting a bit late. Some young man Effie's friendly with has gone to collect him.'

Effie's face flushed as the gaggle of women turned to stare at her, Sue giving her a knowing smile. Blimey, was everyone in on this matchmaking business? Effie was glad to have her attention drawn away by a young boy looking for a book on superheroes.

She rifled through the shelves and presented the child and his younger sister with an assortment of brightly coloured picture books featuring a variety of super-heroes. The little girl held her hands out at a book about a magical unicorn, which the boy made a face at. Effie was just placating him with a book about a monkey with magical powers, when the door of the shop was flung open and her own superhero stepped through, harried, slightly out of breath, but with Christie Kernow right behind him. The shop hushed as Jake's eyes met with Effie's.

Effie straightened up and passed the book to the boy and without her eyes leaving Jake's, crossed the room until she was standing in front of him. 'Thank you so much.' She grabbed his hand and gave it a squeeze. 'I owe you a pint.'

'No worries, it was nothing, really,' he dismissed with a disarming smile, 'but I could murder a cup of tea.'

Effie turned to Christie. 'Hello, welcome to the Polcarrow branch of Books by the Sea, I'm so glad you managed to get here.'

'Me too! I'd have hated to have missed it. What a charming little shop you have,' she enthused as she took in the bright décor. 'It's adorable and that sea view! Divine!'

Effie nodded in agreement. 'Is there anything I can get for you. Are you ready to start or do you need a breather?'

'I'm perfectly ready to begin. I had a nice sit down in the station café, gave me plenty of time to work on my next manuscript, tight deadline on this one, but if you're putting the kettle on, I'd love a cuppa. Milk, no sugar, please.'

'Sure, anything else?'

'Just a glass of water, but I'm hoping there's some of those buns left for after.' Christie gestured at the refreshments table.

'I'll make sure of it. Where would you like to sit?'

Christie glanced around the shop. 'It's going to have to be one of those gorgeous armchairs if that gentleman doesn't mind?'

'That's my dad,' Effie told her, 'I'm sure he'll be happy to move.'

'He can stay and listen if he wants,' Christie said as she made her way over to the vacant chair. 'Hello, ladies, are you here for my talk, lovely, wonderful and oh look, you have all my books! I love it when fans turn up. How are you all doing?'

Effie left Christie chatting to her audience and headed into the kitchen to find Jake had got there before her and was boiling the kettle. 'You don't have to do this.'

'But it's manic out there. Not being funny, Eff, but how does Clive think you're going to run this shop alone? What about breaks?'

This hadn't crossed Effie's mind. 'It's probably only like this because its opening day and the entire village has turned up,' she said.

Jake's jaw clenched. He opened his mouth but thought better of whatever he was going to say and closed it again. 'Do you want one?'

'Yes please.' Effie watched as he found a third mug and dropped teabags into them before filling them with boiling water.

'What is it, Jake?'

Jake took a long time giving the teabags a stir. 'I don't think it's my place to say, but your boss, he's really taking the piss. Sending you here to paint the shop, completely flaking out when his star guest couldn't arrive. I didn't mind going to collect her, Christie is fascinating and interesting company, she was telling me all about where she gets her ideas from, but Clive should've gone to collect her.' He squeezed the teabags, tossed them into the bin and retrieved the milk from the fridge. 'She's the star attraction and he was just going to leave here there.'

Effie's instinct was to defend Clive but instead she sank into herself. 'I know,' she admitted, 'but let's not discuss this today. There's some superhero-obsessed kids out there and Sue is about to combust with excitement at meeting her favourite author. I do this for the readers, not for Clive.' She snuck a glance behind her just to check he wasn't listening. Instead, he was behind the till, merrily serving some customers. 'He inherited the business,' she explained, 'I'm not sure books are in his blood though. You have a sit down and I'll take this through to Christie.'

Picking up one of the mugs, Effie made her way back into the shop where Christie was already holding court, her audience listening in awe as she regaled them with a story about a very precarious trip she'd taken to Tintagel in a gale in the name of research.

Chapter Twenty-Four

Effie flicked the shop sign to 'closed' and sank back against the door, happy but exhausted after an eventful but successful opening day. Closing her eyes, she took a few calming breaths before reopening them to survey the shop.

All that was left on the refreshment table were a few crumbs of book-shaped biscuits, a pile of glasses that would need to be sorted, and a lone hot cross bun. Glancing around the shop, her heart swelled with happiness to see so many vacant spaces on the shelves where customers had purchased the books that had taken their fancy. They looked like gaps in a wide, but happy smile.

Clive had seemed pleased with how well the opening had gone and had managed not to notice the unimpressed glances Jake had been casting his way. Christie Kernow had been a huge success, happily chattering away long past her allotted time and Sue had practically skipped out of the shop clutching her autographed novels. Clive had been right; Polcarrow was the perfect place to open the next branch of his shop. Effie was confident that today wouldn't just be a one-off in terms of business.

She'd just finished cashing up the till when a tap at the shop door caught her attention. Glancing up, her heart skipped a beat when she saw Jake peering through the window. He'd offered to drive Christie to her hotel along the coast in St Ives, where she was meeting another author friend. Hurrying around the counter, Effie unlocked the door and threw it open. The sight of his rugged good looks coupled with the fact that he'd managed to save the day, made Effie throw her arms around him.

'Oh my God, Jake! We did it!' she squealed as he swung her around.

'No, you did it, Effie, you did.' He beamed as he set her back down, his hands on her shoulders, anchoring her.

Grinning, Effie's eyes met his, their faces only inches apart. Electricity buzzed between them, a current running from their eyes to their lips, down their fingertips. An urge to kiss him surged through Effie, making her face flushed in response. It felt so good to be in his arms, like she was being held strongly against whatever life could throw at her.

Flustered and not knowing what to do about the very obvious attraction that was growing between them, Effie loosened her grip on his shoulders and took the slightest step back, just enough for Jake to release her.

'Effie, you were amazing!'

A blush crept over her cheeks at this praise but before she could bat it away, Jake continued.

'I was so impressed. I mean, I knew you'd be great, but I was worried when I remembered you felt anxious around new people, so I didn't know if this would be too much.'

His concern touched her. 'Thanks, Jake, I'm always OK when I'm in shop mode, with the books, it's like I can be a different version of myself. Like my true self.'

Jake frowned. 'There's nothing wrong with any version of you. I hope Clive knows what he's got in you. Honestly, all of this wouldn't exist without you. Where is he?'

Effie shrugged as if it was nothing. 'He's gone home. Family dinner for his mother-in-law.'

Deciding not to push the matter, Jake asked, 'How are you feeling?'

'Honestly? No idea! It's been so full on. Tired but happy, it went far better than I expected, I mean, look at all those empty shelves!' She signalled to where the local fiction area had been cleared. 'I don't think we have a single copy of anything by Christie left! I thought Clive was a bit mad opening a shop here, but now I think it was one of his better ideas.'

Jake's brow furrowed. 'Shame he's not so good at the actual working in a shop. You can't run this all by yourself, Effie.'

'I know,' she sighed. 'We have to see how the next few weeks goes. If he's seen how busy it is today I'll at least have some leverage to take on a part-timer. But I don't want to think about that now. I had a really good day, I made this happen, me! I want to tidy up and go and celebrate.' Effie did a little excited jump for joy.

A smile spread across Jake's face. 'I'm glad to see you're taking the credit you deserve. He glanced around at the mess. 'Right, have you got some bin bags? The quicker we clean up, the quicker we can have that celebratory drink.'

Effie darted into the kitchen and came back with a roll of bin bags. 'The glasses are made of some recyclable or compostable plastic, so they can go in the recycling bin,' she explained as she handed him a rubbish bag. 'Jake, it wasn't just me, you've done your fair share. Painting, collecting Christie, you didn't have to do any of that.'

'Thanks, but I wanted to, it's the least anyone would've done.' Again, he brushed off her gratitude. 'I didn't see Clive offering to go and pick her up. She was fantastic. Fascinating to talk to. You couldn't have an opening without your star attraction.'

'That's true. Shame I was too busy serving customers to listen to her,' Effie sighed as she started to clear the table. 'Thank you, Jake, let me at least buy you a pint tonight,' she said, laying a hand on his arm.

Jake glanced down at it before closing his own hand over hers. Again, the moment between them was charged. 'Thanks, Effie, and it's been a pleasure to help you. I've enjoyed it.'

'And you don't mind helping tidy up?'

Jake began to collect up the glasses for the recycling, 'Not at all. I'll clear this. You can straighten the shelves, then we can head off.'

'I might need to put the vacuum round as well,' she said looking at the floor, which was strewn with crumbs and sand. 'It was impossible to stop the kids trailing biscuit crumbs everywhere. They had a great time though, so I can't complain, I just hope the books aren't sticky.'

'Maye we should get Scruff in to hoover up all the crumbs.'

Effie laughed. 'He'd love that! But he'd probably take ages.'

'We have plenty of time, Effie, we'll have the shop shipshape, or shopshape in no time.'

'We do make an excellent team.' Effie beamed at him. As she watched him make quick work of tidying the refreshment table, she hoped their compatibility would extend beyond the shop floor.

Chapter Twenty-Five

Easter Sunday dawned bright and sunny. Effie rolled over in bed and buried her head into the pillows. The shop opening, followed by an evening celebrating at the pub, had exhausted her. She closed her eyes and willed sleep to return, but her ears had already tuned in to the sound of the seagulls calling and when she reached for her phone she saw it was almost nine. She couldn't remember the last time she'd slept in so late.

With plans to open the shop for a couple of hours that morning, Effie pushed back the covers and padded into the bathroom where she ran a bath. With a contented sigh, she slipped into the vanilla-fragranced bubbles. Lying in the hot water, she replayed the events of opening day.

Jake was right, she couldn't run the shop by herself, it'd be impossible over the high summer season. She didn't think Clive had considered any of the implications of opening the shop other than grabbing a property in an up-and-coming location. In fact, Effie hadn't considered the implications of running it alone. Although she knew she'd have to see how popular the shop actually became and how busy the little seaside village was in high season.

Getting out of the bath and wrapping herself in a fluffy towel and robe, Effie padded into the kitchen, where she flicked on the kettle and sliced a hot cross bun to toast. She'd been so busy the previous day she hadn't got around to having any of the treats Lola had baked, so was looking forward to seeing what was left in the café.

Carrying her breakfast over to the sofa, Effie pulled the curtains back and took in the scene outside. The sea gently lapped at the golden sand, Freya and Angelo were strolling on the beach, throwing a ball for Scruff whilst Alf perched on the harbour wall. Happiness spread through Effie as she sipped her tea. For all her worries about moving away from home, Polcarrow had embraced her in a big welcoming hug. It had been far easier to make friends and be accepted into the community than she'd imagined. There was also Jake.

Effie swallowed at the thought of Jake, with his tousled blond hair and strong forearms with their intricate tattoos she still hadn't asked him about. Heat rose in her as she remembered the intense way he'd looked at her as he'd passed on his opinion about Clive's uselessness or the way he'd taken time to make sure the walls and shelves were perfectly painted.

Most of Effie's crushes had been unrequited – a day-dream about a man with a nice smile, filling in the blanks or creating a life for the gorgeous barman in the pub she'd frequented with Maddie, but never dared ask out. She'd returned home after university wary and bruised by Brad and it had been so much easier to bury herself in books and knitting.

Jake, however, was real, he was showing up for her every day, unasked, and this was something Effie hadn't experienced before. The few guys she had dated had always let her down, cancelling plans last minute or dating multiple women at the same time. Jake was a man who cared about other people, and he clearly liked her, but was it romantic? Could she dare to put her heart on the line for him?

Effie briefly allowed herself to imagine being swept into his strong arms, being kissed by him, before batting the image away. She needed him as a friend; after all, if she was hoping to stay in Polcarrow, she couldn't risk ruining what was beginning to bloom between them. She still couldn't get the phone call from Tara out of her head. Or the restless energy she sensed in him, as if he'd merely come home to plan his next move, rather than put down roots. She had been wrong in the past, thinking guys were interested in her, and she wasn't willing to make that embarrassing mistake again.

It had been a wise idea to open the shop for the morning as a steady stream of holidaymakers ventured in to have a look around, ask for particular books, and Effie even made a few sales and took down a few orders. After the chaos of opening day Effie enjoyed the calm, studious way people browsed the shelves and took a moment to sit in the chairs, commenting on the view. She could forget that it was another arm of Clive's small empire and easily imagine the shop was her own.

One o'clock rolled round before Effie realised and the morning had gone. She was just doing her last-minute tidy when the door jangled open. Her eyes flicked up from where she'd been tidying the children's corner to see Jake propped up in the doorway, two felt buckets in his hand.

'Which one do you want? Bunny or chick?' he asked, holding them out to her.

Effie stood up and made her way over to him. 'Chick please.'

'You're going to make me have the pink bunny one?'

'You're definitely secure enough in your masculinity to use a pink bunny bucket,' she teased.

Jake passed Effie the chick bucket. 'I do secretly quite like pink. Always go for a pink iced cake. Just tastes better,' he said with a shrug.

'Aw, that is so cute! I totally agree. It's always the pink French Fancies for me.'

'Hmm . . . looks like I'll be fighting you for those.' He narrowed his eyes and pretended to size her up.

Effie's heart skipped a beat at the implied future the thought of fighting him over a box of cakes brought.

'Are you ready?'

Effie nodded. 'Let me just lock up,' she said and shooed Jake out of the shop. He took the bucket back from her as she pulled down the blinds then locked the door.

'Good morning?' he asked.

'Actually yes. We probably won't be opening on Sundays normally but since it's Easter and people are on holiday I thought I'd take advantage of it.'

'You are a shrewder businesswoman than Clive gives you credit for.'

Effie beamed at his praise. 'How was your morning?'

Jake groaned. 'I spent it being bossed around by Mum, sorting out stuff for the Easter egg hunt. Doing everything other than hiding the eggs. When I was a kid it was the other way round. Even though I wasn't able to take part my brother and I were sent out at the crack of dawn to hide the eggs all over the village.'

'That is so mean!'

'Tell me about it! Imagine being seven and watching all your friends taking part, winning chocolate eggs, and you're banned!'

'And now?'

'I think we're probably meant to let the kids win. But that doesn't mean I'm not going to try my hardest to find the most eggs.' He grinned at Effie.

'Ah, so you're the competitive type?'

'I had an older brother, so everything was a competition. How many roast potatoes we could eat, who could kick the ball the furthest. What about you?'

'Roast potatoes?' Effie asked.

'No, siblings? But it you want to tell me about the roast potatoes . . .'

Effie laughed. 'I've never counted. What was your best?'

'Fourteen. I had indigestion for days afterwards though. Jason has never let me live it down.'

'That is a lot of potatoes,' she concluded before saying with a sigh, 'I'm an only child, so no siblings to fight with or compete with or even play with. I never felt lonely though.'

'Did you ever wish you had siblings?'

'When I was really little, but as I got older the wish sort of vanished. I was happy by myself with my books. I didn't think I was missing out on anything,' she said contemplatively.

'And now?'

Effie shrugged. 'I still don't think I'm missing out. I'm used to being by myself, filling my time with books or knitting, I enjoy my own company, but it doesn't mean I want to be alone forever.' She slid a glance up at him.

'No boyfriends back in Penzance then?'

'No,' Effie said trying to smooth over the sadness in her voice, 'I'm chronically single. Maybe I should just get a cat.'

'Oh Eff, I think you're too young to be a cat lady.'

She caught his gaze and tried to figure out the meaning swirling in his eyes as he looked back at her. 'Cats are cute though!'

'Hmm . . . most of the ones I've met are complete bastards. My nan's cat absolutely hated me. Come on,

I can hear Mum ringing the bell. These Easter eggs aren't going to find themselves.' With a gentle touch to her arm, he set off.

Effie watched him move away from her before picking up her pace. What she hadn't shared with Jake was that she also had a secret competitive streak.

Chapter Twenty-Six

The people of Polcarrow took their Easter egg hunt more seriously than Effie had imagined possible. When they arrived at the church hall, tables were set up with registration forms on one side and on another someone was patiently waiting for the returners to come in and count their eggs.

'They're not real eggs,' Jake explained as they lined up to register for the event, 'just little wooden ones that have been kicking around for donkey's years. The person who collects the most gets the prize. Mum's had Dad up since the crack of dawn helping to hide them.'

They shuffled to the front of the queue. 'So, you know all the best hiding places?' Effie asked.

Jake nodded. 'I like to think so. Hi, Mum, Effie and I are entering.'

Jan glanced up at them, her eyes swinging from Jake to Effie and back again, something hopeful gleaming in them. 'Jake, you know the rules,' she warned.

'But it's Eff's first year. It's only fair she has a go.'

Jan cast her eye at Jake's bucket. 'You'll have to leave that behind. I don't want to be accused of favouritism.'

'Oh, come on, Mum, just this once. Anyway, I was planning on letting the kids win. They've already had a head start.'

Jan considered the entry lists. 'Oh, go on, but I made sure your dad hid the eggs really well,' she said as she wrote their names on the list. 'Meet back here at four for the grand reveal.'

'Three hours?' Effie asked as they walked away, 'How many eggs are there?'

'Lots. Mum takes this very seriously. It's always been run by the family. My grannie did it before her. Come on, let's get out of here, time to go hunting!'

'Who painted all these?' Effie asked as she plucked an egg out of a flower pot. It was chipped and slightly worn, but the purple dots still showed against the yellow background.

'Mum and Grandad. I spent school holidays helping him touch them up. Mum now does it. Think my great-grandparents were involved as well.'

Effie dropped the egg into her bucket along with the others she'd found. Judging by the scant few rattling around in the bottom, the village children must've swept through already. 'That's really sweet. It's nice to have something like this in the family. Will you carry it on one day?'

Jake paused. 'I hadn't really thought about that. Gosh. I mean, it'd be a shame to let it stop. Mum has a few years in her yet, but she definitely dropped enough hints about settling down and getting involved in village life. I don't know . . . it's . . . a lot. Do you fancy an ice cream?' he asked, changing the subject.

'Sure, I think we've earned one,' Effie said as she followed him down to the harbour where an ice cream van was doing a steady trade. 'What are you having?' she asked as they perused the menu.

'A ninety-nine with chocolate sauce and sprinkles,' Jake said.

'Ooh chocolate sauce? Hmm . . . I'm a raspberry sauce girl.'

'Do you want sprinkles?'

'Why are you even asking?' Effie feigned outrage.

Jake paid for the two ice creams and they wandered down the harbour wall to where it was a bit quieter. Perching on it, they kept one eye on the seagulls as they tucked into their ice creams.

'First Mr Whippy of the season,' Effie groaned happily, 'so, so good. Oi, shoo, shoo, Mr Seagull. So, I take it your mum wants you to settle back here then? What do you want?'

'Yeah, she does. Jason runs a surf school in Newquay, so he's still on Cornish soil. Has a girlfriend but no sign of a ring yet, even with baby Cara on the scene. Mum is desperate for a wedding.'

'Was she disappointed when you split up with your fiancée?'

Jake considered this. 'I don't know. I'm not sure she ever liked Tara that much. Thought she was a bit flash.

And she was. But she knew what she liked and what she wanted, you have to admire that.'

'What happened?' Effie asked gently, curious to know what had really led Jake back home, what had really gone on between them.

'I think I grew out of it to be honest. Everything became more about the brand than who we were. It didn't feel equal. To start with, it was about the two of us, but as commissions came in I was relegated to being the cute boyfriend, I stopped having a personality of my own in a way. Tara's just overtook everything.' He gave a hollow laugh. 'People loved us together but all that did was drive us apart. We met at university, one of those couples who got together in freshers' week and were then inseparable. I know! So annoying,' Jake chuckled as he licked his ice cream.

Effie's heart caught as she watched the fond memories scudding across his face. She felt a sharp pang in her chest from not having found love at university like everyone else seemed to.

'After graduating we tried to settle down, act like grown-ups, but we both desperately wanted to see the world. So, that's what happened. Tara started off with a blog and slowly opportunities to endorse products and places came in. I'm not going to lie, it was fun, so much fun, but after a few years, well, it was a job. Yes, the locations were pretty, but the hours were long. People don't see all that. Early mornings, outfit changes in little Italian alleyways, catching all sorts of flights. Twenty-four hours to fit in three cities, make it look like we were there for a week. Still, we earned enough to buy our own place in Bristol.

'I thought that would slow things down for both of us. We were successful and comfortable. We'd come back to the UK and within weeks, get itchy feet again. I know Tara's contacts helped me develop my photography following, and I am grateful for that, as I wanted less and less to do with being in front of the camera but sometimes I'd have liked to have earned it on my own merit.' Jake turned to Effie and gave her a long look as he considered what to say next.

He paused to lick chocolate sauce off his fingers. 'Mum's been great. I think because she finally has me home. I never thought I'd end up back here. I always wanted to see what was over the horizon.'

'Cornwall can seem very small and far away from the rest of the world when you're younger,' Effie said, her voice strained as she tried to sort out her own feelings on Jake's reveal. 'I'm sorry your relationship didn't work out. It couldn't have been easy.' She didn't ask the questions she really wanted to: was he still in love with Tara? Were they actually over for good? She couldn't help but feel he was holding something back from her.

Jake shook his head. 'No, it wasn't. It's tricky to have to pack up and start again. Find my feet.'

Effie considered him as she crunched through her chocolate flake. Her heart had been swelling more and more each day with feelings for him, but was he ready for a relationship? She had to stop with the wild fantasies until she knew where they both stood. She'd been burned before. Instead, she asked, 'Do you think you'll stay here?'

Jake glanced at her, taking her in, his eyes skimming down her face thoughtfully. 'Honestly? I don't know. I wasn't planning on coming back permanently but now . . .' He trailed off with a shrug. 'I'm weighing up my options. It's tempting to stay, I mean, look at it—' he signalled to the view '—but, am I throwing away possibilities? There's still so much stuff unfinished with Tara. It's not easy to talk or sort it out when she's in different time zones.'

'It must be hard for a relationship to be over after you've been through so much together,' Effie said.

Beside her, Jake shifted awkwardly. 'The thing is, Effie, I don't know if we are over.'

Her heart skidded to a halt. 'What do you mean?'

Jake's eyes skittered everywhere else other than meeting hers. 'The thing is . . . well . . . there is so much to unpack. So much to sort out. We've been together over ten years; it didn't feel right just to throw it all away because I was feeling a bit lost. So, we decided to take a break, see how we felt when everything had calmed down.'

'A break. Right.' Effie swallowed down the truth, her heart sinking as he threw cold water over her romantic hopes. At least she knew where she stood. Realising their split wasn't quite as clear cut as she'd previously believed, Effie drew back. As she fumbled around for the right words, a seagull swooped in and snatched the remainder of her ice cream cone from her hands. With a scream, she jumped, half off the wall and half into Jake's arms.

'Woah!' He steadied her. 'You OK? He was a bruiser.'

Effie righted herself, clinging to his strong arms, feeling safe in the way he was gripping on to her, anchoring her. Her heart raced. 'Yes, I think so now,' she exhaled, her legs a bit wobbly. 'I should've been paying attention.'

Jake cracked a smile. 'I shouldn't have been distracting you.'

'Oh, I don't know, it was a nice distraction,' she dared.

Jake seemed to soften. Effie watched him chew over her words. Their gazes tangled and the heat from his fingers was charged against her hips. Effie leaned in ever so slightly, just at the same time as Jake did. The natural urge to kiss him buzzed on her lips. Jake swayed forward slightly before jolting back.

'Effie, I—' he began, his energy jittery.

Before Jake could finish what he was going to say, another seagull swept in over their heads, cawing and snatching at the ice cream cone Jake had discarded as he'd leapt to Effie's defence, saving her from making a huge mistake by giving in to the temptation to kiss him.

'I think we better get out of here.' He gave her hips a squeeze before stepping back and gathering up their baskets.

Effie watched him head away from the harbour, feeling adrift now that their cosy afternoon of Easter egg hunting had turned slightly frosty. At least he'd been honest, she guessed, albeit in a roundabout sort of way. Effie zipped up her jacket to keep out the chill and followed him, sneaking a glance back at the pesky seagulls as she went, who were devouring the ice cream cones as if they'd never seen food before.

Chapter Twenty-Seven

'Oh, wow Eff, this looks amazing!' Maddie exclaimed as she threw herself onto one of the armchairs. 'How do you get any work done with that view?'

The Polcarrow branch of Books by the Sea had been open for four days and things had calmed to a steady pace following the launch, which Effie was secretly relieved about. She was also thrilled to see Maddie, who had announced via text the previous evening that she was visiting on her day off.

'It's so charming, and these book cushions are adorable.' She plumped one up. 'How did you get Clive to agree to all this?'

'I didn't give him much choice. The shop was in a right state when I arrived so I think he felt a bit guilty.'

'Guilty? Clive? Really?'

'You know what he's like, anything for an easy life.'

'Hmm. So where is this hunky man I've heard so much about? And those scones you keep posting photos of?'

'The scones are next door; we can go for lunch when I take my break.' Effie had decided to close the shop for half an hour each day so that she could have a lunch break. She still hadn't had a chance to speak to Clive about the practicalities of employing someone else. Effie turned her attention back to the postcards she was sorting into the display carousel.

'And this . . . Jake, is it? Eff! You're blushing. Come on! Spill! Is he fit?'

'Maddie!' Effie shushed her, her eyes darting around as if he might pop in at any moment. 'Keep your voice down, please.'

'Why? There's no one here.'

Effie squirmed. She loved Maddie but she had the tendency to be a bit loud, especially at inappropriate moments. 'I know, but, well, I think I like him. Like that, you know. But . . . things with him are complicated. Anyway, he might not feel the same.'

'Clive told me he dashed off to play the hero when Christie got stuck,' Maddie scoffed.

'Yes, well, Clive should've done that, don't you think?' Effie deflected.

'Maybe, but that would be far less romantic,' Maddie pointed out as she hauled herself out of the chair and started to peruse the shelves, even though the shop stocked exactly the same books as the one in Penzance.

Effie said nothing and instead concentrated very hard on making sure the postcards were perfectly lined up in their holders. She could feel Maddie's eyes on her.

'Sorry, Eff, you know me, I get carried away. I just want you to have some real-life romance, not just the stuff you get in books, but a man who can properly look after you.'

'I know,' Effie said. 'But I need Jake as a friend right now. He's not sure if he's staying permanently. He broke up with his fiancée before coming here. Or they're on a break or something.' She shrugged as if to pretend she didn't care, when in reality she'd done nothing other than turn Jake's revelation over in her head since the Easter egg hunt. What on earth did being on a break actually mean though?

Maddie rolled her eyes. 'In that case, keep it casual, have some fun. And don't look so shocked!'

'Maddie! You know I'm a relationship girl.' The fact that Effie had been chronically single hung between them. 'Anyway, she's an influencer. So probably super glamourous.'

Pulling her phone from her pocket, Maddie asked, 'What's her name?'

'Oh Maddie, no, I don't want to know.'

'Are you not curious?'

Effie dropped onto the space beside her. 'Well, of course I am, a bit, but I don't want to go snooping.'

'Pah! It's research. Checking out the competition.'

Effie stared at Maddie's phone, which was open on Instagram. 'Her name is Tara, that's all I know.'

'Hmm, there'll be hundreds of them. What's Jake's surname?'

Effie paused, not sure that she really wanted to go snooping, but Maddie fixed her with a look that dissolved her. 'Jake Penwith.'

Maddie typed 'Jake Penwith' into the Instagram search. Effie leaned over her shoulder as Maddie scrolled through the results until she could identify the profile photo. Effie clicked on it. The first few posts were shots of the Cornish coast, all dreamy sunsets and bright, bursting dawns. Effie held her breath as Maddie scrolled down.

'Phwoar.' Maddie fanned herself as she opened one of the posts showing a shirtless Jake emerging from some tropical waves like a god.

Effie's face flushed. 'Maddie,' she hissed, 'stop it, what if you accidently like something?'

'So, I'll unlike it.' She shrugged. 'Right, here we go.' She opened up a photo that showed Jake with a stunning dark-haired girl almost wrapped around him. 'Found her!'

Effie watched as Maddie clicked on Tara's Travels handle. 'Bingo!' Maddie held the phone up to Effie. The pinned post was one of Tara and Jake. Tara, all flawless makeup and expertly styled long dark hair, was showing off a flashy engagement ring. Effie skimmed through a few other photos, until she'd had enough of eyeing up 'the competition'.

'I really didn't need to see that,' she grumbled as she turned away from Maddie. Tara's profile made it seem that she and Jake were very much still together. Confused as to what was really going on between Jake and Tara, Effie stood up and distracted herself by straightening some already very straight books.

'So, how are you getting on down here, really? It's lovely but very quiet.' Maddie broke the silence.

Effie, relieved by the change in conversation, replied, 'I like it. I've been so busy I've not had much time to miss Mum and Dad. Plus, they've popped down a couple of times. Everyone has been so friendly. I've started swimming again. I feel content.' When she glanced up she saw Maddie studying her.

'You do look a bit different. More confident. No – don't get me wrong, you are more confident than you think you are, but this place suits you. I think you were a bit lost in the old shop with Clive always on at us, or Zach coming in and shifting things around.'

Effie made a disgusted face at Zach's name. 'Is he still away?'

'Yes, as far as I know.' Maddie picked a map up off the shelf, leafed through it and replaced it. 'I don't think he'll be bothering you for a while. So, Clive was telling us you're full of ideas. What's going on?'

'I'm going to do a book club. Not just any book club, I'm going to allow people to come along and talk about the books they've enjoyed. Sue, she's in charge of the village committee and a force to be reckoned with, has wanted to set one up for ages, so we'll be doing it together. I'll also be doing kids story time once a week.'

'Story time? That's brave! Fantastic ideas though.'

'I think I've forgotten the shop isn't actually mine,' Effie admitted. 'It's nice to pretend it is though.'

'Polcarrow suits you, Effie,' Maddie said as her stomach let out a rumble. 'Ooh that's the cream tea alarm. Can we take a break?'

Effie checked her watch. It was only half eleven but there hadn't been a customer for a little while. 'Sure. Let me grab my things.'

Once the shop was locked up and the 'Back in Thirty Minutes' sign hung, Effie walked Maddie the short distance to Lola's café. Pushing open the door, they found Freya behind the counter, bent over a crossword. She quickly straightened up only to relax when she saw it was Effie.

'How's it going?' Freya asked.

'Slow today,' Effie admitted. 'This is my friend Maddie, we worked together in Penzance.'

'Nice to meet you,' Freya greeted.

'I've heard all about these famous scones.' Maddie almost drooled as she took in the goods in the display cabinet. 'Oh, carrot cake, my favourite! Do you have takeaway boxes?'

'We do,' Freya said. 'So what would you like?'

'Two cream teas please,' said Effie. 'We'll just take the seat by the window if that's OK?'

'Sure, go for it, I'll bring them over,' Freya said.

Maddie had already plonked herself down on one of the chairs and was sighing at the sea view when Effie joined her.

'I am so insanely jealous that you got chosen for this gig.'

'Sorry, Maddie, I know it probably wasn't done fairly.'

Maddie batted this away. 'It doesn't matter. I don't think I have your drive and ambition anyway. I'm just hoping Clive lets us come down here and cover when you're on holiday or something. Do you think the shop will be a success?'

'I hope so. It's been quiet today but we're still out of season. I guess only time will tell. There's no way Clive would've invested if he didn't think it'd be viable, you know what he's like.'

'Yes, slightly on the stingy side. Oh wow!' Maddie's eyes grew as large as saucers as Freya placed two cream teas in front of them.

'I know! They are quite big,' Freya said, 'let me know if you need anything else. Enjoy.'

'Thank you, we will,' Effie replied.

Maddie picked her scone up, 'It's enormous! I am so glad I am wearing an elasticated waist. How are you staying so skinny with all this temptation?'

'Daily swims,' Effie said as she sliced her warm scone in half.

Maddie shuddered. 'I don't know how you do it.'

'It's invigorating!'

'I know what else would be invigorating.' She waggled her eyebrows.

'Maddie, no,' Effie groaned as she heaped cream onto her scone.

Maddie dropped her voice. 'A nice sexy, hunky manly man to throw you over his shoulder and carry you up to—'

Before Maddie could finish her sentence, the door opened and Lola stepped in, followed by Jake, who had his camera bag slung across his body.

'Effie!' He beamed as he saw her.

'Jake!'

Maddie swivelled around, her mouth dropping open as she took in Jake's rugged sandy good looks, the spotless white T-shirt, the thigh-hugging jeans, the tattoos.

'This is my friend Maddie,' Effie managed.

'How do you do?' He held his hand out. Maddie almost melted under his attention.

'I'm good, very good,' she purred.

'Nice to meet you. I won't interrupt.' Jake's eyes flitted to Effie.

'No, it's fine,' Effie said, 'Maddie wanted to try the scones.'

'How are they?' Lola interrupted. 'I made them fresh this morning.'

Effie watched Maddie, who didn't seem to know where to look.

'Erm, they're great. Lived up to the hype.' Maddie held up her half-eaten scone.

'Well, I'll leave you to it,' Lola said. 'Thanks for today, Jake. I can't wait to see the photos. Engagement shoot,' she informed Effie and Maddie.

'No worries, Lola, I'll send them over to you later, I just want to give them a once-over. Check they're up to standard.'

'I'm sure they'll be brilliant, and anyway, no offence but it's not like there are any other photographers available. Righto, enjoy your scones, ladies.' Lola waved at them as she headed back into the kitchen.

Jake stood in the middle of the café, not quite sure where to go.

'Flat white, Jake?' Freya asked.

'Yeah sure, I'll have it to go though.'

Effie's face fell, which Maddie caught and saved with, 'Oh don't mind us, there's a spare seat. I've heard all about your heroics, Jake.'

Effie was sure she was as red as a tomato when Jake pulled out the spare chair and asked, 'You have?'

'Umm-hmm. Effie said you're a dab hand with a paintbrush.'

'Oh yeah, that, the shop was awful. What kind of man is your boss? Honestly? I'm not impressed. Cheers,' he said as Freya placed his coffee in front of him. He added one sugar and took a sip.

'How did the engagement shoot go?' Effie asked, desperate to change the subject. She knew Jake had been worried about it, that he'd been feeling the pressure.

'Let's just say Lola knows what she wants!' He exhaled. 'But that made it easy for me. The hardest thing is when the subject has no idea what they want, or how to get it. Look.' He switched on his camera and turned the screen to Effie and Maddie and flicked through shots he'd taken of Lola and Tristan down on the hidden beach.

'Wow, Jake, they are amazing,' Effie enthused as she leaned further over his arm. 'You can really see how in love they are, they're beautiful.'

'Thanks,' he said slightly bashfully. 'I'm hoping Lola will let me use them to showcase my skills. I'm setting up a business,' he explained to Maddie, 'portraits, weddings, birthdays, you know. I've taken some of the shop for Effie.'

'Ah so that's where the social media shots came from?' Maddie said.

'Did you think I'd suddenly become amazing with my camera phone?'

Maddie raised an eyebrow. 'I did wonder. They were far too professional looking.'

'Oi!' Effie exclaimed.

'Would you like me to take your photo?' he asked. 'I want to do a series about the people of Polcarrow and you have such a good set-up here, with the sea view, the light is sitting just right and those cream teas look amazing.'

Effie glanced at Maddie, who nodded. 'Sure.'

'How do you want us?' Effie asked, which earned a smirk from Maddie.

Jake stood up and turned his camera on. 'Just act natural, like I'm not here. I like to catch people in the moment, not posed.'

Effie instantly forgot how to do anything naturally. Maddie picked up the teapot and began to pour. Effie's eyes ran all over the place, from Maddie, to Jake, to out at the sea. She picked up her scone, but her hands shook under his scrutiny, so she put it down again so that she didn't end up dropping it. Although, she assumed that would be very natural, which Jake was aiming for.

'Are you done?' she asked eventually.

'Yes.'

Effie relaxed and took a massive bite of her scone, eyes closed in pleasure at the taste of the jam and cream bursting on her tongue. Just as she did, the camera clicked. Her eyes snapped open. 'Hey!'

Jake was laughing. He turned the camera to Effie and Maddie. 'It was too good to miss.'

They burst into laughter at the blissful look on Effie's face as she bit into the scone.

'Right, I better be off. I'll leave you ladies to it. Effie, I'll see you soon.' He drained his coffee, waved goodbye to Freya and headed out the door.

Effie watched him go. When she turned back, Maddie was looking at her. 'What?'

'Oh Eff, he's dreamy, no wonder you like it so much down here.'

'Only just broken up with his fiancée, remember,' Effie sighed. She took a long drink of tea and wondered how much Jake was contributing to her enjoyment of being in Polcarrow. Would she be so keen to stay if he wasn't around?

Chapter Twenty-Eight

Effie found herself settling into the rhythm of Polcarrow life. Now that the bookshop was open, she had a little more spare time in the mornings for her swim. The bracing water setting her up for the day. Back home in Penzance, her swims had been more occasional so it was bliss being able to indulge her passion every morning.

Effie wasn't the only one to brave dipping a toe. Although she was drawn to the solitary aspect of sea swimming, she had been thrilled when other villagers had turned up to have a go once the spring sunshine was a more regular occurrence. The hot chocolate and coffees they shared afterwards, sitting outside Lola's café, further embedded Effie into the little community.

Effie had almost given up on Jake joining her until one Sunday morning, still yawning, she made her way across the road and saw him lingering on the sand, a towel around his shoulders, wearing only a pair of swimming shorts and a brave smile. She stopped in her tracks, taking in his toned, lightly bronzed body. Following his admission he was on a break with Tara, Effie had shoved her romantic hopes to the back of her brain and focused on their blossoming friendship instead, but it was hard to deny that she was still very attracted to him.

'Hurry up, Eff, I want to get this over with,' he called.

'You don't have to do this if you don't want to,' she told him, remembering him saying he was a summer-only swimmer.

'No, it's fine, I want to. I've been thinking about it for a while. I've just been summoning up the courage. Come on, before I chicken out.'

Laughing, Effie dropped her dry robe. 'How did you grow up by the sea and not swim in all weathers?'

Jake just shrugged as he followed her towards the water's edge. 'I guess I did as a kid.'

'How do you want to do it?' she asked. 'I recommend just going for it.'

Jake sucked in a breath as the cool water eased over his toes.

'Just keep breathing and follow me.' Effie turned to him and as an afterthought, held out her hand.

Jake glanced down before taking it. His hand engulfed hers, but their palms fitted together perfectly, their fingers entwining like tentative roots. Effie relaxed into his touch. It was going to be increasingly difficult not to fall for him further at this rate.

'Ready?' She stepped forward, the sea lapping up over her ankles.

Jake nodded and followed her. Hand in hand they waded into the waves until they were up to their knees.

'How's that?' she asked.

'Cold—' Jake's teeth chattered '—but actually, yeah, it feels good.'

'You don't have to go any further if you don't want to,' she told him. 'I know it's not nice when people try to force things on you.'

'Yeah, but I want to give it a proper go.'

'You do?'

Jake smiled at her. 'I do.'

'OK.' Effie reluctantly let go of his hand. 'You can get out whenever you're ready.'

She waded in further until she could lean forward and allow the waves to take her. No matter how many times she fell into the sea's embrace, it was always like being welcomed home. Turning in a circle, she watched as Jake did the same, spluttering at the temperature as he splashed over to her.

'Keep breathing,' she told him as they swam closer together, 'you're doing great. Are you all right?'

'It's bracing!' Jake sucked in a breath and allowed himself to settle as one with the water. 'It might not end up being my new hobby, but I can see why you do it.'

They swam a few more strokes, Effie getting into her stride, but she was aware of Jake spluttering valiantly along beside her.

'I'm really sorry, Eff, but I think I'm done,' he admitted.

Effie paused, treading water. 'That's fine, Jake, you've done brilliantly for a first-timer. I'll join you in a bit, use my dry robe.'

'Will do.' Jake gave a quick nod before turning for the shore.

Effie watched him until he was safely in the shallows where he emerged like a stunning merman from the waves. With a sigh, she turned back and swam a little further out. With every stroke she tried to erase her attraction to Jake. Falling for a man who had confessed he wasn't sure if he was sticking around and that him and his ex were on a break wasn't dangerous, it was downright foolish. Out in the water, the physical distance between them helped to settle her heart and mind. Finishing her swim, Effie resurfaced and joined Jake on the beach, picking up his towel to dry herself off.

'Eff, I feel alive,' he said in wonder, holding his arms out and wiggling his fingers, 'everything is buzzing.'

'I'm so proud of you for giving it a go.' She smiled as Jake got up from the sand and tried to offer her the robe back. 'No, I think you need it more than me. Are you ready for the next bit?'

'The hot chocolate?'

Effie nodded.

Jake leaned forward and whispered in her ear, sending a delicious shiver down her spine, 'Confession, that's the only reason I came.'

Once they'd dried off, they made their way across to Lola's café. Freya, who was manning the counter, raised her eyebrows as they entered.

'You're both far braver than me,' she said. 'What can I get you?'

'Hot chocolate please.' Effie beamed and glanced at Jake.

'Well, same for me, I'm here for the full experience.' He grinned. 'You've got to try it, Freya, it's life affirming.'

'I'll take your word for it,' Freya said as she turned to make the drinks. 'Glad to catch you, Jake,' she said over her shoulder, 'I've got a proposition for you. No, not like that.' She laughed as she set the hot chocolates down. 'More of the artistic kind. Whipped cream?' She held the can up.

Effie shook her head.

'Ah, go on,' Jake said, 'why not? What's this proposition?'

Freya passed Effie her marshmallow-laden hot chocolate before squirting a generous mound of cream onto Jake's. 'I've finally got permission to use the outbuilding behind the café as a gallery on a temporary basis over the summer. I have no idea how long it'll run for, or if it'll be a success, but I wanted somewhere to display my own paintings, keep all the money for myself. Even Angelo is working on a piece for display. I'm looking for local artists to show their work.'

'That sounds amazing!' Effie enthused as she scooped a slightly melted marshmallow off her drink.

'It does,' said Jake, 'well done. Do you want to use my decorating skills?'

Freya laughed. 'No, I can wield a paintbrush just fine, but I was wondering if you wanted to display some of your photos? Might help you get your business off the ground. What do you think?'

Jake turned to Effie, then back to Freya. 'Erm, well, that's quite something. I'd say I'd love to, but can I have a think about it?'

'Yeah, of course, no pressure,' Freya insisted. 'I've got a couple of weeks before I open. So, let me know in a few days? Then I can get the programme together.'

Jake nodded. 'Definitely, see you soon, Freya,' he said as he followed Effie towards the door. Once they were outside, Jake exhaled. 'What do you think I should do?' he asked as they perched on the harbour wall.

'Jake! It's a fantastic opportunity, of course you should say yes!'

Jake scooped off the whipped cream and spooned it into his mouth whilst staring thoughtfully at the horizon.

'You are going to say yes, aren't you?'

Jake turned to her. 'I should. But I need some thinking time. Hey, are you busy this afternoon? Want to take a walk out across the cliffs? Don't tell Steve, but the pub in the next bay does the best scampi and chips.'

'I never say no to scampi and chips.' Effie grinned at him.

Chapter Twenty-Nine

The low-lying grey clouds from the morning had cleared to reveal the most perfect spring afternoon for a walk along the Cornish coast path. The sun had come out and was bouncing across the sea as if to light the way. Jake was an excellent guide, regaling Effie with stories of his misspent youth.

'Jase had to carry me home after I'd drunk too many beers. God knows how he did it,' he said with disbelief. 'I was fifteen, Mum didn't know whether to tell me off or be glad I made it home.' Jake laughed. 'It's weird coming back and looking at it as an adult. Nostalgic. Maybe it wasn't all that bad.'

'Jake, you grew up in one of the most beautiful places in the UK. I can't understand why you'd be so desperate to leave when everyone else is so desperate to come.'

Jake mulled this over as they began their descent into the next village. 'Maybe it's because it's where everyone comes on holiday. The first time we flew to Spain, I was enthralled. OK, so it might just have been a resort on the Costa del Sol, but the fact there was other places out there fascinated me. To be fair, Mum, Dad and Jase don't get it either.'

Effie sighed. 'I'm trying to understand it. Has Cornwall not lured you back with her charms yet?'

Jake stopped and studied Effie. She squirmed slightly under his gaze, and not in an unpleasant way. It was as if she was part of the equation. She didn't even want to know what that meant.

'It might be, a bit, well, you're having a very good go at twisting my arm. What with the sea swimming, the cute bookshop, I'm seeing it through different eyes. I might see if this scampi is as good as I remember before making any final decisions though,' he joked.

'Oi! You better not have lured me here under false pretences,' Effie exclaimed. 'Scampi is my favourite.'

Effie followed him down the path into an even smaller village than Polcarrow. It clung to the side of the cliffs, balanced almost precariously along the coast. The whitewashed buildings were gnarled with age and fishing boats were scattered across the tiny beach. Effie came to a stop beside Jake, who'd pulled out his camera. She studied the way he framed his shot, searching for the best angle to capture the sunlight glinting off the waves.

'What do you think?' He turned the screen to her.

Effie's head swam at the proximity to him, her face brushing his arm as she leaned over to study the photos. 'They're beautiful,' she said as he clicked through the ones he'd taken on their walk.

'Hmm, I think they'd be better at sunrise. Looks like there's an early morning trip in store for me.' He turned to her, the laughter dropping out of his voice as he took her in.

Effie froze, her eyes hooked on his, neither of them able to step back or close the gap between them. Eventually, Effie stepped back, slightly befuddled. She couldn't fall for Jake. Or fall for him any further, if she didn't know what his future plans were.

'Jake, you have to show some photos at Freya's exhibition. What's holding you back?'

Jake put his camera away. 'I don't know. Maybe I don't think I'm good enough? Or maybe I don't think anyone will be impressed by my photos.'

'Jake, don't be silly, you're definitely good enough – Freya wouldn't have asked you if she didn't think so.'

'True. My posts of Cornwall have been getting a lot of likes online,' he admitted.

'There you go! People love seeing photos of Cornwall, and you're a local and you have an eye for capturing things other people might not notice. You have to do it, Jake, honestly, it's a fantastic opportunity. For your business, too,' she said, playing the trump card she knew would sway him.

Jake mulled this over as they made their way towards the harbourside pub. A table with a view of the sea had just become available and they slipped into it.

'That's true,' he admitted as he pulled the menu towards him. 'So you think I should say yes?'

'Of course!'

Jake flashed her a smile. 'Well, there you go, there's my answer. Scampi?'

'That's the reason I came! But I'll have a lemonade, I don't want to be all wobbly on the way back.'

'I'd carry you,' Jake quipped as he extracted himself from the bench and made his way inside.

Suddenly warm, Effie picked up the drinks menu and fanned herself. It was the sunshine, she assured herself, not the idea of Jake swinging her up into his arms. Definitely the sun.

Chapter Thirty

As well as Polcarrow life, Effie was slowly getting into the swing of things with the shop itself. Running it alone was a huge learning curve and some evenings Effie collapsed into bed, exhausted from trying to do everything alone. Other days, she'd shut the shop and stifle tears that only one customer had been in, and that had only been to ask directions to somewhere she didn't know. On days like that she didn't know whether or not to press Clive for an extra member of staff, yet when it was busy she was rushed off her feet.

Mostly, however, Effie was enjoying running the bookshop and pretending it was her own. After all, she'd done all the hard work, she thought with satisfaction, as she glanced around at the full shelves, the armchairs with the sea view that had been a social media winner, why not indulge in a little fantasy. She rearranged the romance novels she'd set out on the local fiction table, still considering the idea of setting up a romance-only book club.

Effie was just reading a blurb on the back of a book when the shop door opened and Lola stepped inside.

'Just checking numbers for later,' she said.

Tonight was the inaugural Polcarrow book club. Almost all of Effie's suggestions had been steamrollered by Sue, who'd been trying, unsuccessfully, to set up a book club for years and was thrilled to have someone else to back the venture. The opening of the shop had given the residents just what they needed to have their arms twisted by Sue. The original plan had been to host it in the shop, however the number of residents who'd signed up meant they'd had to switch venue to Lola's café. Effie was secretly pleased, it would mean one less job for her, especially as Lola had leapt at the opportunity to host.

'I think there's twenty,' Effie said, 'but Sue was convinced she could persuade some more people to attend.'

Lola laughed. 'Sue's always good at a bit of arm twisting. I have a confession though.'

'Oh, go on.'

'I've not read the book.'

Effie laughed. 'That's OK, most people don't read the full book at a book club, they mostly come along for the socialising.'

'Phew.' Lola pretended to wipe her brow.

'Thanks for offering up the café out of hours, Lola, I know you work so hard already.'

Lola shrugged. 'It's fine, my lovely. You know, when I arrived Polcarrow was this sleepy little village, lost in time, so anything that helps breathe new life into it I'm more than happy to be involved in. Sue has been trying to reinvigorate the community for years, so she's over the moon to have us here.' She was cut off by her phone ringing. 'Oh, it's the florist. I better go, see you later.' Blowing a kiss goodbye, Lola left the shop.

At seven that evening Effie was tweaking the collar of her blue and white checked blouse and wondering if she should apply lipstick rather than lip gloss when a text came through on her phone.

> Good luck! You'll smash it. Managed to convince that hunky photographer that you're the girl for him?!?! xxxxxxxxxxx

Effie smiled at Maddie's wishes and the extreme amount of kisses attached to the end of the message. She sent a quick reply, omitting anything about Jake. In fact, she hadn't seen much of him since their swim and walk two days previously. He'd had meetings with a couple in Newquay about photographing their wedding and had been staying with his brother. She had missed him but didn't like to examine too closely what that meant.

Deciding to forego the lipstick she rarely used, Effie gathered up her copy of Christie's book and the notes she'd made to go along with it. Considering almost everyone in Polcarrow had bought the book, it had been the logical choice as recommended reading. Effie was curious to know what other books people might bring along, not only was she full of recommendations, she loved adding new authors to her out of control to-be-read pile.

After locking up the flat, Effie headed down the stairs and out into the cool evening air. The weather had taken a turn following the glorious golden sunshine of Easter weekend and April was rolling out in muted greys and lazy clouds drifting across whatever sun did show. When she entered the café, Sue, Lola and Freya were already there, all gathered around the counter, peering at something on Lola's phone. Effie hovered, not wanting to intrude.

Lola glanced up, her attention caught by the sound of the door closing. 'Effie, come and have a look. I'm trying to choose my wedding bouquet, what do you prefer?'

Clutching the strap of her bag, Effie made her way over. Being so easily enveloped in the already formed friendships was still taking some getting used to. She studied the photos Lola was showing her. 'I think I like the classic red roses the best.'

'That was my choice, but the others prefer the yellow,' Lola told her.

'Like you were going to listen to us,' Freya playfully jibed before telling Effie, 'Once Lola has her mind made up, there's no going back. I didn't say I didn't like the red, they are more you.'

'Definitely—' Sue nodded '—but I prefer yellow for a summer wedding.'

'Like it's that summery out there. I had to turn the heating on this morning,' Lola replied before slipping her phone into her pocket. 'Right, is this set up OK, Effie. I've done mini brownie and blondie bites and we'll be offering pots of tea and filter coffee, is that all right?'

'That's perfect,' Effie confirmed.

'I've read the book and have lots of thoughts,' Freya said. 'That's why I don't want to spend the evening making complicated lattes.'

'I've made a list of questions and topics for discussion,' Sue said, pulling a notebook out of her bulging bag. Her copy of the book had Post-it notes poking out of various pages.

'Erm, so have I,' Effie said, holding up her similarly annotated copy.

'We can exchange notes, I'm sure we've come up with the same things.' Sue picked up her coffee and headed over to the table by the window.

Effie glanced at Lola and Freya. 'I thought it was supposed to be my book club?'

'Sue just can't help herself,' Lola said, 'you try taking back control. Here, have a consolatory blondie.'

Not sure how she felt about Sue muscling her way in, Effie took the treat and popped it into her mouth. Fresh sharp raspberry burst alongside the creamy white chocolate. 'Oh, that is divine.'

'Look at it this way,' Freya said as she leaned over the counter, 'if Sue is in control, it's one less thing for you to worry about.'

'True—' a smile of realisation spread across Effie's face '—and I do get a bit nervous talking to crowds. I prefer the sitting and reading bit.'

'Then Sue is your perfect co-host. She loves an audience,' Freya said as she started to line up the teapots.

The three women spun around when the door opened and Alf shuffled in, Tristan behind him.

'No Scruff?' Freya asked.

'Didn't like the book, did he?' Alf held up a copy with a chewed corner. 'Left him at home. Effie, my dear, care to join me. I'd be really interested to hear your thoughts.'

'Of course, but I'm meant to be running the discussion.'

'Are you?' He signalled over to where Sue was setting up. She'd even brought a microphone that she was in the process of testing. 'I think you've been ousted. I wouldn't want to fight her for control. Where's your young man?'

Effie was about to say he was in Newquay and that she wasn't expecting him, when the door opened and Jan walked in, Jake a few steps behind her. Effie's heart skipped a beat as he ran his hand through his unruly blond hair and fixed her with a look that pinned her to the spot. A look full of relief at being reunited. A look that scrambled all her senses and made her relieved that Sue had decided to commandeer the first Polcarrow book club. Maybe next time Effie would manage to wrestle it back.

Chapter Thirty-One

'So, you survived being Sue-d last night?' Jake asked as he handed Effie her post-swim hot chocolate.

Laughing, Effie lifted the lid and gave the marshmallows a little stir. 'Just about. Actually, it took the pressure off me,' she said, as she perched on the harbour wall, her dryrobe wrapped around her. The evening had been a huge success, everyone had loved the book and had queued up for Effie's recommendations before leaving. She'd been buzzing too much to sleep properly, so the morning swim had helped clear her fuzzy head.

After a few grey mornings, the sun was starting to peek out from behind the clouds, like a promise of the season to come. Effie took a sip. 'Ah, it doesn't get much better than this.' She glanced at Jake. 'Well, I guess you've seen some better sights.'

Jake paused for a moment. 'Yeah, I guess I have. Ticked off a lot of the bucket list ones, but I was still sort of on a big, long holiday. Being able to live with this view every day, well, yeah, that is something special.'

'So, Cornwall is working its charms on you?' Effie asked.

Jake gave her a look, his expression suddenly solemn. 'The truth?'

The smile slid from her face. Bracing herself for his answer, Effie nodded.

'It's not just Cornwall working its charms,' he said carefully, before taking a sip of his coffee. 'I'm having a nice time. Between helping you and trying to set up the photography business it's great, but I'm not sure if this is the best place for me, to say yes to Cornwall feels like a huge commitment. I'm sorry. But it's more of a seventy–thirty split.'

'What percentage has what?'

'Seventy to stay. Dad said if the photography business doesn't take off, I can help him. That would definitely mean staying here in Polcarrow though.'

'Well, you are a dab hand with a paintbrush,' Effie said, trying to hide her disappointment whilst trying to also convince herself that seventy per cent sure was pretty good going, whilst ignoring the mixed signals he kept sending. 'I was impressed by those skills, but actually your photography is even better. How's it going?'

Jake put his coffee cup down and pulled his phone from his pocket and swiped the screen. 'What do you think?' he asked, passing his phone to Effie.

Effie put her drink down and took his phone. 'Is this your website?'

'Yeah, Jason helped me set it up. He did one for his surf school.'

Effie scrolled through the photos. 'I think it looks fabulous,' she said, passing the phone back to him. There was a nice mix of local seascapes, far-flung land-scapes and portraits.

Relief washed over Jake as he scrolled up and down the screen. 'You really think it's OK? You're not just saying that, are you?'

'As if I would! It looks great, Jake, really. If I was looking to hire a photographer to shoot my special occa-sion, I'd feel confident in what you're showing there. Thanks for including the shop!' Effie tapped on one of the photos from the opening to enlarge it.

'I was running out of non-landscape things to share,' he confessed as he clicked on another image. It was one of the ones he'd taken of Maddie and Effie in Lola's café.

'I can't believe you made what I thought was a snap-shot look like a professionally posed photo,' Effie said, leaning over to take it in, her mind boggling at the composition, the lighting. 'You really have a talent.'

'Thank you.' Jake slipped his phone back in his pocket. 'So now I just wait, I guess. Lola and Tristan have booked me for the end of May.'

'That's awesome news! Have you chosen your shots for the exhibition at Freya's gallery?'

Jake laughed. 'I've been trying to! But striking the right balance is harder than I thought it'd be. There's so many. I've been agonising over it for the last couple of days.'

'Maybe you need a new eye?' Effie suggested as she fished one of the melted marshmallows out of her drink, sighing with happiness as she popped it into her mouth. 'My favourite bit. What?' Effie asked. 'Why are you looking at me like that?'

'You're so cute when you get to your marshmallows,' he said with a smile.

Effie's face flushed.

'But also, you're right, you haven't seen all my photos. Do you want to come over later and help me decide?'

'Me? I don't know anything about what makes a good photo,' she protested.

'I just need a second opinion. I'll cook for you. I make a great Thai curry.'

'Ooh that's one of my favourites.'

'So that's a yes?'

Effie finished her drink 'It is a yes.'

Chapter Thirty-Two

Effie agonised over what to wear for her date with Jake. Hang on, it wasn't a date. Was it? Probably better not to treat it as one, she decided, as she compared two of her favourite tops before choosing the comfiest. After all, Jake had seen her fresh from the sea, hair wild and wrapped in an old towel, so did it matter what she wore? No. Also, he was still lacking commitment to staying in Polcarrow. Plus, there was the small matter of him being on a break from Tara. She really didn't want to have to mend her heart when he decided to carry on chasing new horizons. Friends, she reminded herself, pushing down the bubbles of happiness that always rose up when she thought of him.

Effie slipped on her shoes, took the bottle of wine she'd had chilling in her fridge and let herself out of the flat. The evening light lay low and slumberous across the sea as she made her way round to the back of Lola's café and up the staircase to Jake's flat. She paused before knocking on the door. Music was turned down and her heart rate leapt as footsteps made their way over to the door. Jake pulled it open.

'Good evening.' A smile spread across his face.

'Good evening,' Effie said, a sudden shyness taking over as she stood on the threshold of his home. Even though Jake had been in her flat, setting foot in his felt strangely intimate, as if it could reveal a whole new layer of him. 'I brought this.' She offered the wine.

'Brilliant, come in.' Jake pulled the door back and made space for her.

Effie stepped inside and removed her shoes, despite Jake telling her she didn't need to. 'I feel weird wearing my outdoor shoes in the house,' she told him, 'Anyway, if I end up on your sofa, I like to tuck myself up.'

Jake gave her a look as he processed her long explanation. Their eyes caught and it was as if all the air was sucked from the room.

'Sorry, I'm sure you didn't need to know all that,' she said as she cast her eyes around the small, sparsely furnished flat.

It dawned on her that she wasn't going to uncover anything new about Jake from his living space. The décor didn't give away much of his personality, but the lack of belongings screamed a lack of permanence. Effie's heart sank. She'd tried to kid herself that he'd choose Polcarrow, and maybe even choose her, but the emptiness of his flat was a sobering truth. Out on the seafront when the sea breeze wrapped their worlds together, anything felt possible, but standing in the stark reality of Jake's flat, Effie realised he had been honest when he said he might just be passing through. She had to believe him, not her hopes.

'No, I like hearing all these little bits from you,' he said. 'Do you want a glass of this now?' He signalled to the wine. 'Or with dinner?'

'Maybe a little now,' she said, hoping it'd soothe her nerves.

Jake disappeared into the kitchen and Effie made her way over to the window with the sea view. She watched the gulls strutting on the harbour wall before turning around to study the living room. Jake had made some effort to create a cosy ambience. A red throw over the arm of the sofa, a couple of matching cushions arranged neatly, a coffee table with a lone plant in the middle. Gentle music wafted from the sound system and the lamps were on low. A couple of candles flickered on the half-filled bookshelves. Effie crossed over to them. There were a few sudoku puzzle books, some photography journals and a games console. Jake returned and passed her a glass of wine.

'Cheers.' He held his out to her. 'I'm embarrassed there's no actual books there.'

'Cheers.' Effie chinked her glass against his and then took a sip. It was sharp and crisp, exactly how she liked her wine. She took a longer swallow. 'I'm not judging.' She winked. 'You've really not been here long, have you?'

'Yeah, it is a bit sparse,' Jake laughed. 'A couple of months now. My parents weren't exactly expecting Jase or me to ever move home and you know, living at home at thirty doesn't feel very cool. I was sleeping on the sofa feeling like an intruder when I heard this flat was going free. Did you know Angelo used to live here?'

'Really?'

'Yep. When he arrived last summer, fleeing some drama back in London.'

Effie glanced around the blank walls. 'I like the idea of this being a bolt-hole for the needy.'

'Hey! Well, maybe I was a little needy,' he admitted. 'But I've not done near half as much to this place as you have to yours. A lot of my stuff is still in our flat in Bristol.'

Effie chose to ignore the 'our' and asked, 'Do you still have itchy feet?' Tired of the caginess about his plans, she decided to try and probe further, so that she could make an informed decision about risking her heart.

'A bit. I'm in touch with some of the guys. They're travelling around Cambodia and it looks amazing, so I feel like I'm missing out, but I don't currently have the funds to join them. Otherwise, yeah, maybe I'd be there,' he admitted.

Effie let this sink in. The reality that, despite saying he was seventy per cent sure he'd stay in Polcarrow, the temptation to bolt was still running wild through his veins. 'I've never been anywhere,' Effie sighed, trying to push away the feeling that she was dull and boring creeping in.

'There's still plenty of time,' Jake reminded her. 'Where would you go?'

Effie laughed. 'I don't actually know. I've always had my head too much in a book to think about the outside world. It might sound weird because you've been everywhere, but I'd love to go to Scotland, right up to the other tip of the country. See the Highlands.' She didn't admit this dream had been born from reading *Outlander* one too many times.

'Confession time; I've been all over the Far East, Canada, Australia and if you can get a long haul flight, I've been, but never to Scotland properly, isn't that terrible? Tara had a whistle-stop commission in Edinburgh, but we were in and out in twenty-four hours, although from the photos you'd think we'd been there a week.'

'Was it really hard work?'

Jake nodded. 'Yeah, sometimes. Early mornings. Lots of outfit changes,' he groaned. 'It really changed her. The woman I left was not the woman I fell in love with at uni. And I'm not the same person I was then, either. Coming back here has allowed me to reflect on it all. Sometimes I wonder if what I was searching for all along was always right under my nose. Other times I feel the pull to book a ticket and go far away. There's still so many places I want to go. Do you get that?'

'The travel thing? No, I've always felt happier in Cornwall. I realised that when I was twenty-one and now I'm worried I haven't lived.'

Jake fixed her with a long look. 'But are you happy, Eff? That's what it boils down to.'

She met his eyes and rolled the answer around on her tongue. Had she been happy back then? Certainly not. Was she happy now? 'Yes,' she answered, 'I am, or at least a lot happier than I thought I'd be. I didn't know what to expect from Polcarrow. I thought I'd miss my family too much, but . . . I feel a bit bad saying this, I don't. It's like I've been forced to stand on my own two feet and I'm actually a lot better at it than I thought I'd be.'

'I'm really pleased you're here; shall we toast it? Us both ending up in Polcarrow at the same time?' Jake held his glass out.

Effie caught the look in his eye, the warmth that lingered there like embers. Did he feel what she was feeling? An inexplicable tug forward, like there was a thread wound between them? Would their timing just be fleeting though? Standing up, she took a step forward and tapped her glass against his. 'I'll certainly drink to that.'

Feeling bold, she took a sip without breaking eye contact before a rumble from her stomach cracked through the intensity of the moment.

'Oops.' She giggled. 'I've not had anything since a cheese and pickle sandwich at lunchtime,' she confessed.

'Good thing I've got everything prepped to start cooking. It'll be minutes. Come through. I've got my laptop open – I need you to help me choose the photos.'

'I still can't believe you're asking me.'

'Fresh eyes,' Jake said as he led the way into the kitchen where his laptop was open on the table. 'Have a flick through whilst I get the food on the go.'

Effie slipped onto one of the chairs and couldn't help but feel like she was prying as she tapped the mouse and the screen burst into life. A file full of photos was already loaded. 'Do I just look through these?'

'Yeah, go ahead.'

'I feel like I'm prying,' she told him as she opened the first one which revealed a peaceful pink dawn over a white sandy beach. Effie studied it. It could be Australia, but equally it could be Cornwall. She clicked onto the next, a beautiful autumnal scene that appealed to her cosy girl heart. 'I like this.' She turned the laptop towards him.

Jake peered over his shoulder. 'That was in a cabin in Finland. We were off grid. The colours were amazing. That lake was freezing though. I only dipped my toe out of curiosity.'

'Sounds like I'd love it. It's beautiful, you should use this,' Effie said after studying it for a moment longer, trying to imagine what it would feel like to plunge herself into a cold lake. As she clicked through the other photos, unravelling the itinerary of Jake's life, a lump started to form in her throat. Had she missed out by staying put in Cornwall?

Effie clicked through the rest of the photos. All of them impressive travel shots – cherry blossom in Japan, boats washed up on a Thai beach, the water turquoise and inviting. Jake really had seen everything. They were beautiful yet none of them really stirred her. 'Jake,' she began as something started to sizzle in the pan, 'can I be honest?'

'Umm-hmm go ahead.'

'These photos are all amazing and it's fascinating to see where you've been but I'm not sure they're going to touch the hearts of the locals. I think they'll be impressed, but whether or not they'll think anything deeper about them, I don't know.'

Jake was still for a very long time. Effie watched him with trepidation as he stirred whatever was in the pan.

'Sorry, Jake, I mean, what do I know?'

'Effie, it's fine,' he said with a groan. 'I think you're right.'

'You do?'

'Uh-huh. I think that's why I can't choose. They're impressive but I'm not sure if they have soul.'

'I like the Finnish one,' she reminded him. 'Do you have any you've taken here?' She continued to click through the social media worthy spots he'd photographed.

'Yeah, in the last file,' Jake said.

Effie opened the folder as Jake finished cooking, the delicious aroma of onions and coconut curling up her nose and making her stomach gurgle. Effie snuck a glance at him, his broad shoulders, the trademark white T-shirt, the unruly blond waves she wanted to run her fingers through. Swallowing, she turned her attention back to the photos.

The first shot was of Lola's café in the dawn light, the blind still drawn, anticipation for the day ahead paused in time. The second was of the ice-cream-hued cottages basking in the sun, their windows reflecting like sunglasses. Then came the photos from Alf's ninetieth. The old fisherman and Scruff captured enjoying the celebrations, surrounded by the embrace of the villagers. There were even shots of the bookshop full to bursting on opening day. Jake had managed to capture not only the life that flowed through Polcarrow, but the secret moments others hadn't realised existed.

'What do you think?' Jake asked nervously as he approached her, two steaming plates in his hands.

Effie managed a smile. 'I've not tried it yet.' She pushed the laptop to the other side of the table.

'Not the food, silly, the photos.' Jake placed the plates on the table before taking the bottle of wine from the fridge and topping up their glasses.

Effie scooped up some of the fragrant curry and took a bite, the flavours exploding on her tongue. 'Oh my gosh, this is delicious. Did you learn to cook whilst travelling?'

'Yeah, I always tried to immerse myself in local life. I love Thai food so it was the perfect place to learn to make authentic dishes.' Jake said before looking at her expectantly. Was there also a little bit of nerves furrowing his brow 'The photos?'

'OK, the local ones are so much better, so much more alive. I think everyone will love seeing Polcarrow through your lens. It might even help you drum up some business.'

Jake let out a sigh of relief. 'You have no idea how happy I am to hear that. Landscape was always more my thing but as I've got older, I find more joy in photographing people. Landscapes can be beautiful, but people are far more interesting. You see their layers; everyone has a story to tell. Photographing the locals is totally different from taking shots of Tara.'

'Are you still in touch?' Effie asked, trying to keep her voice light, interested.

Jake pushed his food around his plate. 'Yeah, sometimes. We still talk. There's a lot to unwind from our lives, it's difficult to navigate.'

The seriousness of his tone sobered Effie up. 'Of course,' she said, reaching for her glass to stop herself from asking if Tara was part of the equation for his future. She took a sip and placed the glass back down with shaking fingers. All this confusion was the reason she kept well away from dating. As she went to pick up her fork again, Effie paused. Jake hadn't taken his eyes off her.

'What?' she asked, her voice thick, her nerves feeling as if they'd burst out of her skin.

Jake leaned forward and before Effie had time to realise what was happening, his lips were on hers, a soft invite. Before she could kiss him back, Jake had pulled away.

'Jake!?' She gasped.

'I'm sorry, I just couldn't resist.' He pushed his hands through his hair, agitated, exasperated. 'I shouldn't, sorry. Things are complicated but I'm really attracted to you, Effie, I've been wanting to do that for ages.'

'No, well, yes, but . . . I . . . I'm attracted to you too,' Effie flustered, eyes skittering everywhere before they fell back on Jake. A chance she'd be stupid not to take.

He looked tortured, unsure, as if everything in his life had suddenly unravelled itself and he didn't know how to put it back together. One minute he was treading on eggshells trying to explain that he didn't know what he wanted to do next, the next he was kissing her. Effie knew she should leave. Knew she should take back control of the situation. Knew that staying would only get her heart broken.

Effie pushed her lips together, committing that first kiss to her memory. Jake probably wasn't over his ex. He was undecided about staying in Cornwall. Effie weighed up these truths against the desire that one kiss had sent storming through her. He looked so tousled and gorgeous, she'd had a crush on him ever since he'd swooped in and saved the day with helping to paint. Wouldn't Maddie tell her to live a little? Wasn't it time for her to give in to the desire she felt for him? A seventy per cent chance was still quite high.

Then she did something she would never have thought she was bold enough to do before she arrived in Polcarrow. Effie threw caution to the wind, and leaning forward, kissed Jake gently. Her whole body fizzed with delight, waiting half in expectation, half in anticipation for his next move.

A heartbeat, a moment, an eternity passed before Jake kissed her back. Sweet release flooded through them both. As the kiss deepened, Effie gave in to everything she knew she wanted but didn't think she'd get. Her heart, she figured, would mend.

Chapter Thirty-Three

Jake wasn't around the following morning when Effie finished her swim, nor did he turn up when she opened the shop. Her lips still tingled from his kisses and she'd slipped into bed the previous night high on the feeling of Jake's body pressed against her. She now worried that it had been a passionate, thrilling mistake.

So, it was natural that her heart lurched when he wasn't around that morning. She'd grown used to seeing him waiting for her with her post-swim hot chocolate. The kiss had made her rearrange everything that had happened between them. Effie had previously told herself that Jake was just being kind when he helped her, because he was at a loose end, but it seemed more likely now that the painting and holding her hand through Alf's party had been because he fancied her. *I'm really attracted to you*, he'd said.

Effie's face flushed at the thought. She wasn't the sort of woman men had crushes on. She'd accepted being left on the sidelines a long time ago and all the dates she had been on had never turned into anything more than a lack-lustre second date or a half-hearted promise of friendship.

Effie craved her own happy ending but had resigned herself to only ever finding it in between the covers of her trusty books, rather than in between the sheets. Entangling herself with gorgeous, kind, funny Jake the previous evening had allowed her heart to leap with hope that her own romantic fortunes were about to change.

However, Effie couldn't deny that as the morning rolled slowly on, the lack of Jake's presence was tying her stomach into knots, and not the good kind. What if he regretted kissing her? She'd chosen to ignore the red flags he'd unfurled for her. What if last night meant nothing to him and right now he was sitting in his flat chewing over how to let her down? After all, she was quite clearly hoping to stay in Polcarrow whilst he was gazing wistfully over the horizon, his wanderlust not quite fully sated.

Effie reached for her phone, pulled open the messaging app and hovered over Jake's name. It was only half past ten, she realised, she couldn't text him and ask him where he was. She had to remain cool. Right, she smoothed down her dungarees, she needed a task to take her mind off Jake's kiss and subsequent absence.

There'd been a new delivery of greetings cards the previous morning, so Effie brought the box out from the small storeroom and set it on the counter. They were mostly pastel watercolours of a stylised Cornish coast, but Effie found them charming and knew the customers would love them. She was busy pricing them up when the shop door opened. Glancing up Effie saw Jake standing in the doorway, a nervous look on his face, a package in his hand.

Effie swallowed. She'd known all along Jake was attractive but when had the real feelings started to grow? Was it with every stroke of the paintbrush that brought the shop to life, waking her up from her internal slumber as well? Her mind raced through every moment they had shared: Alf's party, the reassurance he lent her allowing her to slowly dismantle some of the barriers she'd kept herself safe with? The hero moment when he'd rushed out of the shop on opening day to rescue Christie? All those post-swim hot chocolates? Jake had woven himself into her life without her fully realising. She liked him, really liked him. But she didn't like the grave look on his face.

'Hi,' she managed as she nervously shuffled the birthday cards.

'Hi.' Jake's voice was equally awkward. 'I missed your swim.'

Effie nodded. 'The hot chocolate wasn't quite the same.'

'I'll make it up to you,' he said but there was something stilted in his voice.

Awkward silence fell like a shroud between them. Effie placed some of the cards in the holder on the counter whilst Jake watched her, keeping close to the door, his jacket zipped up as if he wasn't staying.

'Jake, are you OK? Are we OK?' she asked, her heart pounding. Were they a 'we'?

His brow furrowed. 'What do you mean?' He took a few more steps into the shop.

Effie studied him. 'You're being a bit weird. Like distant.'

'I was worried about seeing you after last night.'

'Why?' Effie asked, her whole body freezing with dread.

Jake squirmed. 'Oh God, Effie, don't. I wanted to kiss you for so long but now I don't think it's what I should have done.' His eyes met hers gravely.

'Jake, what is it?'

Jake's eyes darted nervously around the shop, trying to look everywhere other than at her. 'Can you take a few minutes? I don't want to do this in here.'

Effie swallowed. 'Sure.' She pulled her cardigan on, one of her favourites, green with little ducks on it, grabbed her keys and followed Jake outside into the fresh spring morning. She followed him across the road to the harbour wall, but he didn't stop, just kept walking away from the village. Effie had to quicken her pace to keep up with him.

Jake stopped at the far end of the beach, just before the path that rose up to the headland. Effie recalled the walk they'd taken over the coast path the previous week. All cider-induced giggles as they exchanged pieces of their lives like tokens. Now, as Effie looked at Jake where he sat on the bench, her stomach sank. She suspected they wouldn't be sharing much more.

'Effie, please sit, I can't do this with you looming over me like that.'

Although she had half a mind to keep making him feel uncomfortable, she didn't want him to see her reactions to whatever he was going to tell her. The awkwardness, the distance, everything about him told her it was going to be bad news.

'I really like you, Effie, I do. I meant it when I said that I'm attracted to you, and I've enjoyed helping you with the shop,' he started, picking over his words as he traversed the emotional minefield he was clearly trying not to detonate. He risked a glance at her. 'Oh God, this is such a mess.'

Effie remained silent, waiting for him to dig himself out of the hole and unwilling to lend him a helping hand.

'I told you at Easter that Tara and I are on a break. I never lied about that. I never lied to you about how hard I found all the travelling and influencer stuff in the end. You're an amazing woman, Effie, but I loved Tara, we had a future planned out. She's, well, she's been in touch this morning and wants to talk.'

'I see,' was all Effie could manage as her mind unravelled everything she had shared with Jake over the past few weeks.

'Eff, I didn't mean to hurt you or lead you on or anything like that. I meant it, I really like you, I'm attracted to you, but I'm not sure if I'm over Tara yet, or if I'm even ready for a relationship. I really need to speak to her, try and sort things out for good this time. I should never have kissed you last night, but I just, well, I just couldn't resist, and I'd been wanting to kiss you for such a long time.'

Effie turned to him, taking in the tortured expression on his face, which matched the way she felt inside.

'I thought you were cute and fiery, and I only meant to offer you a hand at the beginning but the more time I spent with you, the more I enjoyed your company. Everything I said about you being unlike the other girls I've met was true. Ugh, this is so hard for me, I don't know what to do, but I do know I shouldn't have kissed you last night and that I can't lead you on any longer.'

Silence settled in the space between them, filling it up, pushing open the cracks that had started to form.

'Oh God, Effie, please say something.' He rubbed his face in despair.

'Jake, I'm not sure I know what to say,' she admitted, 'it's a lot to process. I thought, well, I thought there was something here.' She gestured between them. 'I'm not imagining that, am I?' She turned to him, searching his face.

Jake met her eyes and let out a long exhale. He looked so serious, so forlorn, like he really didn't know what to do next. 'No, Effie, you aren't. I'm sorry that I got carried away when so much of my life is in limbo. I couldn't resist you but you deserve better. It was never my intention to hurt you, please believe that.'

'What are you going to do?'

'I have a job further up the coast this weekend. I have the exhibition. I'm sorry, Effie, but I need some time to think about what I really want.'

Incensed by his indecisiveness, Effie stood up and turned to him. 'You should've been more careful with my feelings, Jake. Even when we were just friends. Are you just going to keep swanning in and out of here saying you don't know what you want? Are you waiting for Tara to call you up and ask for you back? Or are you actually going to make your own mind up? You couldn't decide about Freya's exhibition. You dithered over your business. It seems to me you're waiting for everyone else to decide your life when it should be down to you.'

The words fell on Jake like a slap of reality. Effie watched them land, sink in. Watched as he processed what she'd said.

'Effie—'

'No! No, Jake, please, just leave me alone for a bit. In fact, I think we could both do with some space.'

Jake stood up, reached for her hand, but Effie had already stepped out of his reach. Pulling her cardigan tightly around her, she took him in, one last long look, his mane of golden hair, his eyes as blue as the Cornish sea, a man who it seemed was only going to be a brief chapter, not her happy-ever-after.

'Goodbye, Jake,' she said squaring her shoulders, then she marched back into the village, wiping away the threat of tears.

She unlocked the shop, stepped inside and leaned against the door, taking deep, steadying breaths. They were only on a break. He'd implied that at the Easter egg hunt, but she'd allowed herself to get swept up in his storm of confusion and possibility.

Once her bruised heart had calmed down, Effie glanced around the shop, at the books, her home and haven. It was time to get on with the reason she'd come to Polcarrow: to sell books.

Chapter Thirty-Four

Effie smoothed the silky midnight-blue material over her hips and wondered if the dress was too much. She'd bought it years ago on sale because she'd fallen in love with the colour but had never had an occasion to wear it. Until now. Although she couldn't help but wonder if it was a bit too fancy for a small gallery opening in a little Cornish fishing village.

A smile spread across her face as she imagined Lola telling her that there was no such thing as too fancy. However, as she put her earrings in and fastened her necklace, Effie noticed the smile didn't quite reach her eyes. She tried again, an attempt to turn the light Jake had dimmed back on. There was a glimmer. It would have to do.

The past week had been difficult. Jake hadn't been into the shop since their talk. Effie had allowed herself the indulgence of one wine-soaked night of tears before pulling herself together and getting back on with her life. Maybe in time her feelings would revert back to simple friendship. Or maybe Jake would head back to Bristol, to Tara and she'd never have to see him again.

Effie didn't know how that made her feel. Filled with a strange sense of loss, of what could have been. Mostly she felt a bit foolish for choosing to ignore the signs he'd clearly laid out.

Jake had been noticeably absent from Polcarrow for the last week, which had helped her heart begin to heal. Effie had caught fleeting glimpses of him as he exited the café, takeaway cup in hand, jumping into his car and heading off to whatever adventure he was chasing. She missed the companionship, the early-morning chats about what they were doing that day. The cups of tea he'd bring her.

Thankfully Lola had been far too busy planning her wedding to ask her too many questions about where Jake was. Effie wanted a bit of time and space to get over the romance that never quite got off the ground. Like all her romances, it had been a brief burst of excitement before inevitably fizzling out.

Tonight, however, there was no escaping the fact that she would be seeing Jake. After all, he was showing his photos at Freya's gallery. Another reason for choosing the dress. It might have been slightly fancier than she'd usually go for, but Effie felt a million dollars in it. She might not be able to compete with a glamorous influencer, but she was determined to show Jake what he was missing.

Effie put on her shoes and picked up her bag. As she let herself out of the flat, she heard voices as people gathered waiting for the gallery to open. Her breath caught a little. *You don't have to stay all night*, she reminded herself as she descended the stairs, enjoying lifting her long skirt like a Regency lady.

This time she didn't feel as nervous as she had at Alf's party because she knew everyone. Polcarrow had enthusiastically embraced her and the bookshop. The figures in the till showed that Clive had been right to trust his hunch on opening a branch in the tiny village.

Slightly wobbly in her high heels, Effie picked her way around the front of the shop and into the alley that separated the bookshop from the café. She paused, taking in the scene before her. Golden light spilled out of the doorway, illuminating Alf as he waited to cut the ribbon. Effie caught sight of Jake standing next to Freya. She held back, listening as Freya made a short speech.

'I think this must be the whole village.' Freya laughed as she tossed her long dark hair over her shoulder. 'Thank you so much for coming. I don't know why I didn't expect this crowd, but I should've known you'd all want to come along and support a local venture. Thanks, everyone! I hope you all have a wonderful night. Alf, can you do the honours?'

Alf took a pair of scissors off Freya and paused before cutting the ribbon to say, 'Scruff sends his apologies. He's not got much of an artistic eye, I'm afraid.'

Everyone laughed as Alf cut the ribbon, and Freya, throwing her hands up in the air, declared the gallery open. Effie's heart swelled to see her new friend achieving her dream. Maybe Lola was right and there really was magic in Polcarrow. Effie certainly believed it as she made her way towards the gallery, drawn along by the tide of villagers.

She was one of the last through the door. Picking up a glass of Prosecco, Effie glanced around. Freya had done an amazing job transforming the outbuilding into an intimate cosy space for artists to showcase their work. Although the space was small, the fresh white walls gave the illusion of it being larger than it was. The light was low and golden, inviting the viewer in towards the work on show. Effie made her way over to where two of Freya's seascapes were hanging on the left-hand side of the room. Effie studied them, transfixed by the soft swirling pastel skies, the way Freya had captured a soft, candyfloss dawn across Polcarrow bay.

'Beautiful, aren't they?' A familiar voice ran like fingers down her spine.

Effie turned to her right and swallowed. Jake was there, his eyes skimming over her face as if he was trying to figure out how to make amends.

'Jake?' was all she managed. He looked utterly gorgeous, and her heart took a traitorous turn. He'd tried to smooth back his wild blond waves and his blue suit brought out the colour of his eyes. She clutched on to her glass to stop herself from reaching for him.

In turn, Jake's eyes skimmed from her head to her toes and back again. 'Effie, you look stunning,' he managed before taking a gulp of his drink.

Rather than lost for words, there was too much between them to still be said and too little that could be done to change what had already been spoken. Effie turned back to the paintings before she said something she'd regret.

'I love these, they're so ethereal, the light, how does she do it? It's perfect,' she said, steering them towards safer ground. 'Freya is so talented. I'd love one of her paintings but I'm not sure my budget would stretch yet,' she gabbled nervously.

'Something to aspire to. I love seeing how artists interpret the scenes I capture on camera. Seeing this makes me feel like a fraud. All I do is point and click.'

Effie glanced at him, noticing his dismissive tone. 'Don't put yourself down. You have a great eye for detail, and everyone likes something different. Photography is its own skill. Anyway, your photos are why I'm here.' Her gentle reminder seemed to break the ice that had formed over their friendship.

'Flatterer.' Jake smiled and his shoulders relaxed. 'Shall we get another drink?'

Effie glanced at her now empty glass. 'Good idea,' she said.

She followed him over to the refreshments table and took the glass he handed her. They chinked their glasses together in a cheers, eyes meeting as they took their first sip, memories of the kisses they'd shared running hot up Effie's neck.

Effie turned to study the activity in the room. On the opposite side from where they were standing, Angelo,

Freya's sculptor partner, was standing next to some twisted metal shapes that reminded her of stormy waves hurling themselves against a harbour wall. Angelo was guarding the piece as if he didn't want anyone to come too close. He'd been a successful artist before his life imploded, and he'd run away to Polcarrow and slowly rediscovered his need to create.

Jake's photos were displayed on the main wall and these were the ones most people were gathering around. Locals mingled with visitors from out of town and Effie was pleased that Freya's social media campaign to advertise the opening night had garnered the interest she'd desired. Effie made to step forward but Jake held her back. The brief touch sent shock waves through them both

'I want to watch them,' he explained when she gave him a questioning look. 'I want to see what they make of the photos without realising I'm watching.'

Understanding what he meant, Effie joined in with his observations. She watched as Alf cackled with laugher to find the photo of him and Scruff from his birthday. Other villagers were exclaiming between themselves that they'd never seen Polcarrow look so beautiful as in the dawn shots Jake had taken, as if the sunrise was breathing new life into the village. Effie glanced between Jake's daybreak photos and Freya's paintings; they complemented each other perfectly.

'I think they like them,' Effie whispered.

In response, Jake drained his glass in one swallow and flashed her a relieved grin. 'I think I'd better go over,' he said, putting his empty glass down. 'Wish me luck.'

'Good luck!' Effie followed him, watching as Jake's dad broke away from the crowd to pull him into a hug.

'Jake boy, these are stunning, honestly, I knew you had skill, but I didn't realise just how talented you are until I saw them like this.'

'They look so much better framed than on a phone screen,' his mum said, planting a kiss on his cheek.

'Thanks, that means a lot.' Jake beamed with pride. Elation surged through Effie to witness his parents' love and support. Her own romantic hopes might have been dashed but she found she still wanted the best for Jake's career. After all, he'd been an ardent supporter of hers.

Effie lingered back slightly until the crowds began to clear from around Jake's photos. Still holding her glass, she made her way down the line, peering at all the details that were more obvious now that the photos had been enlarged and printed. The depth of the colours, the way Jake's eye drew the viewer in, she wasn't surprised to see little red 'sold' stickers beneath half the photos.

By the time she'd taken them all in, exchanging small talk with the locals she was still growing familiar with, Jake was busy talking to a man dressed in a finely cut suit. Not wanting to interrupt, she watched as they exchanged business cards and shook hands. The suited man walked away, and Effie caught Jake's eye. He was barely controlling his excitement.

'Who was that?' she asked as she joined him.

'Simon Cauley, he has a few high-end hotels around Cornwall. Can you believe it, he wants to have a look at my portfolio with a view to me taking some art shots of local scenery for the hotel rooms,' Jake exhaled.

'Jake, that's amazing!' Everyone had heard of Simon Cauley's eco hotels with their sea-view rooms and hot tubs. In fact, Effie had pored over the website on numerous occasions wishing she had the funds for even one night's stay.

Jake slipped the card into his pocket. 'I think I'd better do some more circulating, are you OK if I leave you? I'll catch you later. I need to talk to you.'

Effie's heart sank at the seriousness of his tone. Hadn't they talked enough? What on earth was there left to say? 'Jake, I'll be fine. Polcarrow feels like my second home now. I'll step outside if I need a breather, but go and make the most of this, you deserve it.'

Jake leaned towards her slightly then pulled back. Effie's brow furrowed in confusion before she stepped away, putting some distance between them. As she watched him move away, she realised just how difficult it was going to be to untangle the romantic feelings from the roots of their friendship.

Chapter Thirty-Five

'Well, I think that was a success,' Freya held her glass up as the last few visitors milled around.

'I can't believe I sold all my photos,' Jake said with disbelief as he joined in the cheers.

'Well done!' Effie couldn't help but feel proud of his achievement.

'I think I better start taking this photography thing more seriously,' he quipped, making everyone laugh.

Simon's contact details hadn't been the only ones Jake had swapped that night. One of the perks of being a bit of a wallflower was that Effie could linger, listening to the conversations that were being exchanged. She'd watched as people picked up Jake's business cards, praised his work and sighed over the fact their favourite prints were already sold. She was sure he'd be inundated with requests for reprints.

'Is this going to be a permanent gallery?' Jake asked Freya.

'For the summer and then we'll see what happens. I was fed up of selling my stuff and paying commission, but I needed to see how tonight panned out. Would you be interested in selling more prints?' Freya asked him. She had sold one of her paintings, and had spoken to someone about a commission, so it had been a successful night all round.

'Definitely. It'd be great to have a place to run my business from. Maybe we can talk about sharing the cost of rent or something?'

'I would be up for that! This place is currently owned by the landlord of the café, so I need to do some proper negotiations, but I don't see why we shouldn't have a permanent art space here in Polcarrow, especially as we have a thriving café and bookshop.' Freya turned to Effie and asked, 'How's it going?'

'Better than I expected. I thought it'd calm down after the opening and well, it has, but I'm still getting a steady stream of customers through the door.'

She'd received an email from Clive that morning congratulating her on the figures and the success of the shop but also to remind her that he was going on holiday the following week. Effie had been elated and then a little stressed about the pressure of keeping the shop going. She had some ideas up her sleeve to keep the promotions fresh, but she would be working flat out. When Clive was back from his holiday, she'd ask him about getting some additional help.

'I'm going to start doing a book matchmaking service.'

'A what?' Lola asked as she joined them.

'A book matchmaking service. A bit like a blind date with a book except the customer will tell me the sort of things they like to read, genres, authors and I'll hand-pick a couple of titles for them. I'm thinking of doing it like a gift box. Put in a couple of treats. What do you think?'

'That sounds delightful!' Lola clapped her hands together.

Effie snuck a look at Jake, who was smiling down at her. 'Do you think it'll work?'

'Of course it will,' Jake said softly. 'You can make anything work, Eff.'

They couldn't help it; their bodies were drawn closer in the low lamplight. Effie wanted nothing more than to slip her arms around Jake and sway along to the music that was gently playing in the background, something soothing and classical, flowing as light as a dream around them. Jake gazed down at her and it was as if they were the only two people in the world. Effie sighed before stepping back.

She knew if Jake stuck around it would be tricky to just be friends. Tonight had only shown how they were still naturally drawn together. Effie yearned for the hopeful electricity they'd once shared but didn't want to be burned by it again. Her lips missed the kisses and her heart melted for what could have been. She might have been romantically delayed in life, but she knew she deserved someone who could be fully her own, not someone who was unsure where he wanted to be, no matter how utterly gorgeous he was.

'Did you have a nice time tonight, Eff?' Jake asked.

She nodded. 'Of course I did, but thanks for asking. It was great seeing how much everyone liked your photos. I'm so proud of you. I think you're going to be really successful.'

'Thank you, you have no idea how much that means to me,' Jake said, his voice serious. 'Look, let's get tidied up here and then we can join everyone in the pub, that's if you're OK to go.'

Effie knew they should show their faces at the pub for at least one drink. 'Maybe for one, it'd be nice to celebrate with everyone.'

'Are you sure?'

'One hundred per cent.' She was going to make him work for her attention.

Jake's eyes swallowed her up, full of a desire that sparked in her heart.

'Effie.' Her name caught in his breath as he stepped forward, his finger tugging at one of her stray curls.

Effie closed her eyes, swallowed, tried to compose herself as all the air rushed out of the room. Her feelings were far too strong to be this close to him. 'Jake . . . I . . . We . . . Don't make this harder.'

'Eff, please, I really need to speak to you, can we go somewhere quieter now?' Jake swallowed nervously, as if he wanted to get whatever he needed to say off his chest as quickly as possible.

Effie lifted her face, her eyes catching his, their feelings swirling like a galaxy around them. She wanted to resist, wanted to protect her heart, but he was looking at her in a way no one had ever looked at her before, as if she was the whole universe. Effie opened her mouth to agree when the sound of Jake's name being called shattered everything.

'Jake! Jakey, my darling, I'm sorry, I got lost, didn't I? Wrong village.' The woman laughed.

Jake stepped back from Effie as if he'd been caught doing something he shouldn't. A chill ran down Effie's spine as she turned towards the door where an impossibly sleek-looking woman stood. Her flawless skin was expertly made up, her tan deep and not from a bottle, the black sheath dress she was wearing hanging off her perfect figure.

'Tara?!'

Effie hadn't even needed Jake to confirm who she was. She was even more stunning in real life than the photos.

Jake's eyes bounced from Effie to Tara and back again.

'Jake! Jakey!' Tara bounded over to him as quickly as her skyscraper heels allowed.

'Tara?' You made it!' he exclaimed, as she threw her arms around him in a way that dragged Effie's heart to the bottom of the ocean.

Jake's eyes were full of regret as he caught Effie's over Tara's shoulder. Effie narrowed her gaze and turned her back on him and whatever it was he was going to say. She made her way over to Lola who was tidying glasses at the refreshments table.

'Do you need a hand?' Effie forced brightness into her voice.

'If you don't mind,' Lola said, 'I just need to take these into the café, put the glasses through the dishwasher. Can you grab that tray?'

'Sure.' Effie picked up the tray and followed Lola out and into the brightly lit café kitchen. 'Where should I put them?'

'Just on the counter. That's lovely, thank you.' Lola straightened up and studied Effie. 'Are you OK? You look a bit pale.'

It was on the tip of her tongue to blurt out that Jake's ex-girlfriend had sashayed in. Was Tara an ex though? What did being on a break actually mean? Instead, Effie rubbed her forehead and stuttered, 'Yes, I think I'm going to head home, my head, it's been quite a busy evening.'

Lola's brow furrowed as if she didn't believe her but instead of voicing her doubts, she simply said, 'Of course, you have a good night. Put a cold flannel on your head, that should help.'

Effie smiled her gratitude, for the advice and for being so easily let go. As she hurried out of the kitchen, she glanced around, eyes searching for Jake, for reassurance, but instead she found the evidence she'd needed to remind her to stay well away.

She spied him through the open gallery door, illumin-ated like one of the works of art she'd admired. With hands on hips, Jake was leaning forward listening intently to whatever Tara was telling him, a smile of familiarity on his face. Her gestures were exaggerated, her laughter piercing the night air. Jake didn't even glance up. Was this what he'd wanted to talk about? Effie fled the scene as quickly as her high heels would carry her.

Chapter Thirty-Six

Feeling like Cinderella fleeing the ball, Effie lifted her skirt and hurried between the two properties running up the stairs to her own flat. She unlocked the door and almost hurled herself inside.

Door closed, Effie sank down to the floor. What had Jake said? They were on a break. Had he known Tara was going to turn up tonight? He must've done. Jake must've invited her. Oh gosh, and Effie had allowed her hopes to float dangerously close to the surface. He said he wanted to talk to her, well, there didn't seem any need for that now.

Effie fished her phone out of her bag and opened her rarely used Instagram app. It wasn't her style to snoop, plus she'd been so busy with the shop, so she'd not looked since Maddie had found Tara's profile. However, now her curiosity got the better of her as she typed Tara's name into the search box and pulled up her account.

There were a few pinned posts. The third one was a few years old and showed Jake lounging in a hammock next to Tara in blissful contentment. But it was the first one that hollowed Effie out; a stunning tropical beach engagement shot. She hadn't recalled seeing that when Maddie had been sifting through the page. She opened it up. It had been posted the previous week. So much for them being on a break!

She opened the first few posts, which showed Tara travelling around the English countryside, showing off the first blooms of spring, a fancy afternoon tea in a luxury hotel as well as a sponsored post for a very expensive-looking electric car. In all the photos she looked immaculate, her signature curls shining like dark chocolate, a smile breaking like dawn across her elfin face. Tara didn't look the sort to contort herself into a wetsuit and let her hair dry into wild waves.

Swallowing back all her questions, Effie began to scroll through the comments. Eventually she found a reel titled 'Where is Jake?' Against her better judgement, Effie opened it. Tara was sitting in front of a mirror, hair back in a fluffy headband, doing her makeup whilst discussing the products she was using and explaining where her boyfriend was.

'Hello, my lovelies, I've seen all your comments, and I know you're all wondering where my gorgeous Jakey is. I wanted to make this video to stop all the speculation and reassure you that everything is fine. Really. We're just working on some individual projects but we both have something really exciting coming. I know you'll love it.'

Effie glanced at the date. Seven weeks ago. Just before she had moved to Polcarrow and met Jake. No wonder he'd been cagey about his future plans. Effie was embarrassed to admit that she'd thought the term 'being on a break' had meant the relationship was heading towards its end, not a reconciliation. She pushed aside memories of their tender kisses, his claim that he was seventy per cent sure he'd stay in Polcarrow. When had he decided to get back together with Tara?

Exhausted from the social activity of the evening and from scrolling through social media, Effie put her phone back in her bag and let out a long sigh. Determined not to let some man make her cry, she wiped away the tears, her hands coming away with mascara smears. Her eye caught the time on the kitchen clock. She'd been sitting on the floor for forty-five minutes, lost in her social media doomscrolling. Forty-five minutes and Jake hadn't come to find her. Effie's heart sank when she realised where his priorities lay.

She hauled herself up, padded into the bathroom and removed her makeup, before changing out of her dress and into her pyjamas. The dress, which Effie had felt a million dollars in at the start of the night, looked frumpy next to Tara's sleek sheath. Heading back into the kitchen, she turned on one of the low lamps and set the kettle to boil. She was making a camomile tea, musing sadly on how differently the night was meant to end with celebratory drinks in the pub, when there was a knock at the door.

Effie froze. The knock came again.

'Effie, please, we need to talk.'

She swallowed. She could just pretend she hadn't heard; that she'd gone to bed. Her name came again like a plea. She crossed over to the door and pulled it open, fixing Jake with what she hoped was a steely, unimpressed stare. 'OK, what do you have to say?'

'Effie, I'm sorry, I . . .' he floundered.

'Do you have something to be sorry about?' she asked.

'No. Yes. Maybe. Effie, please, can I come in?'

She stepped aside and let him into her flat, her sanctuary. She regarded him through the moonlight, the distance between them now feeling unnavigable. She wasn't going to start this conversation.

'So, that's Tara.'

'I figured that out.'

'Effie, please, let me explain.'

'I'm not stopping you.' She moved past him, picked up her mug and perched on the edge of the sofa, not inviting him to sit. 'What's going on? Are you still on a break or are you back together? Is this what you wanted to talk to me about?' she snapped.

'Yes.' Jake sagged into himself. 'But it's not what it looks like, honestly, Eff, it's a mess, a huge, huge mess. I was honest when I said I didn't know if I was staying. Tara and I were on a break and we do have unfinished business. But, you have to believe me, it's not of the romantic sort.'

Effie sat back, curling her feet underneath her. 'I don't know what to believe any more, Jake. What's going on?'

'We still have some professional ends to tie up.' Jake dropped into the chair. 'It's one of the reasons I was trying not to lead you on,' he began. 'Things between us are complicated. We decided to spend time apart to see if we missed each other.'

'And do you?' Effie asked even though she knew the answer would sting.

Jake considered this. 'Maybe. At least in the beginning, but now, I don't know. I didn't think I'd meet you and that made things complicated. Effie, I'm not explaining this very well, am I?'

Sipping her tea, she shook her head.

'You see, it was all true, all the stuff about me being burned out by the travelling. The putting our relationship on a break. The not knowing what was going to happen. We've been in touch recently, trying to resolve things. There's still so much to sort out. I've always tried to be honest with you, Effie, but it's been difficult when I've not known what I want. But the longer I was here, the less appealing going back became. But it turns out, I have to go back with Tara.'

'Why? What do you mean?'

'We have one last contract to see through. A joint one. In the Maldives. We can't get out of it. Believe me, I've been trying.'

Effie stared at him in disbelief. 'What?'

Jake squirmed. 'It was all organised before we went on a break. If we cancel, Tara will have to pay back the fee she's been paid and she's already spent it.'

'Can't you just not go?'

Embarrassed, Jake shook his head. 'I spent my fee too.'

Silence spread between them.

'I spent it on the flat, the website, printing those photos,' he explained. 'I saw it as a way to start again. I was just planning to be here a few months to decompress, make some decisions. Meeting you has confused things for me.'

'Don't blame this on me, Jake.' Effie's voice was cold. 'So that's it? She turns up and you ditch everything here to go and play fake boyfriend?' Effie couldn't help her hurt spilling out. 'You are going to be a fake boyfriend, aren't you?'

'Effie, I know it's hard but please try to understand, I can't not go,' Jake's voice was strained. 'I need to do this. We both do. We were together ten years, we built a brand, we have a lot to discuss and sort out. This is the perfect opportunity to do so.'

Effie sipped her tea, trying to process what Jake was telling her. 'You didn't answer me, Jake, are you and Tara getting back together?'

'I don't know,' he admitted in a small voice. 'We still have a lot to talk about.'

'In the Maldives? Such a hardship.' Effie rolled her eyes.

'Eff—'

'When?'

Jake's eyes were pained as he looked at her. 'Tomorrow. I'm leaving with Tara tomorrow. We have an early-morning flight the day after.'

Effie studied him whilst trying to process everything he was trying to say. Realisation that she was exhausted by all his excuses washed through her. Yes, that flicker of attraction still lingered between them, but Jake's commitment to everything seemed as fragile as a pattern in the sand.

'I'm so sorry, Eff, this wasn't meant to happen.'

'Us? Or Tara coming back?'

'Everything in the way it has. Us was a good thing. You have to believe me. But the timing . . .'

Effie drained her tea and stood up. 'In that case, I think you'd better go. Since you've got an early start. And a big decision to make. Just make sure you make your own mind up, Jake, that you do what you want, not what anyone else thinks you should do.'

Jake flinched at the hardness in her voice before standing up. As he moved, he reached for her, but Effie stepped back, folding her arms into her body to keep herself held together. He moved across the flat, cutting through the moonlight. He pulled open the door, paused to look back at her. Regret flickered over his face. He opened his mouth, but whatever he was going to say, to make it better or worse, was trapped within him.

Effie flinched as the door clicked shut. Silence flooded in as the tears overflowed.

Chapter Thirty-Seven

After a terrible night's sleep, Effie knew the only thing that would set her right was a swim. After hauling herself out of bed, she pulled on her wetsuit, tugged her hair into a braid and stomped out of the flat. A flat grey sky hung over the harbour, so at least that matched her mood. Crossing the road, she froze as her name was called.

'Effie.' Jake's voice was strangled with emotion.

She paused, pulled by the longing in his voice, which reached into her heart and squeezed tight. Effie inhaled a breath before exhaling powerfully, as if to breathe him out of her. Risking a glance over her shoulder, she saw him standing on the pavement by a flashy white car, a smart suitcase at his feet, his camera bag across his body. He looked as wretched as she felt. *Good*, Effie thought, pulling herself up to her full height, holding her head high, pleased that he was suffering with his choice. Although she was sure once he was on the plane heading to a tropical island, he'd forget all about Polcarrow, and about her.

Tears pricked at her eyes as she watched the scene unfold. Tara dashed out of the café. Even her casual wear was stylish.

'Jakey, I got you a flat white and a bacon bap. I've got to come back here, babes, I want to show everyone that café, and that bookshop looks adorable. Jakey, are you listening?' Tara's exasperation was laced with intimacy, a tone she'd clearly used on Jake numerous times during their relationship. 'What are you—Oh.'

Tara's eyes met with Effie's, held like a challenge. Effie was determined not to be the first to look away.

Jake finished loading his bags into the boot and took his coffee. 'Cheers. I'm all done.'

'Good, come on, we've not got all day, got a flight to catch. Got your passport?'

Jake patted his top pocket and rolled his eyes. Effie couldn't help but watch as he fell back into easy familiarity with Tara. Jake took one last look at Effie and called, 'I'll be back in two weeks.'

Two weeks? Effie winced, that was a long time, longer than he'd implied. She didn't have time to respond because as soon as he was in the car, Tara pulled away from the kerb and sped along the harbour front as if she was trying to win first prize in the Grand Prix.

Effie watched them go before setting her shoulders and heading onto the beach. She shrugged off her dry robe and waded into the sea, enjoying the way the cold water tugged her back into the present, focused her back on herself. She submerged, allowing herself to become one with the sea, but as she swam, her brain crowded with all the things she should have told Jake. Not just how much she liked him but that, in fact, she was falling in love with him, no matter how hard she'd tried not to. She held that thought; it was life altering and all consuming. Maybe it would have made him stay if she'd told him? Or maybe it was better to keep it to herself, just in case he rekindled his romance with Tara. After all, they had a whole history built together over years, all Effie had were some rickety, thrown-together foundations.

Falling in love had always been the dream but never the plan. Love existed like something ethereal, just out of reach, an abstract thing she read about in books and lay in bed dreaming about. Effie had yearned for it but hadn't really expected to find it. Now she had she didn't quite know what to do. Not that she could do anything with Jake jetting off to the Maldives with his ex. If she even was still his ex.

Effie briefly wondered if she should've just asked him to stay but the rational part of her understood that he had obligations, commitments. She also knew she couldn't make his mind up for him and it was best to retain her own dignity. If he got back together with Tara then clearly he wasn't the man for her. Or even the man she thought he was. Maybe she just had to trust him, trust that he was telling the truth, that this really was one last hurrah for Tara and Jake, something to please the fans.

Still, that didn't sit right with Effie. She'd become wrapped up in Jake, swept off her feet by his kindness, his bright blue eyes. After a fortnight of jet-setting, would sleepy Polcarrow really be enough to tempt him back?

What could she offer him really, other than a rented book-shop with a sea view and a love of swimming. Would Jake choose luxury over simplicity? Effie pondered this and realised, with dismay, that she didn't really know him well enough to guess.

Tired of her own negative thoughts and before they could drag herself any further under, Effie swam back towards the shore. Rubbing her hair with a towel, she glanced up to Jake's flat window, a traitorous smile tugging at her lips as she remembered him thinking she was a seal. After throwing on her dry robe, Effie made her way up the beach, pleased that the swim had been invigorating and restorative.

'What's going on?' Lola asked the second Effie walked through the door. Her face was etched with concern. 'Who was that woman?'

'Tara. Jake's ex.'

Lola's mouth fell open and she was struck speechless, which was something Effie guessed didn't happen often.

'His ex?'

Effie nodded.

'Where on earth did she come from?'

'Bristol, I think. They only split up earlier this year. Or they were on a break. I no longer know which,' Effie explained. She didn't think it was her place to tell Lola about the broken engagement. Jan, Jake's mum, could fill her in on the details if she felt inclined. 'They've gone to do some work in the Maldives. They are, were, influencers.'

'Influencers? Well, I never!' Lola gave a disapproving 'hmm' as she reached for a mug. 'The usual?'

'Please.' Effie sat down. 'And can I have one of those flapjacks too, please.'

'Of course, and extra marshmallows after all that. So, are they back together?' Lola asked as she placed Effie's breakfast in front of her. 'I thought you two were getting really close. I had my money on you getting together. You make such a sweet couple.'

Effie swallowed the compliment. 'Thanks, I thought Jake was a good one too. I don't know if they're back together. They were, or are, on a break. He said it's just a job that they're both contracted to do. But . . . they were together for a long time and they're spending two weeks together. She's so glamourous and I'm . . .' She signalled to her swimwear.

'Stop right there, young lady! It's got nothing to do with looks, it's what's inside that counts. And you are utterly gorgeous inside and out, never doubt that! If they split up, they would've split for a reason. Jake seems a sensible lad, I doubt he'll go rushing back to her, even if she does try it on. Which I'm sure she will.' Lola slapped a hand over her mouth.

The flapjack was suddenly dry in Effie's mouth. 'Thanks, just what I needed to hear. Anyway, he told me he's not ready for a relationship.'

'Oh, honey, I'm sorry, what a shitty thing to say! Men, sometimes, honestly, they don't know a good thing when it hits them round the head.' Lola pulled out the chair opposite Effie and sat down. 'Now, you have to decide what you're going to do. He's away for two weeks, how are you going to spend the time? Pining? Wallowing? Or just getting on with keeping the bookshop going? Jake likes you because you get stuck in. Don't let that feisty girl vanish because he's gone off with some fake-tanned ex, OK?'

Effie stared at Lola, slightly terrified but also slightly empowered by her speech. 'Okay, I promise won't,' was all she managed.

Chapter Thirty-Eight

Trying to put whatever Jake was up to with Tara out of her mind, Effie refocused her attention on the reason she was in Polcarrow: The Bookshop.

Now that it had been open a few weeks Effie had settled into the rhythm of the shop. Saturdays were always the busiest and Mondays the slowest, which she used to make sure the shelves were stocked, that everything was clean and tidy and the window display updated. Changing it every week had given the customers something new to look forward to, with some even trying to guess what the next theme would be.

As the days stretched towards summer, Effie knew she'd have to ask Clive for some help, even just so that she could have a proper lunch break. She fired off an email to him, asking to meet to discuss the shop moving forward. His out-of-office bounced back. It seemed that everyone except Effie was jetting off to warmer climes.

As she stepped back from arranging the latest window display, which was fairy-tale themed, Effie reflected on how far she'd come. When Clive had given her the opportunity to open the new shop, she'd been daunted, worried she'd never be able to move away from home and do it all alone. Of course, in the end she hadn't done it all alone, Polcarrow had swept her up in its warm, slightly nosey embrace, and carried her along. She knew she would've collapsed at the first hurdle if Jake hadn't shown up wielding paintbrushes.

Jake felt as intrinsic to the shop as the yellow chairs and the cosy kids' corner. He'd been by her side every step of the way, white paint, hot chocolates and afternoon teas. Jake had held her hand and intuitively known exactly when to step back to allow her to shine. Effie knew he'd given her a much-needed push to step into her own light. Every morning she looked forward to unlocking the shop, greeting customers, chatting books and seeing the locals swing by. Effie had made a whole life in Polcarrow without even realising it.

As full as her days were with the shop, Lola bustling in with a new cake to try or Alf stopping by so that Effie could give Scruff a fuss, she missed Jake. Even if it had only been a few days. She missed his sparkling blue eyes, the way he made her feel grounded, she missed the feel of his reassuring presence around her and mostly she missed the possibility of the future she'd become wrapped up in. Yet she also knew she couldn't pine for a man who was still making his mind up about what he wanted his own future to look like. Effie's future now felt firmly rooted in Polcarrow, and she knew she'd thrive even without Jake.

'You have to keep hold of that future,' Lola had told her one morning, 'you have to trust him. The cards never lie. You're meant to be!'

'Thanks, Lola,' Effie had sighed, appreciating Lola's sunny positivity but unable to quite believe it for herself.

Effie lasted about four days before she cracked and searched for Jake on social media. The last photo on his page was still of the Cornish waves, which made Effie's heart race with suspicion. It made her feel like he'd vanished. He was meant to be working, where were the tropical paradise photos?

Knowing she shouldn't, but unable to resist, Effie typed in Tara's handle and crumpled as she took in the photos. Tara in a stunning white bikini draped over a sun lounger, sipping sunset cocktails and snorkelling in crystal-clear water. However, it was the final photo Effie saw that twisted the knife; Jake emerging from the sea, Tara in his arms like he'd rescued her. The complete contrast to the morning he'd swum with Effie stung. The post had the most likes, the comments were insane. There was no mention in the caption of the break-up, in fact, they looked happily reconciled.

Just about remembering to lock the door behind her, Effie darted out of the shop and round into the café, where Lola and Freya were behind the counter, restocking the scones.

'Effie, what's up?' Lola asked.

Effie held the phone out to them. 'This.'

Lola and Freya peered at the photo. Lola pursed her lips as if trying to hold in whatever was going through her mind. Freya reached out and scrolled through the comments.

'I know he said he wasn't ready for a relationship, but he said they were on a break, that it was complicated.' Effie hated the way her voice sounded, the way she felt she was clinging on to Jake.

Throwing a look at Freya, Lola came round from behind the counter and ushered Effie over to the window table. The next thing Effie knew, Freya was setting down a tray of tea and three slices of lemon sponge.

Effie couldn't help but laugh as she wiped away a tear that was threatening to spill. 'Tea and cake?'

'Solves everything,' Lola said, 'or at least, takes the sting away.'

Effie took a bite of cake, the contrast of the sharp lemon and the sweetness of the cake dancing on her tongue. 'I think you might be right.' She took another bite. 'What should I do? I'm not very experienced with dating. Jake's the first person I've ever really liked, the first who I thought was serious about me too. Have I got it all wrong?'

Lola shook her head. 'No, that boy was smitten, honestly, he was. He'll be back. These photos, they aren't all they seem,' she said cryptically.

Effie glanced at her warily.

'If it helps, Angelo did a runner just after we got together,' Freya explained, 'and look at us now, happily ever after. Or something like that.' She picked up the teapot and began to pour out the tea.

'Stop looking at his or her social media, there's no need to torture yourself. You have to trust him,' Lola said gently. 'You also have to accept that they do have history, but that's what it is, history. I feel it in my bones, Effie. You have to let him figure out what he wants. Do you want their past to ruin your future?'

Effie studied Lola. 'But there is no Jake and me. It never really got off the ground.'

Lola looked as if she didn't know what to say, an occurrence Effie didn't think happened often. Thoughts shifted across Lola's face until eventually she patted Effie's hand reassuringly. 'It'll all be fine, you have to trust. Trust is all any of us have.' Lola reminded her.

Effie nodded but her heart wavered and her mind spiralled. However, there was nothing else she could do other than take Lola's advice and try, against her own nature, to trust that if Jake wanted a future with her then he would be back. Only then would she be able to decide if she truly still wanted him.

Chapter Thirty-Nine

Effie hopped from foot to foot feeling like a spare part as Sue set up the second Polcarrow book club. She knew in her heart she should concede defeat and delegate to Sue properly, but the book club had taken off due to Effie's enthusiasm, so she was clinging on as best as she could. Effie's heart warmed to see so many people crowding into Lola's café, clutching their books, chattering away about what they had been reading.

Just as everyone had settled down, hot drinks in front of them, Sue clapping her hands to get everyone's attention, the door opened and in slipped someone who made Effie's heart grind to a halt, and not in a good way.

She gasped to see Zach looming in the doorway like an ominous shadow.

'I hope I'm not late, I've come to see what Effie has been up to.' His voice was low with menace.

The whole room fell into silence. Sue threw Effie a confused look.

'It's fine. This is Zach, Clive's son, you know, owner of the shop,' Effie explained, watching as everyone shifted to welcome him, unaware of how much of a snake in the grass he was. Only Lola picked up on the change in atmosphere.

'Are you OK?' She pulled Effie aside.

'Yes, fine,' Effie lied whilst wondering what had brought Zach to Polcarrow. What did he have to check up on? Clive had been happy enough the last time they'd spoken. 'Shall we get going?'

The evening ran smoothly with lively discussions about the book, copious cups of tea. Alf and Jan had a very heated debate about the ending, which Lola had to referee before it got out of hand. When the subject of the next meeting's read came up, everyone had very strong opinions and no one was afraid to voice them. In the end it came down to a vote between a thriller that had been at the top of the charts for several weeks and a travel memoir.

'Raise your hands for the thriller,' Effie did a count, 'now, all for the memoir.' She totted up the numbers. 'Ah, I'm sorry thriller lovers, but the memoir has beaten you by one vote. But we could do the thriller next time? How does that sound?'

'Good to me.' Alf nodded, which had everyone else nodding in agreement.

After that, the meeting began to break up, people gathered belongings and lingered outside the door to continue their conversations and discuss what they might bring next time. Effie imagined the next meeting might be a very lively event judging by some of the conversations taking place. She began to help Lola tidy up but Zach stopped her, laying a hand on her arm, which made her suppress a shudder.

'I'll see you in the morning.' It sounded like a warning. 'I want to inspect the shop.'

'Oh, OK,' Effie said, glad to feel Lola's presence lingering like a protector. 'We open at nine thirty.'

'I know, it's my business after all,' he said, before turning and heading out of the cafe.

His business? Effie's stomach sank. Was there something Clive hadn't told her?

After a night of tossing and turning, Effie threw back the covers and got out of bed just after six, knowing that the stress of Zach's impending visit was disturbing her sleep. Yawning, she reminded herself she only needed to get through the next few hours and then he'd be gone back to Penzance. She picked up her phone, but it was too early to text Maddie. She also managed to stop herself from checking Jake or Tara's social media. Instead, Effie did what she always did when she was stressed: she swam.

Although the waves didn't wash the worry away, they did smooth out the jagged hackles that had risen. Satisfied that her soul was calm, even if her brain was still racing, Effie went to collect her morning hot chocolate.

'Are you OK, Effie? I didn't get a nice vibe from that Zach last night.' Lola shuddered as she sprinkled the marshmallows on top.

'Yes, I'm fine now I've had my swim. He's not a nice guy,' Effie replied as she paid for her drink. 'He's Clive's son. I'm sure he'll be gone once he's seen the shop. He was always popping in and out in Penzance, but he can be a menace. Gosh, I'm nervous.'

'You'll be fine. You've done a wonderful job, I'm sure he'll be impressed.' Lola pushed the cup across to Effie, then dropped an extra marshmallow on the top.

Effie sipped her drink. She hoped so too but her stomach still churned as she headed back to her flat for a shower.

Worried Zach would be waiting outside, Effie hurried down the stairs just before half nine, her damp hair in a braid. Relief washed over her to see he hadn't arrived yet. Effie opened the shop a few minutes early, wanting to feel in control of the space. As she raised the blinds she couldn't help but smile to see the bay spread out before her. Coming to Polcarrow had definitely been an unexpected blessing, it was such a lovely community and she couldn't imagine ever leaving.

Effie was just waving off a couple who had popped in to buy a book on Cornish coastal walks when Zach arrived, standing hands on hips in the doorway, surveying the shop with a sneer. Taking a few calming breaths, Effie reminded herself that she was in charge, this was her shop.

'Good morning,' she chirped with a brightness she didn't feel.

Zach stalked in, takeaway cup of coffee in hand, and peered down his nose at the interior of the shop. Anger flashed in Effie; how dare he not even greet her?

'How can I help you, Zach?' she asked, thinking it was more polite than 'What on earth are you doing here?'

Zach sat in one of the chairs. 'Good view. Did my father sign all this off?' He waved his hand at the chairs, the pretty blinds, the general décor.

'Yes. I also had to decorate it all myself,' she told him.

Zach let out a laugh. 'I've heard that's not true. You got one of the local men involved. I'm not sure that was sanctioned.'

Sanctioned? What? Effie stared at him in disbelief.

'Why is everything yellow when the company colours are blue?'

'Yellow looked fresh for the spring opening. It's been a hit on social media. Your dad liked it.'

'So, you've been spending all your time on social media rather than working?'

'No, but it is important to drum up business, especially in a holiday destination. The shop has been a success. Your dad congratulated me on it last week. Turns out his idea to open here was a good one. I'm pleased with what I've done.' Effie pulled herself up proudly.

Zach stood up and stalked around the shop, running his disapproving eyes over the shelves. 'What's this? Book matchmaking?' He pointed to the poster on the wall.

'It's my new idea, like a gift box for readers. They tell us their favourite authors and we match them with new books,' she explained, 'I've had several enquiries already.' She didn't tell Zach that she had one box all ready to go for Sue's daughter, Mattie's, birthday. It had been such a pleasure to choose new books to inspire the teen.

'Did Dad say this was allowed?'

'Er, I don't know, I didn't ask. He seemed happy for me to do as I wish.'

'Do as you wish? Effie, this is not your shop and you're clearly treating it like it is. I don't see how Dad can be happy with you deviating from the business plan so much. Yellow door? That has to go, so do those chairs, we don't want people sitting here just to put their photos online. We want them buying things. It's a business not a hobby.'

Effie's jaw hung open in outrage. She spluttered back some expletives before gathering her wits enough to say, 'The business is doing well. People come because it looks nice and then they buy books. You can check the figures.'

'I have,' he said ominously before crossing over to Effie. 'Look, I came down here as a favour to Dad while he is away to check what you are up to. I was worried you were taking the piss and taking advantage of his good nature. Then I find out that is exactly what is happening. You're running this shop like it's your own rather than his or mine.'

'What?!'

'I've heard all about you joining in with the locals, getting them to do your work for you. You're more concerned about yourself than the shop. I'm really not happy and I'm sure if Dad knew what was really going on, he'd agree with me.'

'What are you talking about? Clive is happy,' Effie insisted.

'But I'm not. You're forgetting that you're just an employee, this business will be mine one day so it's in my interest to protect it. That's why you need to go back to the main shop and I'll be taking over running this one.'

'Sorry, what?'

'Pack up, you're leaving, I'll call a mate with a van, he can take you and your stuff home.'

'But I've relocated my entire life here to open the shop. I've worked hard.'

Zach shrugged. 'I don't care. Dad just asked you to set it up, it's your fault that you went beyond that remit. He never said it'd be permanent, did he?'

Cold ran down Effie's back. Zach was right. Clive had only asked her to get the shop up and running, there'd been some vagueness between them about the permanence. 'I just assumed,' she stuttered.

'Well, you assumed wrong. Thanks for what you have done, but I'm here to put everything right.' Zach pulled his phone out of his pocket and pressed a number. 'Yeah, Dave, can you get that van down here in a couple of hours? Great, cheers, see you soon.' He ended the call and fixed Effie with a cruel look.

'Get packing.'

Chapter Forty

'Come on, van's here, we haven't got all day,' Zach hollered up the stairs.

Effie bit her lip to stop the tears from bubbling over as she glanced around the little flat she'd turned into a cosy home. Her belongings were now stuffed into cases and hurriedly shoved into boxes. Her heart lurched to think she wouldn't be waking up to the view of the bay, or skipping over the sand for her morning swim and hot chocolate at Lola's.

Zach appeared in the doorway and gave the flat a once-over. It looked very much as if he was eyeing it up. Effie narrowed her eyes, he had his own place already, what could he want with it?

Zach grabbed her case. 'What have you got in here? Rocks?' he said, before he hauled it down the stairs.

Grabbing her bags, Effie followed him. She knew she should fight this, but she was completely frozen under his glowering glare. From the way Zach had had the van on standby, Effie had a suspicion he'd come here with this plan all along. She couldn't even call Clive as he was on a cruise. Although this whole charade stank of Zach's malicious, petty nature, Effie couldn't be one hundred per cent sure that Clive would back her. She didn't want to think that maybe Zach was telling the truth.

Effie shivered at the thought of Zach taking over the business when Clive decided to retire. He'd wreak more havoc than he was currently as he threw Effie's case into the back of a waiting van. The driver watched dispassionately as he smoked a cigarette.

'What's going on?' Lola demanded as she hurried out of the café. 'Effie?'

'It's none of your business,' Zach snarled at her.

Lola pulled herself up to her full height and fixed Zach with a withering look. 'As a member of the Polcarrow village committee it is my business. Also, as Effie's friend. What are you doing?'

'Lola, it's—'

Zach cut her off. 'It's my business. Well, my dad's,' he admitted, 'but I've done a check and nothing Effie is doing is in line with company policy, so I'm here to get things back on track.'

'What do you mean company policy?' Effie exploded. 'I came and set this shop up with my own hands, it's doing a roaring trade.'

'It certainly is,' Lola reinforced.

'"Set up", that's the key phrase, you came here to set it up, which you've done and now you can go back and leave this branch to a professional.'

'You? A professional?' Effie scoffed.

'Be careful or you won't have a job to go back to in Penzance.'

'How dare you talk to her like that!' Lola exclaimed, stepping forward.

Effie sensed a crowd growing. There was nothing she liked less than a big fuss. She also didn't want Zach to accuse her of having the village gang up on him.

Effie stepped forward and placed a hand on Lola's arm. 'Thank you for everything,' she said quietly. 'I'll try and come back, soon, I promise.'

'I don't like that man,' Lola said through gritted teeth.

'But he is the owner's son. Please, don't make it any more difficult for me. I'll chat to Clive when he's back.' A look passed between them; they all remembered how useful Clive had been at the book launch.

Instead of saying anything, Lola bundled Effie into a hug.

'I'll miss your hot chocolates and flapjacks,' Effie said, wiping away a tear as she stepped back.

'What about Jake?'

She knew she'd miss him too, but instead she shrugged. 'He's probably back with Tara. Maybe this is for the best.'

Lola didn't need to say anything, but Effie knew she disagreed with every word.

With a quick glance over her shoulder and a wave at the loyal villagers and customers, Effie made her way round to the passenger's side of the van and climbed in. The driver merely grunted at her and turned the ignition, speeding out of Polcarrow before Effie could even say a proper goodbye.

Chapter Forty-One

Zach's henchman drove them through the winding Cornish roads as if Effie wasn't there. He didn't even acknowledge her, not even a glance or a single word. Although she was grateful he was keeping his eye on the road, she didn't like the feeling that she'd been packaged up and sent away. The radio wasn't even on. The silence in the van was oppressive as they lurched around corners. Effie wound the window down a notch in an attempt to relieve the tension.

She should have stood up to Zach. After all he was nothing more than a bully, but something about him had always put her on edge. It baffled her how someone as placid as Clive could have such a nightmare son. However, with the van on standby, Effie didn't think any of her protests would have changed the outcome. Maybe this had been the plan all along? Maybe Clive just didn't have the heart to tell her. She'd have to wait to speak to Maddie and hopefully her friend would have some information.

The Cornish countryside gave way to the outskirts of Penzance and soon the van was turning into Effie's parents' street. She gulped back a sob at the sight of it, the garden in full bloom, the cheerful gnomes beside the front door like a welcoming party. She hadn't realised how much she had been enjoying her own flat, her own life, until now. Coming home felt like a massive step back.

The henchman stopped the van and pulled the hand-brake up with a crunch. Effie wondered if he'd say something now, but instead a few more moments of silence passed before she opened the door and jumped out, glad to be out of the oppressive atmosphere. She pulled her bag onto her shoulder and made her way to the front gate. As she pushed it open, the front door opened and her dad stood there, a mug of tea in his hand and a puzzled expression on his face.

'Effie, what on earth has happened, love?' He placed the mug of tea down on the step as Effie hurried up the garden path, relief washing over her as he pulled her into a hug. It was only then that the tears rushed over the dam she'd built since pulling away from the shop.

'What's going on?' Brian asked the driver, who was unceremoniously dumping Effie's bags on the path.

His only answer was a shrug before he jumped back into the van and sped away, leaving Effie standing in her childhood garden, her hopes and dreams packed up in bags around her feet.

'Go inside. I'll bring in your things,' her dad said gently.

Sniffling, Effie stepped into her home, her heartrate instantly calming at being surrounded by the familiarity that had shored her up her entire life. The warm yellow walls, the bright paintings on them, the smell of the fabric softener her mum used. It was like stepping into a hug. Effie helped her dad pull the bags into the hallway before following him into the kitchen where he flicked on the kettle.

'I think there's some chocolate cake left in that tin,' Brian said as he made two mugs of tea. 'I think this situation necessitates a slice.'

Effie lifted the lid of her mum's red and white spotted baking tin, and a divine, rich aroma arose. Sure enough, inside was a chocolate loaf cake. Effie cut two large slices, placed them on plates and carried them over to the table.

'I thought you were enjoying Polcarrow,' Brian began gently.

'I was. I actually really loved being there, but Zach turned up and apparently I'm not running the shop correctly. He had the guy in the van on standby to bring me home.'

'What? But you were doing wonderfully.'

Effie shrugged. 'I know but it's sort of his business. Well, his family business.'

Brian narrowed his eyes. This wasn't the first time Effie had brought woeful tales of Zach's bad behaviour home. 'Does Clive know about this? At the opening he was telling us how well you'd done and how he knew you'd be the best person for the job.'

This made the situation even more confusing. Especially as he'd said the same to her. Effie shook her head.

'No. He's on holiday. I don't know what to believe. I don't think Clive would've changed his mind without telling me himself but maybe he couldn't face doing it. Zach is a bulldozer.' She sipped her tea. 'I should've put up more of a fight but it was such a shock.'

Brian gave her hand a squeeze. 'I'm sure it's a misunderstanding. You'll find out more when you chat to Clive. He'll sort it out, I'm sure.'

'I hope so. I'll have to go back to work at the main shop now, I guess,' she said. 'Maybe the others will know what's going on. I think I'm only fired from the Polcarrow branch, not the entire company.' At least she hoped that was the case.

However, the prospect of returning to a shop that had been her haven didn't feel as appealing as it once had. If anything, Effie felt as if she'd been forced to take a giant step back. Again.

Chapter Forty-Two

The following morning Effie stood at the seafront, eyes closed against the sea spray and against the sinking feeling that she was right back where she started, her dreams once again in tatters. She sipped her takeaway tea, summoning up the courage to head to the main shop. It was like London all over again. All that excitement evaporating into nothing.

The previous night Effie had had to stop her mum from jumping in the car and driving down to Polcarrow to give Zach a piece of her mind. After another round of tears and a large bowl of her dad's delicious mushroom risotto, Effie had settled onto the sofa under a blanket, pleased that she had somewhere to go and parents who cared so much about her. Yet at the same time it felt as if by taking that step to move away, she didn't quite fit back into her old life. She missed her flat, her new friends and, although she was trying not to, Jake.

Yes, she'd been anxious about going to Polcarrow, had doubted that she'd be able to set the shop up, but she'd embraced the opportunity. She'd rolled up her sleeves and got stuck in. With every stroke of the paintbrush, every swim in the sea, every book she'd stacked on the shelves, every morning coffee she'd shared with Jake, she'd built up a life that felt more her own than any other time in her life.

Jake. Effie still hadn't heard from him. She'd also been completely unable to stay away from scrolling Tara's social media, taking in the cosy tropical paradise photos of them together. Effie had known their life-long bond was worth more than the few weeks she'd spent with Jake. Maybe being sent back to Penzance was for the best? Her previous feelings that Polcarrow would still be home without Jake were suddenly hollow. Jake was woven into every memory of the little fishing village.

Finishing her tea, she tossed the cup into a nearby bin and, turning her back on the choppy grey sea, made her way into the town centre. Her feet retraced the familiar steps towards the front door of Books by the Sea but it was as if she was walking on autopilot.

As the familiar blue door came into view, Effie paused. Outside sat the box of damaged or old books they sold at cut price. She'd always loved watching people rummage through it hoping to turn up literary gold. She hadn't got around to setting up such a box in Polcarrow because all the stock had been brand new.

Taking a deep breath, Effie crossed the road and after a brief pause, where she wondered if Zach had opened the Polcarrow shop, pushed open the door.

The familiar worn-in aroma of polish and old books greeted her, a smell she'd always found comforting. Paper and ink, the faint aroma of the coffee Maddie always brewed first thing, the gentle timbre of classical music sounding from the radio. Beside the door were the familiar shelves of beautifully bound classics and in the middle of the room a table stacked with an eclectic mix of local non-fiction and fiction. There was a strange, not unwelcome sensation of coming home.

As Effie pushed the door shut, the bell jangled.

'One minute,' Maddie called from somewhere behind the counter.

Effie lingered by the display table, feeling both at home and out of place. She watched as Maddie heaved a box onto the counter and swept her hair off her face. Her mouth dropped open as she clocked Effie.

'Effie, what are you doing here? Not that I'm not pleased to see you, but shouldn't you be in Polcarrow. What happened?'

Effie's lip trembled. 'Zach happened.'

'What do you mean?'

The tears spilled from Effie's eyes and Maddie rushed out from behind the counter and bundled her into a hug. 'Come on, come through. I'll stick the kettle on and I think there's some cookies left that Zoey made.'

Effie allowed Maddie to usher her into the tiny staffroom and into one of the uncomfortable but practical plastic chairs. Maddie thrust some tissues at her and set about making the tea whilst Effie sniffed and dabbed at her eyes.

'What has Zach done?' Maddie asked as she plonked the tea down on the table and lifted the lid from the biscuit box.

Effie took one of the chocolate chip cookies and nibbled at the edge. 'He just turned up at the book club, glowered at everyone, you know how he does.'

Maddie furrowed her brow and puffed out her chest, which at least cracked a smile from Effie.

'Yes, exactly like that!' She sipped her tea. 'Then he turned up yesterday morning at the shop, completely tore apart everything I'd done. The yellow chairs – told me customers should be buying not sitting down and I wasn't running the business properly. The next thing, he'd told me to pack up the flat, called a van and practically manhandled me out of Polcarrow.'

'What?' Maddie's mouth fell open in disbelief.

The shock on Maddie's face answered Effie's next question; clearly her friend had no idea Zach was back on the scene. 'I feel so stupid. I should've stood up to him. But you know what he's like.'

'Uh-huh. A complete bulldozer. But why did he do this?' Maddie dunked her cookie.

'He told me Clive wasn't happy with the figures, which doesn't make sense because the last email I had was full of praise.' Effie shrugged. 'He told me I shouldn't be running the shop as if it's my own. That I'd gone against company policy.'

'What?! How?'

Effie shrugged again. 'He just said I wasn't trusted to run the business properly. I don't understand. Clive was really pleased with what I was doing. Or I thought he was. If he wasn't happy, he should've told me. I ran all my ideas for decorating the shop past him. He was happy for me to have free rein on some things. I didn't think Clive would be this underhand.'

Maddie shook her head. 'This isn't Clive. Can't be. He's been singing your praises so much it's been driving me and Zoey mad. He's even talking about changing the blue to yellow here.'

'What?'

'This is Zach. It's got him written all over it.' Maddie chewed thoughtfully. 'He split up with that girl he was dating, you know, the one whose dad owns that chain of seafood restaurants. He's been clattering around here in a foul mood for the past week. When he wasn't here yesterday, I just assumed he'd found someone new to amuse him. I had no idea he was heading your way.'

Effie let this sink in. 'So you think this has nothing to do with Clive?'

'Can't have. He's on holiday anyway. Halfway through that cruise. Probably somewhere in the middle of the Atlantic sipping a pina colada. Let's call him.'

'We can't disturb him on his holiday!'

'Effie. We can. Something isn't right about this.' Maddie reached for her phone and dialled Clive's number.

They watched as it rang out. It didn't even go to voicemail.

'I'll try again.' Maddie pressed dial but again it rang out.

They sat back, sipped their drinks and studied the phone. Still no connection.

'So, what are you going to do?' Maddie asked.

'Come back and work here, I guess. I don't think I'm completely fired.'

Maddie narrowed her eyes at her. 'You're not going to put up a fight?'

'Over what? He is Clive's son. It will be his business one day. I'm sure it'll sort itself out when Clive is back. Anyway, what if Zach is right? What if he is doing his dad's dirty work? Clive hates confrontation.'

Maddie considered this. 'True. But it still doesn't feel right. What about that hunky photographer?'

'Back with his ex.'

'What? No way! Seriously? Shit, Effie, I thought he was well into you with all that helping and not being able to take his eyes off you. What is it with modern men?'

Effie shrugged. 'No idea. It's been a brutal week, Mads, can we not keep hashing it out, please? The great Polcarrow experiment is over and clearly another failure to add to my list. I'm gutted to be honest.'

'I know, hun, I know, for what it's worth you were brilliant.' Maddie squeezed her hand and cast her eye at the calendar. 'Anyway, it's not long until Clive is back and we can sort this mess out.'

Effie smiled her gratitude at her, but neither of them needed to remind the other that Clive was a total pushover when it came to his spoilt, entitled son.

Chapter Forty-Three

Effie settled back into the familiarity of home more quickly than she had anticipated or liked. It was like pulling on a comfy sweater and being embraced by its softness. Working beside Maddie was always fun, and although Effie had enjoyed having free rein in the Polcarrow shop, it was nice to be able to bounce ideas around with her friend and colleague. Over cups of tea and boxes of Zoey's baking, they planned out pirate- and fairy-tale-themed events for the local children and reorganised the stockroom, filling up the bargain boxes with an eclectic mix of folklore and military history that had been gathering dust.

Her evenings were spent nestled back in the family home. They took it in turns to cook depending on their schedules, sharing bottles of wine and after-dinner games of Scrabble. Effie had never minded living at home but as she crawled into bed each night she couldn't help but admit to herself that she had liked the freedom of having her own place. She'd got used to it far more quickly than she'd expected. Effie took some comfort in this. Perhaps she'd look for her own flat in Penzance. The thought no longer terrified her.

What she missed the most, though, was her morning swim. Yes, she could pack a bag and traipse down to the seafront but it wasn't as convenient as just crossing the road in her flip-flops and then warming up with a hot chocolate in Lola's. Effie's heart ached when she thought of her friends in Polcarrow. As they'd practically lived in each other's pockets Effie didn't have anyone's number to check in with how things were going. She sometimes brought up Freya's social media and hovered, tempted to message, but Effie also didn't know if she wanted to find out what Zach had been up to. What if he was making a better job of the shop than she had?

The other issue with Polcarrow and social media was Jake. Effie had really thought there was something growing between them, but the more she looked, all she saw were posts of him and Tara looking very much in love. She was embarrassed to admit, even to herself, that when he'd said he wasn't ready for a relationship, she'd hoped that in time he'd change his mind, and she'd finally get her fairy-tale happy-ever-after.

Effie typed out numerous messages to Jake but never sent them. In the end, she blocked both his and Tara's profiles to save her sanity, then deleted his number to remove the temptation to text. Polcarrow had been wonderful, but Effie couldn't help but think that chapter of her life was over. It had allowed her to grow, given her a chance to realise just what she was capable of. Now, she just had to make sure her roots didn't take too strong a hold back home. Home was comfort but now she knew there was a lot more out there, a host of adventures and possibilities over the horizon. Effie wasn't sure what she wanted, but she knew it was something different from the safe life she'd lived since graduating from university.

Chapter Forty-Four

'Your loyalty is remarkable,' Maddie said as she placed a cup of tea in front of Effie.

'Thanks. What do you mean?' She glanced up from where she was flicking through a supply catalogue, marking up some accessories they could buy to shore up the summer reading campaign she was planning on running. Effie thought adults, not just kids, deserved a reward for spending the sunny season with a book. Despite everything, she was looking forward to spear-heading the campaign.

'All this.' Maddie gestured to Effie's lists and mood board. 'Just playing devil's advocate here, but, what if it isn't just Zach being Zach? What if you're right and Clive is unhappy and couldn't face telling you?'

Effie pressed her lips together. 'I've been trying not to dwell on that possibility. How likely do you think it is?'

'Not very,' Maddie admitted. 'If he wanted Zach to run the shop, he'd have asked him first. But – we know Clive doesn't have much backbone when it comes to Zach. And he doesn't like confrontation.'

Effie considered this. 'True.' She cast her mind back to the shop opening, Clive dodging as much responsibility as possible. 'He allowed me to run with my ideas and he liked them.' Even to herself, Effie felt like she sounded as if she was clutching at straws. Then it crept up on her like a rising tide. All the terse phone calls at the beginning of the venture. Had Clive really given her free rein or had she got swept up in the vision she'd had since childhood? Her own cosy little bookshop with sea views? Had she pushed her own agenda onto him because the premises were in such a mess?

'Clive will be back soon so we can find out then,' Effie said firmly.

'What will you do if this was his idea?'

It was as if Maddie had thrown a bucket of cold water over her. What would she do? She wouldn't be able to stay working at the shop after such disappointment, would she? 'I don't know.' Effie managed a weak smile. 'Let's think about that when it comes to it.'

Effie turned back to her summer reading mood board to distract herself from the possibility that, underneath all his amiable bluster, Clive wasn't happy with how she'd been running the shop. Maybe it hadn't been doing as well as Effie had thought? She had been somewhat distracted by Jake and everything else that had been going on in Polcarrow. Maybe she had really messed it all up?

Suddenly, the plan to fill the Penzance shop window display with a deckchair and beach balls seemed less enticing. So did the summer romance reading list she was compiling. Effie pushed her notes aside and buried her head in her hands. She cast her mind back over everything she'd done since heading off to Polcarrow, trying to find the moment she'd managed to get it wrong enough to be demoted.

She was so engrossed in wading through memories that she didn't realise Maddie was calling her name until she placed a hand on her shoulder and jolted her back to the present.

'What is it?'

'Effie, there's some people out there for you.' Excitement radiated off Maddie as she inclined her head and wiggled her eyebrows as if trying to communicate something using an indecipherable facial code.

'Can't you deal with them? I'm really not in a people mood.' She leaned back in the chair.

Before Maddie could say anything else, Effie heard her name being called by a voice that stilled her heart.

'Effie!' It came again, kick starting her into action.

She froze. It was a voice she'd hoped to hear again but never expected to.

'See,' Maddie said with a satisfied smile.

'How do I look?' Effie leapt up, smoothing her hands over her dungarees, brushing off biscuit crumbs. Why hadn't she'd had the foresight to put on a dress or makeup.

'You look fine.'

'Only fine?' She panicked.

'Effie,' Maddie sighed, 'you look like you and if I'm not mistaken, that guy has seen you in a wetsuit? This is definitely several step ups from that.'

'OK, OK.' Effie stepped around Maddie, took in a deep breath and exhaled. She held her hand out; it was shaking. 'I need to get a grip,' she muttered to herself as she made her way out of the office, Maddie hot on her heels.

The short walk from the office to the shop had never felt longer. Her heart pounded and her went mouth dry, all her senses on high alert. She didn't dare even imagine what Jake being back in Cornwall might mean.

Stepping into the shop, Effie's heart almost skittered to a stop. Jake. Jake was there. She took him in, his sun-kissed skin and tousled hair which was pushed back from his face where an anxious, concerned expression ran across his features. Effie gaped at him in disbelief. Lola had been right. He'd come back. But why?

'Jake?' She blinked as if she was seeing things.

A dog barked and Effie's attention was caught by the rabble of people filling up the tiny shop. It wasn't just Jake, but Alf and Scruff, accompanied by Lola, Freya and Sue, who was half listening, half perusing the crime shelves.

'What are you all doing here?' she asked, bewildered.

'Well, I wanted to come on my own,' said Jake, shifting from foot to foot, 'I didn't really want an audience, but they all insisted. You know what it's like, I don't think Lola and Sue understand the word "no".'

Effie laughed as the two women protested.

'Scruff wouldn't be left behind, didn't want to miss out on all the excitement,' Alf said, 'so of course I had to come, keep my eye on him. You know what he's like.'

Emotion bubbled up in the form of happy tears at seeing her friends crowded into the shop, but mostly it was the sight of Jake, his sleeves rolled up to reveal the tattoos on his strong golden arms, the earnest expression on his face that told her he really would have preferred to have come alone. Effie swallowed down all the feelings that were engulfing her, all the questions that were swirling like a storm. She steadied her breathing and focused just on Jake.

'Why are you here?' Somehow she kept her voice steady, emotionless.

Jake took a deep breath before exhaling; Effie was almost pleased to see him looking so nervous.

'We really need to talk. Properly. I never got to tell you what was going on the night of the gallery. But, the long and the short of it is, I've decided to come back.' He shrugged at the simplicity of it. 'The Maldives might be nice but they aren't a patch on Polcarrow.'

'Glad to hear it, son,' Alf interrupted.

Effie really wished she wasn't having this conversation in public. She floundered around for something to say but she was uncomfortable with everyone listening in. She sensed Jake was too. He was right, there was a lot more to say than they could currently voice with an audience. She slipped a glance at Maddie, who was hanging on to every word like it was the juiciest bestseller. Lola, Alf and Freya were waiting for the next instalment. At least Sue was pretending to look at some books. Effie threw Jake a warning glance.

'Effie, when I got back to Polcarrow and you weren't there, I didn't know what to do. Zach—' Jake spat his name '—only told me you were gone. Wouldn't give me any information. We had to work it all out together that you'd come back here.'

'He's ruined the shop,' Sue butted in, 'cancelled story time and repainted the door. The kids hate going in now.'

'Actually, no one likes it anymore,' Alf said sadly.

Effie stared between them all, trying to process what they were telling her.

'You need to come back,' Jake said, stepping forward and taking her hands.

Effie met his gaze, their bodies swayed closer together, but she pulled her hands away from his. Any possible reconciliations could come later. 'I don't know if I can. It is his family business,' she reminded everyone, 'he probably has more rights than I do.'

'We'll all support you turfing him out,' Alf called, Scruff barking in agreement.

Effie glanced around at the assembled crowd, all watching as she decided what to do. Silently willing her to come and save their bookshop. Her bookshop. The natural desire to protest fought with the injustice of being kicked out of a shop she had so lovingly set up.

The fact that the shop meant so much to the residents of Polcarrow lit a flame within her.

'He probably won't listen,' Effie warned them as the door opened, the bell tinkling.

'Listen to who? What's going on?'

In unison they all turned towards the shop doorway to find Clive standing there, slightly sunburned and wearing a Hawaiian shirt.

'Effie, what on earth are you doing here?' he asked as his eyes fell on the rescue party. 'What's going on?'

Chapter Forty-Five

'Clive! I should ask you the same. I thought you were on holiday for another week.' Effie stepped around Jake and Maddie stood to attention behind the till.

Realising there was an audience, including a dog, in his shop, Clive ran his eyes over them and repeated, 'What's going on?'

'We've come to get Effie back,' Alf said.

Clive dropped down onto one of the chairs beside the door. 'I think someone needs to explain what's going on. Effie, why are you here and not in Polcarrow?'

'Because you weren't happy with how I was running things. Zach came and told me. He's taken over the shop,' she explained, her stomach churning in case Clive confirmed this was the truth.

'Zach? I didn't even realise he was back home.' Clive paused as he tried to make sense of what she was saying. 'What's he doing interfering with my business? Never been interested before.' The penny dropped. 'That would explain what's happened! You know, I was watching the accounts and couldn't understand why a thriving shop was suddenly taking no money. I came back because I thought you were struggling, Effie, and I find you here. What on earth is he playing at?'

'Kicked her out of the flat too,' Sue interjected, 'and cancelled story time. He's scared the children off.'

'And he's painted the door blue,' Lola said before adding, 'very badly. It's an eyesore.'

Clive ran his hand through his thinning hair. 'Dear me. Effie, why didn't you contact me?'

'Because you were on holiday! Maddie did try. Also, I thought he was right. That I was running the shop differently to here and that maybe you didn't have the heart to come and tell me yourself. I think I got carried away turning the shop into my own childhood dream and not in keeping in line with the business.'

Clive looked at her in disbelief. 'You really think that?'

Effie nodded. It now seemed so preposterous.

Clive pulled his phone out of his pocket and clicked onto the shop's social media. 'People love it. Or they did. Effie, it was going so well that when I was away, I was thinking we could incorporate your ideas into refreshing this place. This shop has felt like a burden for so long, I will admit that. It was so easy to just let you girls sort it out and run it, but seeing how much everyone loved the Polcarrow shop gave me a boost and helped me believe in the business again.'

Silence fell over everyone as they took in Clive's words. Hope began to rise in Effie as she thought of the shop, her little flat, the sea view and early-morning swims. Jake slipped his hand back into hers. It felt natural, right, even without the talking, she sensed that things were going to turn out for the best.

'So, what are we going to do?' she asked.

Clive hauled himself up. 'I think we need to go to Polcarrow and sort this mess out. That's all I need after the flight I've just had.' He ran a hand down his tired face. 'What was your plan?'

Effie glanced around at everyone, 'Erm, we hadn't got that far yet.'

'But we have come to take Effie home,' Jake said, stepping closer to her.

Effie glanced up at him, feeling safe wherever he was, knowing he had her back in whatever she faced. *Home*, she liked the way that sounded.

Chapter Forty-Six

Effie desperately wanted to talk to Jake alone. She sensed there was much more he wanted to say than he'd been able to voice in the shop. It thrummed between them like a live wire. However, as Sue had driven them over to Penzance in her seven-seater, which they were all now crammed into for the return journey, there was no space for a private conversation. The car was full of unspoken desire, unuttered explanations and anticipation over what would happen next. Everyone pretended that they weren't dying to hear if Effie and Jake were getting together.

Effie snuck a glance at him across the back seat. Jake reached over and linked his fingers experimentally through hers as they hurtled around the twisty country lanes. When Effie gave him a small, encouraging smile, Jake squeezed her hand rather than pulling away. Clive was bringing up the rear in his sports car, Maddie in the passenger seat, having proclaimed they could close the shop for an afternoon as she was not missing out on all the excitement.

'I hope Clive knows we're all doing this for you, not to save his arse,' Jake said.

'We've all missed you,' Lola said. 'Polcarrow isn't the same without its resident mermaid. All the kids are scared of going into the shop because Zach banned them from picking up the books. Doesn't want them getting dirty.'

'I didn't realise Zach cared about books,' Effie said dryly, 'only the money they make.'

'He's not been making any money,' Alf put in. 'He opens late, shuts early, glowers at anyone who comes in until they leave.'

'Empty handed! Honestly, Effie, the amount of people I've had complain that the shop isn't at all what it looked like on social media,' Lola said. 'His attitude is affecting all our businesses.'

'Lola refused to serve him,' Freya said.

'What?'

Lola shrugged. 'If he doesn't want to serve anyone then I don't want to serve him.'

Effie smiled as she thought about how full and rich her life had become since she'd arrived in Polcarrow with her bags of books and baskets of knitting. She cast a glance around the car. Jake, Alf and Scruff, Lola and Freya, even Sue, all of them cared deeply about a business they'd known for about five minutes. Not just the business, Effie realised, but her as well.

'Thank you, honestly, I didn't realise how much this all meant to you. In fact, I didn't realise how much this all meant to me either.' Her voice was choked with emotion.

'We've learned to be more accepting of incomers,' Sue explained as she took a bend at far too high a speed, jolting everyone over to the left-hand side of the car. 'Sorry! Especially incomers who embrace being party of the community. If we want to revive the village, then we need a little bit of outside help.'

'Watch it,' Alf warned, 'she'll have you on the committee next!'

Everyone laughed and began to chip in with tales of Sue's various hare-brained schemes, from reinstating the Fisherman's Fair to a lobster pot Christmas tree. Effie snuck a glance at Jake only to find him watching her, his expression soft.

'Do you know what you're going to do?' he asked.

Effie shook her head. 'Nope! I'll make something up.'

Jake brought her hand to his lips and kissed her knuckles. 'You can do anything, Effie, you've got this.'

When Effie stepped out of the car, legs wobbly and stomach churning from Sue's driving, she wasn't so sure that she did have it. Wandering over to the harbour wall, she dragged in some calming breaths of sea air and waited for her stomach to settle.

'Give her some space.' Jake held everyone back, including Maddie, who jumped out of Clive's car the second he pulled up.

Jake took a step forward and lightly touched her arm. 'Are you OK?'

Effie nodded. 'Sue's driving,' she explained.

'Erm . . . yes,' Jake laughed.

Eyes closed, Effie inhaled the sweet sea air before opening them and being greeted by Polcarrow bay spread out before her, welcoming her home. She fixed her gaze on the horizon, steady and sure, to be relied on. Her eyes moved over the waves as they washed onto the sand, then over and up the beach, the tiny grains worn down into softness over thousands of years. All this had existed before them, and it'd be there long after they'd all passed.

Turning around, she fixed her eyes on the shop, her stomach churning for a different reason. Her beautiful springtime window display had been cleared, the blinds pulled halfway down, and the cheerful daffodil yellow door hastily slapped over with blue paint. Even from this distance she could see Zach had done a bad job. Seeing how he'd ruined her vision, Effie balled her hands into fists and stormed across the road, then pulled open the door.

Effie glanced around. The shop looked familiar and completely unrecognisable at the same time. The yellow chairs had been moved and Effie really hoped they hadn't ended up in a skip, they'd been expensive but worth every penny. There were gaps in the shelves where stock had not been replaced and a layer of dust on top of the till. The rainbow-print rug she'd bought for the children's area had been removed. The whole shop looked sterile, its atmosphere oppressive and warning people away. No wonder takings had been down.

Where was Zach? She'd been inside long enough to have grabbed books, maybe even the till and run off. How dare he preach about the importance of running a shop and then leave it unmanned.

'Zach?' she called, her voice flaming with anger. She gave him enough time to emerge from wherever he was hiding before calling his name again. This time she made her way through the shop and found him lounging in the kitchen, headphones in, watching something on his phone.

Incensed, Effie reached across and pulled the headphones from his ears. Momentarily startled, he shot to his feet in a panic, before narrowing his eyes at Effie.

'That's assault,' he growled at her.

'So, have me arrested then.' She shrugged, taking a step out of the kitchen, back into the shop, Zach matching her step for step. 'Personally, I'd be more concerned about how you've left the shop unmanned. Something could've been stolen.'

'Unlikely. Not like anyone comes in here.' Zach shrugged. 'Why are you here? Didn't you get the message, you're not welcome in this shop.'

'What? The message that the shop was doing badly because of my management of it?' Effie folded her arms, no longer intimidated by him. 'Looks like you're doing an even better job than I was of running a shop badly.

Where's all the customers, Zach? Have you scared them all away?'

'People don't care about books, Effie. It's about time Dad realised that, got rid of the business, sold it off. I don't want to keep running it after he's retired.'

'You were pretty keen on running it a couple of weeks back,' she pointed out.

'I was trying to help Dad. You were doing your own thing, and I didn't like it.'

'But your dad did,' Effie said as it dawned on her. Zach was jealous that she had been trusted to open the new shop, not him.

'You might think books are boring, Zach, but they're important. They offer escapism and information, and they've kept a roof over your head and food on your table for a long time. Your dad might not have his heart fully in the business but that's because he has people like me, Maddie and Zoey to keep it going, people who love books. I've come back to Polcarrow to take back this shop and my flat.'

Zach laughed. 'Effie, you can't be serious. You can't tell me what to do, you're just an employee, you're lucky I didn't just fire you. I let you go back to the Penzance branch, why can't you just be happy with that?'

'Because this is where I'm happy,' Effie said in a moment of weakness.

However, she should have known Zach would seize any vulnerability and try and use it to his advantage.

'Not happening, Effie. After your behaviour today I think you need to be fired. You've assaulted and insulted the owner of the business.'

'You're not the owner, Zach.'

'I will be one day, and I'll start as I mean to go on,' he said chillingly as he reached into his pocket and pulled out his phone and pressed the screen.

Effie could hear it ringing in the silence between them. They never took their eyes off each other. Effie scowling, Zach looking smugly down at her.

'Hi, Dad, yeah, yeah, are you having a good holiday? Uh-huh, uh-huh, you just got back? Oh, wasn't expecting that but actually, it's a good thing, you see I've got a bit of a problem with one of our staff members. Effie, yeah, I know, well, she's turned up, shouting at me, insulted me and really, it's time she was fired, we can't be putting up with that.' Zach turned his back on her as he continued his tirade.

Effie stood and listened as he spoke lies down the phone, a smile spreading across her face as the shop door slowly opened and Clive stepped in.

'Yes, Zach, I agree, we need to discuss this in person.'

Zach froze. He dropped his phone from his ear and, as if in slow motion, spun around, horror washing over his face to see Clive standing in the shop.

'Dad? What are you doing here?'

'I could ask you the same thing,' Clive said with a level of steeliness Effie hadn't known he possessed. 'What have you done, Zach?'

'Dad, I can explain, honestly.'

'Effie told me you kicked her out the shop and told her it wasn't doing well, is that true?' Clive asked gently. Even Effie could see that he was trying to give his son a way out of this mess.

'But she wasn't keeping in line with our scheme,' Zach insisted.

'*Our scheme?* You've not shown any interest in the business until now. What happened with the paddle board business?'

Zach shifted uncomfortably. 'Didn't take off.'

'And the cocktail bar?'

'The same,' Zach admitted.

Clive glanced around as if looking for somewhere to sit, but without the chairs, there was nowhere to perch. He rubbed his forehead wearily. 'Zach, you and I need to talk. If you are serious about setting up a business, or being involved in this one, which I don't actually believe you are, we need to talk properly. This shop was my idea and I trusted Effie to get it going and she did really well. I know you told her that it wasn't making money, but that wasn't true, the shop was a success. I was pleased with what she'd done. But look what you've done to it.' Clive indicated the shop that had had its soul stripped out.

Effie shifted awkwardly as she watched father and son regard each other. Knowing she was intruding on something that should be private, she made a step towards the door. Clive stopped her.

'Effie, wait, I want you to hear what I have to say too. I was thinking of retiring, but two things have happened. One, how beautiful this shop was gave me a new passion for the business I didn't think I'd get at this age. Two, Zach, you're not ready to take over and I don't even know if that's what you want. I need to trust you and if this is what happens when I go on holiday, then I dread to think what would happen if I stepped away fully.

'This shop is all our lives whether we love it or not. Zach, like I said, we need to talk, but not today, I'm knackered from my flight and just want to go home. Effie is having the shop and the flat back as of now. And the shop goes back to how it was. OK?' He looked at both of them.

Effie nodded.

'Yes, Dad.'

'Right, let's get home. Give Effie back the keys.'

Zach reached into his pocket and threw the keys onto the counter. Effie didn't make a move to take them. Her triumph sat uncomfortably on her. She watched as Clive pulled open the door.

'Where are the yellow chairs?' Effie asked.

'Someone had them for some studio thing, I think,' Zach said.

'We can get some more,' Clive reassured her.

Effie nodded and watched them walk past her rescue party. As Zach passed, she swore she heard Scruff growl.

Once she'd heard Clive's car disappear around the corner, she made her way over to the counter, picked up the keys and, holding them tight in her hand, brought them to her heart.

She was home.

Chapter Forty-Seven

After Effie had regaled the growing crowd on the harbour for the third time about what had transpired between her, Zach and Clive, it was decided that the celebrations should be moved to the pub. Effie was happily swept along the seafront by the villagers and almost carried through the pub door.

'There you go.' Steve placed a pint of local cider on the bar in front of Effie. 'On the house. Never did like that bloke. Came in here sniffing at my wine selection like he was some sort of connoisseur.' The fact that Zach probably couldn't tell his Merlot from his Shiraz didn't need mentioning.

Effie sipped her drink and turned to everyone. 'Thank you. It looks like I'm here to stay.'

A cheer went up, and Effie beamed. Other than being tucked up in the safety of her parents' house, she had never felt like she belonged anywhere as much as she did in Polcarrow. The fact that the residents had mounted a rescue mission to bring her back brought a tear to her eye. She shook their hands, allowed them to bundle her into hugs and repeated the story to anyone who'd missed it. Through the melee her eyes met with Jake's. Time slowed as he raised his drink to her. Effie couldn't even begin to get her head around what him being back in Cornwall would really mean.

Once everyone had a drink in hand, they moved outside to the beer garden, having decided it was too nice an afternoon to spend indoors. The sun had peaked out from behind the clouds like a blessing for Effie's return. Effie sighed at the sea view as she slipped into the bench of the picnic table. Jake threw a few bags of crisps on the table between them and asked, 'Is it OK if I join?'

'Of course,' Effie said, waiting until he'd sat down to chink his glass against hers.

'Effie, we really need to talk,' he said, glancing around nervously.

She nodded. 'Later, I don't think we're going to get a moment unobserved for a while,' she said, cracking into a bag of cheese and onion crisps. Anxious about what he might say, Effie didn't want anything to spoil her triumphant glow.

'I'm not intruding, am I?' Maddie asked as she joined them, pint in hand. 'Only Daniel can't make it until he finishes work, and I didn't fancy sitting in the back of Clive's car with that frosty atmosphere. Sounds like you kicked arse. I liked having you back in Penzance but I can see this place suits you better.' She gave a not-so-subtle indication towards Jake.

'Yes,' Effie said, catching his eye before replying to Maddie, 'I didn't realise how much being here meant to me until I saw what Zach had done to the door. Lola was right about it being horrendous. I'm glad I have some yellow paint left. That's my first task tomorrow. I just wish I knew where the chairs had gone.'

'The chairs?' Freya called over from where she was sitting with Angelo and Alf. 'The yellow ones?' When Effie nodded, Freya continued, 'They're in my gallery. He was going to throw them in a skip, so I paid him fifty quid to take them off his hands.'

Effie's heart sank. At least they'd gone to a good home. 'Oh, that's great. I'm relieved they didn't go in the bin.'

'I saved them for you,' Freya explained, 'I knew you'd be back. Lola said.'

'What?'

'I did the cards,' Lola told her as she joined them. 'Zach's reign of terror was always predicted to be short lived.'

Tears welling in her eyes, Effie glanced between Lola and Freya, overwhelmed by their kindness. 'Thank you, I don't know what else to say.'

'We can move them back as soon as you're ready,' Freya said.

Effie glanced around the small gathering of friends, who'd once been strangers, who had gone out of their way to save her dream. 'I'd like to say something,' she said, standing up, her voice wavering and her resolve almost vanishing as everyone turned to look at her.

'I've always been content with staying at home. I went away to university but didn't like it. That made me feel like a failure. I felt like I didn't know how to do life. Now I know I was just trying to do life the wrong way with the wrong people. I was scared of leaving home for so long but Clive's proposition was too good to turn down and I'm glad I didn't because if I had I wouldn't have met all of you.

'I know everyone talks about stepping out of your comfort zone, like the comfort zone is a bad thing, which I don't agree with, but I stayed in mine too long. You've all made me feel so much more welcome than I'd ever imagined I'd be and I'm grateful for all your support, not just today, but when I opened the shop. I really couldn't have done it without you.' Effie exhaled and caught Jake's eye. 'Phew, that's the longest speech I've ever made.' She could feel her cheeks colouring. 'So I'll stop wittering on and just say thank you again.'

With a little bob of her head, Effie sat down and took a long slug of her cider as everyone erupted into applause. As she put her glass down, she caught Jake's eyes. He was beaming at her as if she was the most wonderful woman on the planet. For the first time in her life, Effie felt as if his assessment of her was correct.

Chapter Forty-Eight

The evening drew in and Effie realised, as she waved Maddie off, that she was now stuck in Polcarrow and all her things were back home in Penzance. Grabbing her phone from her pocket she almost called Maddie, asking her to come back and collect her, but she remembered Jake and. the conversation they needed to have.

She'd phoned her parents earlier that evening to explain the situation and they were both outraged at Zach's behaviour and gutted that they hadn't been there to witness Effie's moment of triumph. As she'd hung up, Effie glanced around the busy pub garden and over at the lazy evening sea, her heart swelling with just how loved she was. How lucky she'd been to be able to reclaim her dream life. She would never have felt confident to fight her battles if it hadn't been for how much Polcarrow had got behind her.

Slipping her phone back into her pocket, she caught Jake's eye and watched as he nodded towards the garden gate. Everyone was engrossed in their own conversations, so didn't pay much attention when Effie slipped away. Jake was waiting outside the pub, bouncing nervously on his toes. He was here, in Polcarrow, that had to be positive, didn't it? Her heart lurched and she tried to hold it back, needing to hear what he had to say before she got carried away with a romantic fantasy.

Effie walked slowly over to him, setting the pace of whatever was going to happen next. She stopped a foot's breadth between them. They each drank the other in, desire for the truth and for each other thrumming between them. Effie shivered and Jake unzipped his hoodie and handed it to her.

'Won't you be cold?' she asked as she snuggled into it, the residual warmth of his body wrapping around her. She just about managed to stop herself from lifting it to her nose to inhale his scent.

'I'm fine,' he said. 'Effie, we need to talk.'

'Now?' she asked and hiccupped from her second cider. She felt nicely blurred around the edges but not drunk, just enough to soften any blows. 'Yes, now, of course, of course we do.'

She turned away from the pub and headed back along the harbour, Jake following. The sound of everyone else trying to decide if they should order fish and chips carried on the air. Effie's stomach grumbled. Chips sounded good, but clearing the air with Jake was more important.

Effie made her way down onto the beach, and perched on the bottom step. Jake dropped down beside her. The sun was setting in a slow, gentle, golden way. The cool evening air was laced with the briny scent of the sea. Effie inhaled it, allowing it to ground her. Here was where she was happiest, but what about Jake?

'I missed this view,' Jake admitted, breaking through the moment.

'What? Even when you were on a tropical island?' Effie asked, her words coming out harsher than she had meant them to.

Jake flinched at them. 'I missed it more when I was on a tropical island. All that white sand, turquoise sea, yeah, it's good, it might be paradise, but it's not as good as growing up with this on your doorstep. It took me too long to realise that.'

'I agree. Well, about this being on the doorstep. I've never been to a tropical island.'

'You're not missing much.'

Effie turned to him. 'Really? You'd pick this over the Maldives? I've seen the photos, Jake.'

He swallowed at this. 'Right, the photos. Effie, I'm sorry, I should never have gone. The second I got into Tara's car I knew I was doing the wrong thing. I made a mess of everything. I didn't explain it very well to you before I went. I thought you'd understand that Tara and I had an obligation, that I'd tried to be honest with you, but I didn't do it very well. I think needed to go away again to see what I really wanted.'

'And were you undecided about Tara the whole time?' Effie asked, even though she wasn't sure she wanted the answer.

Jake hesitated.

'You were?' She swallowed.

'We'd been together a long time. I had once thought we'd be together forever and I didn't want to throw that away so easily. Maybe we got engaged because it was what was expected more than because we really were still in love with each other,' Jake admitted.

Effie nodded. 'And when you were away?'

'It was nice to slip into the familiarity of being with her. We had a lot to talk about, figure out and unwind between us. After she'd spent the flight going on and on about the contracts she was bringing in, all clothes and makeup and boutique hotel stays, I realised I wanted more from life than jumping from place to place. The same boredom that had made me leave her set in again.'

'You didn't look bored in the photos.'

'It wasn't real, none of it. You have to believe me, Effie . . .' he paused before saying '. . . Eff, look at me, please, don't shut me out.'

The desperate tone in Jake's voice made her turn towards him. Effie's eyes flickered over his face but she remained silent. There was nothing for her to say. Jake reached out and took her hand. Effie tried to resist the way her fingers curled into his, the link between them that felt so safe, so right. She swallowed. The lowering sun flicked golden across his face, lighting him up, softening all the sharp edges she'd got herself caught on.

'I missed this. I missed this view, but mostly I missed you. Meeting you, Effie, changed my life for the better. I spent so long running away from village life, thinking I was living a better, more exciting life than everyone else. Yeah, maybe I was a bit smug about it. It was a huge shock when things ended with Tara. We'd both invested too much to call it quits, hence the break,' he scoffed. 'Either way, I never expected that someone who had spent her entire life devoted to Cornwall would help me see that it has more charms than anywhere else I've been.'

Effie stared at him, heart hammering, hardly daring to believe what he was telling her. 'What's happened with Tara?'

'You didn't see the latest post?'

Effie shook her head and admitted, 'I blocked your profiles.'

If Jake thought this was an overreaction, he didn't say. Instead, he reached into his pocket and pulled out his phone. Effie watched as he clicked on the app and brought up a video that had tens of thousands of likes and hundreds of comments. He pressed play.

Effie wasn't sure she wanted to look but she leaned over anyway and saw Tara perched on the edge of a very luxurious-looking hotel bed, Jake beside her looking as if he wanted to be anywhere else but there.

'Hi, everyone.' Tara waggled her fingers at the camera. 'This is just a little, long-overdue life update from Jakey and me. I know, I know you've been asking where he's been. Well, he's been back home in Cornwall. You've all been such wonderful supporters of us together that we were both very nervous to tell you that we've parted ways. Professionally and romantically. I'm sorry! I know you thought we were true love and all that. Maybe we were once. But everyone grows and changes, that's what life is about and sadly after many happy years together, we've grown apart. But we're both happy, honestly, and hope you'll continue to support both of us in our new ventures, you guys literally mean the world to us.' She blew a kiss and the video ended.

Effie stared at the blank screen, then at Jake. *Could this mean . . . ?*

'I got home this morning to find that bully in the shop. I went to Lola and she told me what had happened. Within minutes, Sue was bundling us into her car. I couldn't believe I'd been so careless with you. For a split second I thought I'd lost you, that'd you'd left because of me.'

'It wasn't because of you,' Effie said, 'but I did wonder if it was for the best. I didn't know if I could stay here if you were with Tara.' She turned to him. 'Jake, what is your plan?'

He entwined their fingers tighter and tugged Effie towards him. 'I'm staying here. In Polcarrow. There's nowhere else I'd rather be.'

Effie stared up into his eyes, melting under the intensity of his feelings shining back at her, hardly daring to trust the edge they were teetering on.

'Nowhere else I'd rather be, Effie, because you're here. When I first came back, I was at a complete loss over what to do. I was floundering. All that photography business stuff was a way of trying to get myself grounded. I just floated about looking for something to moor myself to.

Then one morning I got chastised by an angry mermaid and I was transfixed. I loved helping you in the shop. It was the best thing I'd done in years, it even made me think about joining Dad's business again,' Jake laughed.

'I've had some really positive enquiries from people wanting my photography skills, and I'm meeting with the hotel from the showcase on Thursday. It's all promising enough to make me think it could be a viable business, that it's really worth a shot. Of course there's Lola and Tristan's wedding in a couple of weeks, my big break—' he exhaled '—not nervous at all.'

Effie laughed. They both knew Lola had some very exacting demands.

'Effie, please say something, anything to make me feel like you're not mad at me about the Tara thing. Even though you have every right to be.'

'I'm not mad. I never was. I was sad. Sad, because I thought we had something. OK, so it hadn't really got off the ground, and I suspected you weren't ready for a relationship before you even told me. I respected that but I felt safe with you, comfortable, which I've never felt before. I could be me, and you didn't judge. When you left with Tara, it made me feel I wasn't enough. Look at her, all glamourous and jet-setting, and I'm walking around with sea-frizzed hair and dungarees. I just didn't think it meant to you what it meant to me.'

Jake pulled her into his arms. 'Oh, Eff, I'm sorry I made you feel like that. I never meant to. You're perfect as you are. You're beautiful with your wild mermaid hair and I love how excited you get when a new shipment of books arrives. How you inhale the smell off the pages. I love how you put yourself out there even though you are absolutely terrified and somehow you manage to win every time. You really underestimate yourself, Effie, if you think I was going to run off with Tara when I've fallen head over heels in love with you.'

Jake tucked a stray strand of hair behind her ear. His eyes beseeched her, vulnerable and sparkling with desire. Effie allowed everything he'd said to wash over her. He loved her! It spread a smile across her face. She leaned in and kissed him, slowly, as if for the first time. Jake loved her, it bloomed in her chest, unfurling like petals on a rose. She pulled him in closer, deepening the kiss.

They pulled apart and snuggled into each other as the sun ducked behind the horizon, a shower of gold over the sea. Somehow it felt like a blessing.

'I know I did the wrong thing, Effie, and I know you shouldn't just change your mind because I love you. You can take whatever time you want or need, I'll be here, waiting.'

Effie thought about it, about being angry with him, about being upset, but it was her he was with watching the sun set in Cornwall, not on a tropical beach with Tara. He'd made his choice. How could she keep him waiting when she already knew her answer?

Turning to him, she kissed him again. 'I don't want to wait, Jake. I know I shouldn't have done, and I tried not to, but I couldn't help it, I've fallen in love with you too,' she said, the words forming like a smile on her lips.

Jake let out a sigh of relief as he pulled Effie in tightly against him. 'I don't deserve this but I'm not going to protest and risk you changing your mind. Effie, I am the luckiest man alive.' He beamed down at her.

'Jake, I'm not going to change my mind. Anyway, I need somewhere to stay tonight.' She glanced up at him in what she hoped was a seductive way.

'Oh.' Jake caught her meaning. 'Of course, if you're sure, we don't have to do anything you don't want—'

She silenced him with a kiss. 'I want to,' was all she said before standing up and holding out her hand to him. 'But can we also get some chips, I'm starving.'

'Anything for you,' Jake said, pulling himself up to his full height, and instead of taking her hand, he swung her up into his arms. Effie let out a surprised squeal of delight as Jake carried her up the stairs and across the road, into their future.

Epilogue

Pulling open the church hall door, Effie slipped out into the cooling evening air. It was the last Saturday in May and Lola and Tristan's wedding reception was in full swing. The whole village had been involved in the wedding in some shape or form. The village committee had decorated the church with gorgeous red and white summer flowers to match Lola's bouquet and set up the hall for the reception. Effie and Freya had been honoured to be bridesmaids and taken the organisation of catering upon themselves. However, Lola had still insisted that she made the cake, after all, no one else's baking was quite up to scratch.

Lola and Tristan hadn't wanted anything too formal, just a celebration of their love, and of the happiness they had found in Polcarrow. The wedding had been beautiful, Lola and Tristan's families had been bundled into a friendly embrace by the locals. In fact, the whole day had felt like a celebration of Polcarrow's future and Effie had loved being swept up in being part of the village she now considered home. However, needing a few moments to herself, she had snuck outside.

From her vantage point by the village hall door, Polcarrow was laid out before her, sweeping like a letter S towards the sea, which glittered in the evening sunlight. She recalled the day she'd arrived, trundling down the streets with her dad, the car stuffed to the brim with books, balls of wool and all her dreams. Opening the bookshop had been hard, the biggest challenge she had ever taken on, other than giving Zach a piece of her mind, but she was immensely proud of her achievement. Every morning when she pulled up the blind, she couldn't quite believe that, with Clive's help, she'd made her childhood dream come true. Her own bookshop. Well, almost.

Then there was Jake. A smile spread across her face to think of him, her own happy-ever-after. Kind, funny, gorgeous Jake. They were taking things slowly, building their relationship in Polcarrow, finding pieces of themselves to fit together in harmony, like a jigsaw of their lives. Effie was enjoying constructing it, even the wrong fits had somehow turned out all right. From early-morning swims, to hiking the coast path and tentative plans to travel to Scotland, it was all coming together beautifully. They'd been officially together for a month, and Effie was enjoying the beginning of their story.

Just as she was about to turn and head back inside, the door opened and there he was, her Jake, taking her breath away in a dark-blue suit that highlighted the colour of his eyes. His tie had long been discarded, along with the jacket, but he still looked divine enough to make her catch her breath.

'You OK?' he asked, concern furrowing his brow as he joined her.

Effie nodded and snuggled against him. 'Yes, I just needed some air. Some time to reflect.'

Jake kissed her forehead. 'I understand. It's been full on.'

'More so for you with all the photography.'

'But I'm loving it, Eff, this is definitely what I want to do.' He switched on his camera and skimmed through some of the shots he'd taken of the speeches. 'Look at this, capturing all those private moments that passed so quickly, that Lola and Tristan can now have forever.' He turned the camera off and focused on Effie. 'They're gearing up for the first dance. Are you ready?'

'Of course! I've heard they've been practising for weeks to get it right. We can't miss that!' She shooed him back towards the hall door.

Back inside, Effie glanced around. The whole of Polcarrow was waiting for Lola and Tristan's first dance. Even Scruff was sitting patiently by Alf's feet, a bow around his neck. Effie joined them whilst Jake got his camera equipment ready. Steve dimmed the lights from where he was running the music decks, and an excited, expectant hush went through the hall.

'Give a round of applause for Lola and Tristan for their first dance as husband and wife.'

The applause, accompanied by cheers and whoops, was wild as Lola and Tristan emerged from where they had been waiting, hands clasped, true love plastered across their faces. Lola beamed at everyone as they took their place in the middle of the hall, before focusing her gaze on Tristan, who looked slightly more worried about being centre of attention.

The opening bars of Elvis's 'Can't Help Falling in Love With You' filled the hall. Effie swayed along as she watched Lola and Tristan's tentative dance steps grow in confidence. Jake was not the only person capturing the special moment. As the song ended, other couples joined them on the dance floor. Angelo dragged up by an enthusiastic Freya, Sue and her husband, until the dance floor was almost full.

Effie was bobbing along happily on the sidelines when Jake appeared in front of her. Holding out his hand like a Regency gentleman, he asked, 'May I have this dance?'

Meeting his eyes, Effie bowed her head. 'Of course.'

Jake pulled her hand up to his lips and kissed the back of her knuckles before leading her out onto the dance floor, their gazes never breaking.

As they swayed around the room, locked in their own private moment, happiness filled Effie. Jake kissed her slowly, gently, leaving a lingering promise of the future on her lips. Effie snuggled into him. Their perfect moment, existing only in that instant and only for them.

Jake glanced around as the whole of Polcarrow swayed and danced together. Leaning down, he kissed Effie before whispering, 'And we all lived happily ever after.'

Kissing him back, Effie smiled. She truly believed that Polcarrow, a tiny forgotten little fishing village tucked away on the Cornish coast, was a place full of magic where fairy tales and dreams really did come true. After all, it had brought her everything her heart desired.

Acknowledgements

Whether or not this is your first, or third, trip to Polcarrow, I'm going to kick off these acknowledgements by thanking you, the reader, for choosing this book. I've had so much wonderful feedback from you all about how much you love escaping to the seaside village of Polcarrow, so thank you for your support and I can't wait to take you on more adventures.

Thank you to my wonderful agent, Saskia Leach, you are an absolute star. Thank you for supporting me through some tricky mid-plot wobbles whilst everything outside of Polcarrow was very difficult for me. Thank you to everyone at the Kate Nash Literary Agency for everything you do.

Claire Johnson-Creek, it has been a pleasure to work with you to bring a bookshop to Polcarrow and therefore grow the village not only for the residents, but for the readers. Thank you for all your encouragement and support through the development and writing process. Thank you to everyone else at Zaffre for your work to bring this book into the hands of readers.

Thank you to everyone at Luton Library who have been terrific champions of my books, your support is heartwarming. Thanks also to everyone at Brown Books, Luton, you may recognise the yellow arm chairs!

Special thanks to all my Surrey writing buddies, you fabulous bunch. I always come away from our catch ups feeling inspired and supported. I'm so pleased to have found such wonderful friends in you all.

Thanks to all my friends and colleagues for all the love and support during my writing journey. Special mention to Lucy for all the plotting talk and for coming up with the meet cute in this book! Thank you to Carla, Essi, Helen, Laura, Liz, Sarah and Susan for your friendship. To Margaret for being a number one fan! To Desiree for the support and book chat, always a pleasure to discuss plots with you. Thank you to colleagues at the University of Bedfordshire, I know 2025 was difficult, but somehow we made it!

Last but not least, thank you to my family. Special mention to my uncle John Rowley, who we sadly lost during the writing of this book. Thank you to my parents John and Diana for all your love and support, not just with the book stuff but for looking after me post surgery. To Chris and Kristina, and my gorgeous niece and nephew, Amelia and Henry, your interest in the world and imagination never ceases to amaze me. I love you all. xx

Return to Polcarrow in . . . .

CHRISTMAS AT THE COSY CORNISH INN

Coming Christmas 2026

'The perfect festive romance' Heidi Swain

**A cosy Cornish village. A baker with a broken heart.
And the community who piece it back together.**

After a crushing breakup and the loss of her beloved grandmother
Ruby, Lola escaped to the charming Cornish village of Polcarrow to
start over with just her dreams of opening a café to keep her company.
But Polcarrow has other plans. With the help of her spirited best friend
Freya, a surrogate grandfather in Alf and a community that quickly feels
like family, Lola finds herself drawn into village life – and straight into
the path of Tristan, the disarmingly attractive local vicar.

As sparks fly and Christmas magic fills the air, long-buried family
secrets begin to surface. A hidden chapter in Ruby's past could change
everything Lola thought she knew about love – and herself. And with
the festive season in full swing, complete with fairy lights, Christmas
bakes and a lobster pot Christmas tree, and Tristan's ex back in town,
Lola must decide: will she protect her heart, or take a leap of
faith for a love that could be written in the stars?

Available now

Loved this book?
Join the Memory Lane Community

A welcoming home for all readers who love heart-warming tales of family, romance and history.

Sign up to our newsletter via the QR code below for book recommendations, giveaways, deals and behind-the-scenes writing moments from your favourite authors.

https://geni.us/memory-lane

Or you can also join the conversation in the Memory Lane Facebook Group.